Maniacal

A Detective Jade Monroe Crime Thriller
Book 1

D1736329

C. M. Sutter

AUTHOR'S NOTE

This book is a work of fiction by C. M. Sutter. Names, characters, places, and incidents are products of the author's imagination or are used solely for entertainment. Any resemblance to actual events or persons, living or dead, is entirely coincidental.

ABOUT THE AUTHOR

C.M. Sutter is a crime fiction writer who resides in the Midwest, although she is originally from California.

She is a member of numerous writers' organizations, including Fiction for All, Fiction Factor, and Writers Online.

In addition to writing, she enjoys spending time with her family and dog. She is an art enthusiast and loves to create handmade objects. Gardening, hiking, bicycling, and traveling are a few of her favorite pastimes. Be the first to be notified of new releases and promotions at: http://cmsutter.com.

C.M. Sutter

http://cmsutter.com/

Maniacal:

A Detective Jade Monroe Crime Thriller, Book 1

Sleepy little North Bend just woke up.
The newly promoted Sergeant Jade Monroe and her partner,
Detective Jack Steele, have just been informed of an
unidentified male body found at a local lake. The town is in
an uproar. The victim was nearly decapitated, and murder
simply doesn't happen in North Bend.
As more bodies turn up, the single connection between all of
the victims becomes clear—it's Jade herself.
With each new victim getting one step closer to Jade, time
begins to tick away. She must find the person responsible
before the killer targets her loved ones—or herself.

Stay abreast of each new book release by
signing up for my VIP e-mail list at:
http://cmsutter.com/newsletter/

Find more books in the Jade Monroe Series here:
http://cmsutter.com/available-books/

Chapter 1

He didn't like driving into the worst area of Milwaukee, but he had someone to meet. Tonight, Morris King would be the victim—just another statistic in a city with record murders for the year. He drove down streets riddled with broken-down vacant houses. He stared out the driver's side window at the dark, deserted street—he was getting closer. The bark of an occasional dog in the distance interrupted his thoughts.

The area was more than sketchy. Nothing good ever happened there, especially at that time of night. He wanted to get in and out quickly and undetected.

As he drove, he picked up his phone from the console and called.

A man answered, "Hello."

"Are you alone like I instructed?" he asked.

"Yeah, I'm alone, man. When are you getting here?"

"Soon. Do you see anyone out on the street?"

"Nah… I haven't seen anybody."

"Good." He abruptly ended the call.

Morris knew him only as "Dime," and that was the way he liked it. Anonymity was a necessity going forward.

His headlights reflected off the sign on the corner—Meinike Street. He turned right. His destination was only a few houses away. Dime killed the lights and turned into the driveway. He saw the orange glow of Morris's cigarette burning brightly when he looked toward the front stoop. The sound of gravel under his tires broke the quiet as he tucked his Jeep against the shed at the back of the driveway and got out.

Dime watched as Morris rounded the house and took a final drag off his smoke—the last one he'd ever take. Morris flicked the cigarette, and it spun when it hit the sidewalk.

Doing his best to blend in with the night, Dime wore a black hoodie and dark pants. He stood against the car with his hands jammed deep into his pockets. He gave Morris the once-over. "Let's go inside," he said and pushed himself off the vehicle.

"What's your deal, man? You don't fit the type," Morris asked with a nervous crack in his voice.

"Resale, and don't worry about my type. Do you want my money or not?"

"Yeah, but maybe I'm not charging enough for the oxy."

Dime headed up the three steps to the back door and waited for Morris to follow. He did a quick scan of the neighborhood. Dead silent, save the occasional buzz of a flickering streetlight ready to burn out.

"It's too dark in there. This will only take a minute," Morris said.

"Yeah, but I'd rather make the exchange inside. I have a flashlight. Let's go." Dime watched the kid. His body language said he was reluctant to follow. Dime gave him a wave over the shoulder and entered. He glanced back to see Morris following.

Dime elbowed through the broken back door into what used to be the kitchen. The door banged against one of the many piles of garbage scattered throughout the abandoned house. Sounds of what were likely skittering rodents filled the room.

Morris walked to the counter. "Where's that flashlight?"

Dime reached into his sweatshirt pocket and pulled it out. The darkness concealed his gloved hands. He pointed the light at Morris then set the flashlight down on the counter. "Show me the oxy. You get the cash after I see the goods."

"Sure, man, I got it right here." Morris dug the baggie out of his pocket and placed it on the broken tiled counter next to the flashlight.

Dime stood behind him and hesitated briefly.

The voices in his head came to life and stirred him back into the moment. *Remember the cat? You were only ten but so brave. The knife is your friend. Do it—do it now!*

Dime reached into his pocket and felt the cold steel. He thumbed the release on the switchblade as he pulled it out. He reached from behind and, with a hand on Morris's forehead and a quick, silent swipe, it was over.

Morris King's throat was slit from ear to ear. The freshly sharpened knife sliced through his flesh like butter. His head dropped to his chest like a heavy weight as blood pumped from his carotid artery with each remaining heartbeat. Blood spray hit the cabinets and ran down to the countertop, settling in the grout between the tiles.

Dime breathed a deep sigh and shrugged. "Sorry, man, it wasn't personal. I just needed the practice—it's been a while. You're a means to an end, I guess one would say."

He lowered Morris's body to the floor, careful to keep his own feet out of the blood pool spreading across the linoleum. With the flashlight in his hand, he walked to the door and glanced out. The street was still quiet with nobody in sight. He opened the tailgate, hoping it wouldn't squeak, and pulled out what he needed.

Dime walked back to the house and into the kitchen. He laid a plastic tarp next to the body and rolled Morris on top of it. Morris's head flopped precariously, as if held in place only by a string.

Dime shoved the bag of oxy into Morris's front right pocket. Pills were no good. They were the enemy and would distract him from the job he had to do. He removed the wallet and pulled the battery out of Morris's cell phone and placed those items in a bag. "What's this?" Dime pulled a pocket knife out of Morris's front left pocket and grinned. "What a coincidence." He put a lone dime into the pocket in its place.

Dime smirked at his own cleverness. "There, I'll give you cops something to start with. Try to figure this one out."

With Morris wrapped in the plastic tarp, Dime changed

clothes and placed his blood-spattered ones in the bag with the cell phone, knife and wallet.

He pulled the corpse through the kitchen and down the steps toward the Jeep. A muffled thump sounded each time Morris's body hit a step. Dime dragged him across the driveway to the six feet of space between the garage and his vehicle.

The back of the Jeep had been prepared in advance—lined with another plastic tarp as an extra precaution. He didn't want blood in his vehicle. Dime lifted Morris's lightweight body and rolled him in, then closed the tailgate quietly behind him. He hopped into the driver's seat, clicked the Jeep into reverse, and backed out of the driveway. With a quick glance in both directions—and seeing nothing amiss—Dime drove slowly down the street and turned on his headlights a block away. He already had the perfect place in mind to dispose of his first kill in a long time.

The voices in his head spoke up again. *See, that wasn't so bad. Quick and easy—hardly any effort at all.*

"Mom isn't going to be happy about it," Dime said.

Mom has no say in your life anymore, remember?

Dime chuckled. He continued on and drove north another forty minutes on Highway 41 before he turned off onto a country road. He knew the area well, having grown up there as a kid. Dark, quiet roads and the absence of cameras made the location the perfect place to dump a body. A row of ten mailboxes, some leaning and forgotten, stood at the intersection of Lakeview Road and the short street that led to the water's edge. Old, weathered newspapers and flyers were jammed inside the green plastic newspaper tubes below the mailboxes. Nobody had emptied them in months. Once Dime passed the ten darkened cottages, mostly used as vacation rentals and currently vacant, he continued on, driving his Jeep farther into the woods and off the blacktop road.

"This looks like the perfect spot." He killed the engine and pulled the wrapped body out of the back of the Jeep. He flung Morris over his shoulder. "No problem. You can't weigh more than a buck twenty."

Dime walked to the water's edge, carefully stepped in up to his ankles, then continued on until he found the perfect spot.

With Morris's body placed among fallen branches and reeds, and partially submerged in the water, Dime rolled up the plastic tarp and took the same path back to his vehicle. With a little effort, he jammed the tarp into the same bag as his bloody clothes and Morris's cell phone and wallet. He checked his surroundings for any light coming from homes or vehicles and was satisfied when all he saw was blackness. With the night's mission accomplished, he climbed into the Jeep, pulled out onto the main road, and headed east.

She popped into his mind as he drove. He hated women more every day. It was her fault he had to do this—the bitch. He'd get the attention he deserved, one way or another.

Chapter 2

I reached my desk in the bull pen and sat down. The napkin I had just unfolded would hold the hot number-three breakfast meal I anticipated leisurely eating. Steam wafted off the egg breakfast sandwich and hash browns as I unwrapped them, ready to dig in. Jack walked in right after me carrying a jumbo cup of coffee with the words Pit-Stop written across the plastic refillable cup.

"Is gas station coffee actually any good?" I asked, taking note of his daily routine.

"Try it sometime. It can't be any worse than your morning drive-through joint."

Lieutenant Clark opened the glass door that separated the bull pen from his office. He was a man that couldn't be ignored. In his heyday, the lieutenant had been big, muscular, and brash. Today, he was just big. At fifty-four, Chuck Clark had seen plenty during the last seventeen years as acting lieutenant of our sheriff's department. His naturally brown hair had turned gray years earlier, and his hard edge had softened just a bit. He smacked the doorframe with his open hand and called out to us.

"Monroe, Steele, saddle up. We have a floater on Cedar Lake. Two men casting close to shore found him when their line got tangled in the weeds. The crew is already onsite. Call them for the exact location. Take your breakfast with you, Monroe, and keep me updated."

"Right away, Lieutenant." I pushed back my roller chair, threw my breakfast back in the bag, and stood. "Damn it, you're driving, Jack. For once, I want to eat my breakfast before noon."

The sheriff's department in our small town didn't offer the luxury of a covered parking lot. The cruisers, unmarked cars, Crown Vics, and our personal cars sat outside. We each grabbed a department-issued rain jacket as we headed toward the door. That morning, a light mist cloaked the cool spring air, making me shiver. We climbed into our unmarked car and headed west.

Jack's cell phone rang, and Kyle was calling with directions.

"Do you think you can find the exact spot?" I asked after Jack ended his call.

"Yeah. I guess the area is already taped off. We can't miss it. Kyle said to take County Road P to Scenic and turn south. A half mile up, there's a gravel road that turns right near the public boat launch. Apparently, the body is partially submerged but tangled in the shoreline weeds."

"So he floated to shore?"

"Possibly. We'll know more once we get there. Kyle said to walk in. They don't want our tire tracks messing up the path getting back there. They're considering it a crime scene."

"Really? Did he say why they think that instead of an accidental drowning?"

"Yeah, he said we'd understand once we view the body. Plus, the lieutenant did say a floater, not a drowning victim. Anyway, they all walked in. We should see their cars along the road in just a few minutes."

"Sounds bad." I pointed through the windshield. "Looks like the vehicles are up ahead. This must be the place."

The medical examiner's van, forensics van, and four sheriff's department white cruisers with green-and-tan stripes down the sides, sat on the shoulder of the road. I checked my watch—just after eight o'clock. I patted my right-side jacket pocket to make sure my notepad and pen were there along with my cell phone and lip balm. Jack parked behind the other cruisers, and we followed the gravel road in on foot. We stayed on either side of the path, walking only on the weeds. We reached the team a quarter mile back at the edge of the lake.

"Boys." I nodded to the two-man forensic team, Kyle Miller and Dan Brent, as we approached.

The collars of their royal-blue polos peeked out of the black department-issued rain slickers Kyle and Dan wore. The back of their jackets had FORENSICS written from side to side in large yellow block letters.

Kyle had been with the team six years. He was a nice-looking single man, twenty-nine and with a pleasant personality. He wore his dark brown hair in a buzz cut.

He'd always said he didn't like to fuss with it. Dan, on the other hand, had chin-length naturally blond hair and blue eyes. He was a tall, slim young man and, at twenty-seven, had been in the forensics department three years. Kyle had taken Dan under his wing when he joined the department, and they became fast friends.

"So, what do we have?"

"Not what we expected, Jade," Dan said as he tucked his hair behind his ears.

"Really? Can you expand on that a bit?" I glanced at Jack and saw his eyebrows rise.

"Sure. You do realize that every house along this lake and within a five-mile radius is probably worth over a million bucks, right? I was certain we'd find the typical entitled twenty-one-year-old mama's boy that lives on the lake and accidently drowned after a night of partying and too much booze."

"And you found what instead?"

"Come on back and take a look."

Jack and I followed Dan the fifty feet along the wooded shoreline. We seemed to be on a natural path, likely from deer going to the water's edge to drink. We arrived to find Doug, our chief ME, and Jason, the associate ME, looking over the body they had pulled from the water. They wore rain slickers too, with MEDICAL EXAMINER written across the back. A white blood-stained tarp lay beneath the body, allowing us to see the horrific injury that had taken the individual's life.

I knelt down on the edge of the tarp and stared at the young man lying there.

"Wow, that's pretty gruesome." I leaned in to get a closer look.

Jack whistled and pressed on his temples. "I don't think we've come across this in the past. This poor guy's head is almost sliced clean off."

We stared at the gaping wound that went from ear to ear. The man's neck hung wide open, as if it were on a hinge. A closer look showed the cut was so deep it had nearly severed his spine. There wasn't much tissue left holding his head on, and the spine appeared to be the only thing that kept the head and body connected.

"Looks like gang tats too. We're not in Kansas anymore, Dorothy." Jack pointed to the arms and what was left of the man's neck.

I stood and elbowed him in the ribs but had to agree. "Yeah, I saw the tats too. He's likely from the city." I looked toward Doug. "Did you find his ID?"

Doug was a large man, around six feet tall and husky. He wore his blond hair cropped short. At forty-three, he had been our county ME for longer than I could remember. Jason was fairly new. He started working with Doug a year ago. He was a nice guy, newly married and thirty-two. He had short brown hair and wore stylish tortoiseshell glasses. Jason was friendly, ambitious, and easy to like.

Doug turned his head and looked up at me. "Well, that's going to be a problem, Sergeant. There wasn't a cell phone or wallet in his pockets. We'll pull his prints once we get him on the table."

I thought out loud. "So possibly robbery and murder?

The injury seems too extreme for that. What's in the baggie next to the body?"

"Forensics will check it out, but I pulled it from his front left pocket when I was searching for identification. Not much left of whatever it was. I'm guessing some pills that dissolved in the water."

"Anything else?"

"Yeah, his mouth was full of lake scum, and he had a dime in his pocket."

"That's it—one dime?"

Doug nodded. "Yep, just a dime."

Jack glanced around our immediate area. "Who would even know of this lake if they didn't live near here?"

"Good question, partner. What happened to the guys that called it in?" I asked.

Jason jerked his head to the left. "They're over by the boat launch with Detective Clayton. The lieutenant sent him out along with a handful of deputies this morning before you two got in. They're just a couple of retired guys looking to catch some bass this morning but found this guy instead. It's a real shame."

"Can we get a rough estimate of TOD?"

Doug swatted a fly away. "Hard to say. Rigor is just setting in. Being submerged in water makes a difference, Sergeant. I'll know more after I get him on the table. If you want a rough estimate"—Doug pulled up his sleeve and glanced at his watch—"I'd say he's been dead for six hours, maybe more."

I buried my cold, wet hands in my pockets. "Okay, let's

keep moving. Has Kyle or Dan checked for footprints or tire tracks yet?"

"Kyle's working on it. Once he clears the path, Jason can pull the van in, and we'll get this guy loaded up," Doug said.

Jack and I backtracked to where Kyle and Dan were taking pictures of the area and looking for tread marks on the path.

Kyle saw us approaching. "You're good to go, guys. No tire marks or shoeprints in the gravel that we can see. We'll keep looking for evidence in the brush and weeds too. I'm sure most of us will be out here all morning."

Something was on my mind that I needed to ask Kyle. "One quick question before we go. Why don't you think there were footprints leading to the site? It's been raining, and the ground is soft."

"There's a lot of ways to enter this lake. My guess would be the perp walked through the shallow water with the body. He could have entered the lake anywhere and stayed along the shoreline. It depends on when the body was dumped too."

"Meaning?"

"I don't think it started raining until early this morning. We've got Donnelly, Silver, Ebert, and Lawrence searching everything that is cordoned off. They'll do a thorough job."

"Okay, thanks. We're going to talk to the eyewitnesses now." I pulled the hood of my rain jacket up as we walked to the boat launch. The mist was heavy enough to instantly turn my smooth black hair into frizz. "I'm going to give Clark a heads-up. What we found wasn't the norm in this neck of the woods." I dialed the lieutenant as we walked and turned left at the end of the gravel road. The boat launch with a small restaurant lay straight ahead. I noticed the lights were on in the restaurant, and a green neon Open sign hung slightly tilted from the window. "Hey, Lieutenant, I'm just calling to give you the initial update."

"Go ahead, Jade. What have we got besides what Kyle told me earlier?"

"It certainly isn't the typical drowning, but somehow I think you knew that. We have an African American male whose head was almost severed. That doesn't fit the neighborhood, and I doubt if he lived around here." I wiped my wet forehead. "We saw gang tats on the visible parts of his body too, and there could be more. I think we should keep the actual cause of death off the media's radar, at least for now. In this quiet, upscale neighborhood, the residents will go into a tizzy if those details get out. There wasn't a wallet or cell phone on the body either."

"That creates a problem."

"The only thing we can hope for is fingerprints, if he's in the system."

"Okay, so the witnesses?"

"Jack and I are walking up to them as we speak. I'll catch up with you later, Lieutenant." I hung up, put my phone on vibrate, and zipped it into my jacket pocket as we introduced ourselves to the two older men talking to Clayton.

Chad Clayton was another daytime detective that was usually partnered with Adam Billings, but Billings had stayed back to handle things in the bull pen.

Clayton had dark blond hair and a neatly trimmed mustache. He could use a little more time at the gym, but all in all, he was a great guy. He had been with the sheriff's department for nine years and was a happily married man. His eleven-year-old twins, Megan and Matt, were his pride and joy.

"Clayton." I nodded in his direction. "Gentlemen." I extended my hand, and Jack did the same. "We're investigators with the sheriff's department. I'm Sergeant Jade Monroe"—I pointed to Jack—"and this is my partner, Detective Jack Steele."

The men introduced themselves as Bob Shultz and Leo Moroni. They both appeared to be a little shaken. They looked to be in their late sixties and the type of guys who lived the comfortable, retired lifestyle. Abruptly, their idyllic fishing excursion that morning had turned into something not easily forgotten. I gave them each the once-over after the initial introductions. Bob was short and pudgy, with chafed, windburned cheeks and short white hair. His plaid shirt and fishing hat reminded me of the typical Wisconsin retiree. I assumed Leo was Italian because of his last name, Moroni. He had a large nose, dark eyes, and olive skin. The hairline at his temples showed a tint of gray, but most of his hair was still wavy and a beautiful shade of black.

"How about we sit inside where it's dry?" I smiled to put them at ease. "We have the usual questions to go over with you. I hope we can wrap this up within a half hour or so and let you get on with your day."

We entered the warm, cozy restaurant. A long lunch counter was directly ahead of us with ten stools against it. A few were occupied. Five tables were scattered throughout the room, and four booths lined the wall. I motioned toward a booth. Jack and I took one side and faced Bob and Leo on the other. A waitress approached with a welcoming smile, apparently unaware of what had taken place just across the lake from the restaurant. We ordered a carafe of coffee, and I began the questions. Jack pulled out his notepad and pen.

"What time did you gentlemen get out here this morning?" I asked.

Bob looked at Leo and shrugged. "About six thirty. Right, Leo?"

"Yeah. We launched the boat right as the sun cleared the tree line around the lake. It clouded up almost immediately and started misting. I'm thinking we fished for forty-five minutes or so before we discovered the body."

"And can you explain that to me?" I asked.

"Well, ma'am, I cast close to shore." Bob rubbed his forehead then continued, "That's where the bass usually hit. Lines tend to get tangled in the weeds in the shallow water, you know."

I nodded.

"We rowed in closer so I could pull my lure out of the weeds. That's when we saw him. I swear we almost capsized the boat. I've never seen a sight like that, not even in Nam."

"I'm sure you haven't, Bob. Did either of you touch the body?"

16

"No, ma'am," Leo said. He shook his head. "I'll admit, I upchucked right there in the water."

I frowned at his distress. "I understand."

Jack filled each cup with more of the hot brew and continued with his notes.

"Was there anything besides the obvious neck wound that stood out? Can you think of something that our officers wouldn't have noticed from your point of view, being on the water side of the scene?"

Leo added as he scratched his chin, "I'm sure he was placed there. Bodies don't float across a lake and put themselves halfway up on dry land. The man was in the water up to his chest, but his shoulders and what was left of his head were on the bank. It appeared like he was dumped there. There's no vehicle unaccounted for near the boat launch. The guy didn't drive himself here in that condition and throw himself in the lake."

I paused, waiting for Jack to catch up with his notes. "Good point, Leo. Do you two fish here often?"

Bob answered, "Yep, several times a week. There's nobody that knows this lake like we do. Only guys fishing for bass go back near that shoreline. It's too easy to lose your bait. This is a large lake, and we know the prime spots. There aren't a lot of people that go back to the holes we fish at."

"Okay. I think that's all we need for now. We appreciate your help. Please call us if either of you think of something else, no matter how trivial it might seem. If you wouldn't mind, we'd like to keep the gruesome details quiet. I'd hate to have this incident start a countywide panic." I gave the waitress a ten and told her to keep the change.

Jack wrote down their full names, phone numbers, and addresses. We stood, gave them our cards, shook their hands, and left.

"What do you think?" Jack asked as we walked back to the scene.

"I think this entire area needs a thorough going-over, even beyond the police tape. I'm going to talk to Kyle some more."

The coroner's van was backed to the water's edge. Doug and Jason zipped the young man into a body bag, placed him on a backboard, and carried him to the van.

"Kyle, got a minute?"

"Sure, what's up?"

"Do you really think this was the actual dump site? There's no way the guy floated along the bank to this spot?"

"I doubt it. His body was partially on the shore, which doesn't happen naturally when one drowns. I'm pretty certain this was the site. We've searched for trampled grass and any evidence that a body was dragged to the water, but everything looks normal. The grass is too short to fold over, but the deputies will keep looking. Lieutenant Clark told them to stay out here all day."

I remembered Leo's statement being almost verbatim to what Kyle had just said. "Would it be possible for somebody to carry a body from the road? It's a quarter mile back to the water."

"He'd have to be big and strong, but it's certainly

doable. Like I said before, he could have entered anywhere along the lake and walked the shoreline. Keep in mind, Jade, that there are numerous short streets that take you to the cottages along the lake. The killer could have parked anywhere, not just at the main road."

"Yeah, I know, just thinking out loud. How long before we can print the body?"

"We'll do that first when we get back to the station. I'll give you a call if we get a hit."

"Thanks, Kyle. Jack and I are going to knock on a few doors around the lake. Maybe somebody saw a car parked out here last night. We'll catch up with you at the station later."

Chapter 3

We spoke to four homeowners on the west side of the lake and five from the area nearest where the body was found. Six other homes looked to be weekend retreats or rental cottages. We saw no signs of anyone at those residences. The curtains were drawn, and the driveways were void of cars, boats, or Jet Skis. We kept our conversations short and vague, hoping somebody had information for us, but nobody did. Not one person had seen an unfamiliar car, or any car for that matter, parked along the road or in the parking lot of the boat launch last night. We thanked the people we spoke to and left.

"Three hours of asking questions and we have zilch," I grumbled as we climbed back into the car and headed out. "In all honesty, I wasn't expecting much given the remote area and likelihood of this being a late-night dump. I guess hoping for anyone that could ID an unfamiliar car was wishful thinking on my part considering how dark it must be out here at night."

Jack wiped his forehead with his wet jacket sleeve.

"Remind me to carry a few towels when we go door to door in this kind of weather."

I nodded.

"Anyway, I bet a good number of these folks turn in right after the ten o'clock news. Still, it seems like the perp would have to be familiar with the area. It isn't like there's a sign advertising Cedar Lake off the interstate, you know," Jack said.

I looked out the car window as Jack drove back toward town. Around us were neat, clean houses sprinkled a half mile apart with a lot of farm fields in between. Parents raised their kids there. School buses picked up those same youngsters at the end of the driveway. Violent crime was uncommon in Washburn County. North Bend, the largest city in the immediate area—and the county seat—was still considered primarily a rural, folksy town. Maybe that was what the killer was counting on.

We drove in silence for a few minutes. Different scenarios popped in and out of my mind, and I felt a headache coming on. My temples began to pound.

"Are there any aspirin in the car?" I opened the glove box and began a fruitless search.

"Doubt it."

I groaned and rubbed my damp head. "Does Doug seem off to you lately?"

"You mean more than usual? Like how exactly?" Jack glanced in my direction, his right eyebrow raised.

"I can't put my finger on it, just more matter-of-fact, I guess, and since when does he call me Sergeant instead of Jade?"

"Yeah, that's a recent change, but you were just promoted."

"I think he's still humiliated that I turned down his dinner invitation. I mean, for God's sake, two days after Lance moved out, he asked me on a date. I'm so over men… nothing personal."

Jack laughed. "I'm not taking it personally, but now that you mention it, you could be right. Don't forget, it was his wife who climbed the corporate ladder and divorced him. Doug makes good money, but Linda's income dwarfed his. I think he was actually envious of her, then she moved on without him. I bet he thought he'd have a shot with you."

I laughed. "Yeah, I don't think so. According to what everyone said, Doug and Linda weren't the best match anyway."

"Right, but maybe he feels you knocked him down a few pegs by dismissing his dinner invite."

I gave Jack a stare. "Coworkers shouldn't fraternize anyway. I just wish he'd go back to calling me Jade like he used to."

"You might be overthinking this, partner. Doug's an all-right guy. He's probably getting tired of the daily grind."

"But he's been the ME forever."

"Exactly. Speaking of Lance, how's it going with him anyway?"

I smirked. "Were we?"

"His name came up ten minutes ago. Anyway, what's going on with him?"

"He drives me nuts. He calls or texts almost daily to see

if I've set up an appointment with a Realtor yet. He can't wait to get the house sold so he has his half of the money. I'm sure his little girlfriend is anxious for him to propose so they can start a family. He's a pain in my butt."

"You still sound bitter."

I jerked my head to the left and stared at Jack again. "Seriously? Our divorce was just finalized two months ago. I actually thought I was going to be married to that man for life. I think I'm allowed to be bitter, at least for a few more months. There isn't a handbook for the way to feel after a betrayal, you know."

"Sorry. I didn't mean to be insensitive."

"I'm sorry too. I didn't mean to bite your head off. How's the Internet dating going? Find any hot babes yet?" I laughed when I noticed Jack blush.

"It's going…very slowly." He shrugged. "I never knew how much people exaggerate until after I met a few gals. They say they're single yet somehow forget to mention they have four kids under the age of ten." He shook his head and smirked. "So far, I've struck out in the romance department. For now, the online dating is getting shelved. It looks like we might be busy with this case anyway."

"You'll find the right girl when you least expect it. So the saying goes."

I gave Jack a thoughtful gaze. At thirty-five, he was a handsome man and a really good friend. Short, nicely styled black hair and dark eyes mixed with that dimpled grin made him more than appealing. His muscular body and six-foot frame always made me feel safe in his presence. I was thankful to have Jack as my partner. He had two fun-loving brothers and really sweet parents. We knew each other's families well, as close as we were. Someday, he'd make a good husband for a lucky lady.

We turned left onto Schmidt Road and pulled into the sheriff's department parking lot. Jack killed the engine, and we exited the car. The sheriff's department was located in a tan stucco building. Located on the east side of the city, our part of the government complex included the sheriff's department, jail, morgue, ME's office, forensics lab, and the technical department. The impound lot sat within a chain-link fence behind our building. The large county courthouse with all the annexes faced south on Washington Street.

We shook out our wet jackets as we entered the vestibule through the heavy glass double doors. We hung them on the few available hooks just beyond the front reception counter. The glassed-off dispatch area was directly behind that, with a security door leading to the bull pen and our lieutenant's office. Anyone wanting to visit inmates would sign in at reception and be taken down a hallway to the right and up a flight of stairs to the jail. A visitation room resembling a cafeteria was available for inmates and their guests to spend an hour at a time together, twice a week. Turning left from the reception counter led down a narrow hallway to the stairs. Pictures of previous sheriffs going back to 1922 lined the walls on either side of the hallway. The ME's office, morgue, crime lab, and tech department were located on the lower level of the building.

Jack and I turned left. Eight Italian marble steps down and a stainless steel handrail took us to a hallway on the bottom floor. The first room on the right was the crime lab. We pushed through the glass door and saw Kyle seated in front of his computer. He had returned early with Doug and Jason to work on the fingerprints.

"Got anything?" I asked.

We grabbed a couple of roller chairs and pulled up alongside him.

"Yeah, we have a fingerprint match. I was just about to call you. Take a look. This guy has plenty of priors. His rap sheet is extensive for a kid"—he paused to scroll the sidebar—"that's only twenty years old. Name is Morris King, and he's been around the block a few times, starting with juvie at age eleven. Petty theft, burglary, battery, and most recently he spent six months in jail for distributing controlled substances, primarily oxy."

"Where did he live?" I leaned over Kyle's shoulder to take a closer look.

"Milwaukee. Address is in the inner city off North Avenue. Nothing good ever happens in that neighborhood. A lot of gang-related activity like drive-by shootings, robbery, battery, and rape. It's all par for the course in that area."

"Did you figure out what was in the baggie?"

"Yeah, OxyContin. As far as the body goes, he looks relatively clean on the initial exam, according to Doug. The autopsy hasn't begun yet, but the kid doesn't have any track marks or other obvious signs of substance abuse. Toxicology will take a few days."

"Hmm… okay. Print out the home address for me. Ready for a drive, Jack? It looks like we're off to Milwaukee to notify his family." I checked the time on the analog clock above the bank of computers stationed at the back wall—almost two p.m. "Maybe we can grab something at a drive-through on our way."

My cell phone rang just before we headed out. Clayton was calling.

"Hey, Jade, just checking in."

"Clayton. How's the search going?"

"Still nothing. Found a few old rusty chunks of metal in one field. Looks to be something that fell off a tractor. Other than that—zilch."

"Yeah, sounds like our perp covered his tracks pretty well. You've got four deputies out there with you?"

"That's right."

"Okay, give it another hour or so, then call it quits. Report in to the lieutenant when you get back. Jack and I are headed to Milwaukee to inform the next of kin."

"So the boys found a fingerprint match?"

"Yeah, they sure did. It looks like the kid has been in the system for a while."

"Roger that. Okay, talk to you later."

At three o'clock, we pulled up along the curb in front of a modest, worn-looking clapboard bungalow on Garfield, just south of and parallel to North Avenue. Plastic sheeting covered a broken window, and the peeling paint curled upward from sun damage and years of neglect. Fallen roof shingles lay in the unattended weed-filled yard. The neighborhood was littered with vacant boarded-up houses mixed in with the occupied ones. Images of criminal activity filled my mind thanks to the unkempt area and the number of people lingering at street corners and on stoops as they watched us exit our unmarked cruiser. That was one of the most run-down, crime-ridden areas of Milwaukee.

I knocked on the door twice before I heard footsteps approaching. A deep growl came from not more than ten inches away. Only a front door that had seen better days separated us from what sounded like a large, angry dog. The curtain to our right shifted. A man's face stared out at us, giving us the once-over. He looked to be a tall, skinny man in his midforties, I'd guess. He resembled the type of person that got most of their needs fulfilled with beer and cigarettes rather than healthy meals.

"Sir, we're with the Washburn County Sheriff's Department." Jack and I showed him our badges through the glass. "We need to speak to somebody about Morris King. We'd like to come in, but the dog will have to be removed from the room first."

"What's this about?"

"Are you related to Morris King, sir?"

"I'm his uncle and his legal guardian. What do you want?"

"May we come in? We have information about Morris."

He dropped the curtain back, and I heard him call the dog away. The sound of footsteps returned, and he opened the door to the end of the chain lock.

"Is the dog secure in another room?"

"Yeah."

"May we enter?"

He closed the door, released the chain lock, and opened it fully.

"Sir, I'm Sergeant Jade Monroe, and this is Detective Jack Steele. We're from the criminal investigations unit of the sheriff's department. We'd like to talk to you about Morris. Your name is?"

"The name is Terrance King. Criminal investigations unit? What did Morris do now?"

He pointed to the sofa. He took a seat on the rocking chair facing us from the other side of the small living room. I did a quick assessment of the area I could see. The smell of stale cigarettes and garbage filled the house. I wished a window had been open. Dirty ashtrays sat scattered about on every flat surface. Disarray was rampant. What looked like years of stacked newspapers and magazines sat in the corner of the living room. Most of the window blinds had broken slats, and the beige carpet was threadbare and filthy. A quick glance into the kitchen told me the dishes hadn't been washed in who knew how long. They overflowed the sink onto the countertops, and the table was just as bad. I turned my attention back to Terrance King.

"Does Morris legally live here? You said you were his guardian."

He smirked. "This is his address on record, but is he ever around? No, ma'am. I see that boy now and then when he comes home to shower and put on clean clothes. He's out with his crew most all day and night."

"Does Morris have a job?" I asked. I watched Jack jot down everything Terrance was saying.

Mr. King laughed and slapped his knee. "He sure does. That's if selling drugs and stolen goods is a job."

"Mr. King, I don't want to prolong this more than I have to. We're here to inform you that Morris has passed away. We'll need to know everything you can possibly tell us about his friends, his hangouts, and so on."

"Oh my, my, my, dear Jesus… did he overdose on something?" Terrance wiped his eyes and shook his head. "It was only a matter of time."

I stole a glance at Jack and let him continue for me.

"Mr. King, we need to know if Morris had enemies or if anyone has threatened your family."

"What… enemies? I don't know. Like I said, he hardly comes home anymore. Why are you asking about that?"

"Morris met up with foul play, Mr. King. He was murdered," Jack said.

Terrance hung his head and whispered what sounded like a prayer.

Jack waited out of respect, then continued, "We're going to need you to identify the body since you were his guardian. We have a picture with us today, but you'll still need to come to our county morgue for an official ID."

I opened my iPad and brought up the picture Doug had taken of Morris on the autopsy table. We made sure he was exposed only from the chin up.

Terrance studied the photo while a tear rolled down his cheek and fell to his shirt. He reached for a tissue, blew his nose, and cleared his throat. He nodded. "It's Morris."

"Mr. King, the reason we're here is because his body was found in our county. Now keep in mind, Washburn County is thirty-five miles from here. Do you know if Morris knew anyone out our way?"

"Can't say that I do. That boy didn't talk much, especially to me, even though I was his only kin. He was court ordered to live with me when his mama died ten years back. She was a junkie, nothing but bad news. His old man, my brother, Leonard, has been in the system for fifteen years."

"Prison?" Jack asked.

"Waupun. Haven't seen the man since he was sent up. He's no good."

Jack wrote it down. "No other siblings?"

"Nope, it was only Morris."

"What about his boys—the crew Morris hung with?" I asked.

"I only know first names, but they all live nearby. Devon, Kev, Marshon, and James come to mind. That's all I know."

Jack wrote down the names.

"Did Morris have a cell phone?"

"Cell phone? Yeah, sure he did."

"Would you happen to know what service provider he used? There wasn't a cell phone on his person, but we could order up his records if we knew the provider and number."

"Give me a minute."

Mr. King rose and walked down the hall, his shoulders

slumped. He entered the second room on the left. There were sounds of drawers opening, papers shuffling, and drawers closing before we heard footsteps walking the hallway back toward us. Mr. King had a phone bill in his hand.

"Morris's phone bill came last week. Guess he won't be needing it now." He handed it to me.

"Thank you, sir. This should be a big help. Did Morris have his own bedroom here?"

"Yeah, sure, that's where the phone bill was. I put all his mail in his room."

"How often do you think he actually came home?" Jack asked.

"Once a week, I suppose."

I gave Jack a hopeful glance. "Would you mind if we took a look in his room? I'd hate to go through the red tape of getting a warrant if we don't need to. There may be something in there that could help us."

"It's a mess, but go ahead. He won't care anymore." Terrance led us down the hall to Morris's room. "This is it."

"Okay, thank you. We won't take too long." Then I told Jack, "We better glove up."

Jack and I entered the small, darkened room. I flipped on the light. Only one bulb lit up in the three-bulb ceiling fixture. I looked up. The other two were definitely burned out. The bed was unmade, clothes were strewn across the floor, and the room was a mess. We opened drawers, looked under the bed, and checked the closet. A shoebox on the top shelf caught my attention. The dozen or so shoes in the closet were tossed on the floor as though they meant nothing. Why keep a box?

"Jack, can you reach that shoebox? Let's take a look inside."

"Yeah, sure."

He pulled it down and opened it on the bed. Inside was a .22 Ruger revolver, a stack of cash, and plenty of bagged pills.

"Yeah, that's not good." I took several pictures with my cell phone. "Crap—now what? This isn't our jurisdiction."

"Call the lieutenant and see what he says. We haven't had a predicament like this before."

I agreed and made a quick call to Lieutenant Clark and explained the situation. I told him the room didn't appear to be a crime scene, yet the things we'd found so far could be considered evidence related to Morris's murder.

I looked around as I spoke. "The room is a mess, Lieutenant. What should we do?"

"Okay, I'll make calls to the proper authorities in Milwaukee. I'll explain the situation and have them meet you at the residence. Turn over the evidence you found to them and they can take it from there."

"Will do."

Jack and I found Terrance sitting in the kitchen on the only chair that wasn't covered with an accumulation of junk. We stood.

"Mr. King, we found some illegal items in Morris's room that are going to be confiscated. As long as your fingerprints aren't on any of those items, you're in the clear.

The Milwaukee PD is coming by to take what we found and to fingerprint you. It's in your best interest to cooperate with them. It shouldn't take long."

Terrance nodded. "I never go in that boy's room other than to set his phone bill in there. I don't know what he has, and I sure haven't touched anything illegal."

"We understand and appreciate your cooperation. We'll wait here for them to show up. Should only be a few minutes."

"Mr. King, do you have a pastor or someone to contact for funeral arrangements?" Jack asked.

"Yeah, Brother Tate Johnson at Calvary Baptist Church two blocks away. He's a good man and our local minister. I'll take care of it. When will Morris's body be brought home?"

"It might take a while, but we do need the official ID as soon as possible. This is a criminal case, Mr. King, and we have investigating to do. As soon as we have something concrete to go on, we'll let you know when the body can be released."

"I'll come by tomorrow," he said.

I saw the cruiser pull up to the curb. We handed Terrance our cards, and I told him we'd be in touch.

"Please call either of us if you think of anything else that might help. We want to apprehend Morris's killer as soon as possible."

We shook his hand and went outside with the shoebox to explain the situation to the officers.

My phone buzzed, and I pulled it out of my pocket. The lieutenant was calling back.

"Hey, boss."

"Jade, here's how we're going to do this. I talked to the third district PD, and they want you to stop in before you head back. You'll go over everything you guys know up to this point with them. Ask for a Detective Lindstrom. Apparently he knew Morris and the boys he runs with. It looks like this may end up being a joint effort, but they're fine with taking the house off our hands."

"Got it. I'll update you after we talk to them. The officers just arrived, and we're explaining the situation to them. We're giving them the items we found as we speak."

I hung up, and we left. From there, we had only a six-block drive to the third district police station.

"This looks like the place," I said as Jack pulled up. "Let's see what Detective Lindstrom knows."

Jack parked, and we walked up the sidewalk to the Cream City brick modern-looking police station. The curved facade held green-tinted windows that spanned the entire front of the building. We entered at the ground level, approached the reception counter, and introduced ourselves to the officer. I told him we were there to speak with Detective Lindstrom. He nodded, asked us to wait, and disappeared through the gray steel door behind the counter.

The lobby was nice, clean, and brightly lit for a police station. Black granite floors sparkled beneath our feet, and the cushy green guest chairs in the waiting area were comfortable. Matching potted ficus trees flanked each side of the double glass entry doors that bore the police department logo facing the street side.

Five minutes had passed, and the door finally opened. A fortyish looking tall gentleman walked toward us and extended his hand. I sized him up immediately. He was dressed nicely in a starched white shirt tucked into black pleated trousers. A dark blue paisley-patterned tie was double Windsor knotted around his neck. He had a thick head of blond hair and pretty blue eyes. He looked like a decent guy.

"Nice to meet you. I'm Detective Bill Lindstrom," he said as he vigorously shook our hands.

I introduced Jack and myself, then we followed him back to his desk. Their bull pen was huge. Twenty desks filled the room, with plenty of activity going on. Each desk faced another, likely partners grouped together. A guest chair sat to the left of each desk. Glassed-in offices surrounded the bull pen, and the hallway to the right led to the interrogation rooms and holding cells.

"Have a seat." He pointed to the chair closest to his desk and pulled another one over for Jack. "Lieutenant Colgate is out right now. He would normally be sitting in on this, but I'm sure you'll meet him later. Anyway, I took the liberty of making you copies of each of Morris King's known associates that has a jacket with us. I know these characters, and most of them are nothing but trouble. Hopefully you can get a little information that might help, but they're a tight-lipped group. It sounds like we might be working together for a bit."

"Anything you can do to help us would be appreciated. We've never had a murder case that crossed county lines."

"I understand. So Morris died yesterday, huh?"

"Yes. We have a window putting his TOD in the early hours of yesterday morning, most likely a little after midnight. Two men fishing on a lake in Washburn County came upon his body against the shoreline. They called it in shortly after seven a.m."

Detective Lindstrom glanced in each direction before continuing. "Lieutenant Clark said his throat was slashed?"

"I'm afraid so. The scene was pretty horrific, yet we didn't find a shred of forensic evidence."

He rubbed his chin and raised his brows. "That makes me think the murder would have been from someone else. These knuckleheads Morris knows aren't that smart. There would have been something left behind just from clumsiness if nothing else. Plus there are plenty of places right in the city to dump a body. It doesn't sound like the work of the punks in this neighborhood. They aren't that ambitious to drive to another county to dump off a dead body. Seems like someone thought this one out."

I shrugged and looked toward Jack. "He has a point, you know."

"Have you heard of any chatter about Morris? Bragging, posturing, and the sort? Anyone with a beef against him?" Jack asked.

Detective Lindstrom leaned back in his chair and rubbed his eyes. "Around here, everyone has a beef against somebody. There's a lot of gang activity in these parts. They could have been your boy's best friend yesterday and his killer today. Depends on what's in it for the person doing the dirty work, if you know what I mean."

"I imagine this is one of the busiest police stations in Milwaukee," I said.

"Oh, yeah, that's for sure. Every year it seems like the number of murders goes up. Anyway, here are the jackets. The names, current addresses, and crimes they've committed are enclosed. Give them a once-over and think about what I said. These gangbangers really aren't that bright. I guess I can close out Morris's active jacket. For now, I'll just list him as deceased. Here's my contact info. I'm sure we'll catch up in the next day or so."

We stood and shook Detective Lindstrom's hand, gave him our cards, and left.

"Let's find a decent place to stop," Jack suggested after we pulled out of the parking lot.

"Sounds good. We'll look these jackets over carefully and think things through. Tomorrow we can hit the ground running with a better idea of the people who stand out the most."

I checked the time—five o'clock. We gave the jackets a quick read and shared a carafe of strong coffee.

"None of these guys look like saints," I said, "but they're supposed to be Morris's friends. No matter what, we'll have to talk to each of them to find out who their enemies are."

Jack agreed.

By the time we got back to North Bend, it was nearly six thirty. Lieutenant Clark was shutting down his office when we walked in.

"Jade, Jack, anything else to report?" He pulled his office

door closed and gave the knob a shake to make sure it was locked.

"Only that Detective Lindstrom gave us the jackets on several of Morris's boys. That will make tracking them down a whole lot easier. Hopefully they'll tell us if Morris had enemies too and give us a few names. Usually a crime of passion or rage comes from a person the victim knows, doesn't it?"

The lieutenant nodded. "Yeah, most of the time."

I glanced at the clock on the wall. "Maybe a good night's sleep and a fresh set of eyes in the morning will help."

Jack tipped his head toward the hallway that led downstairs. "I'm going to give this phone bill to Billy and Todd in tech. They can call Verizon and have them pull up the records from Morris's last night alive. The times and people he spoke to yesterday might lead us down the right path. Once we find out who he spoke to last, we'll rattle some cages with Morris's known associates. Jade and I are going to head back to Milwaukee tomorrow, but we'll catch up with Doug before we leave. He might have more to tell us by then." Jack started for the door. "Also, Mr. King is stopping in tomorrow to make a positive ID of Morris's body. I'll let Doug know that too."

Clark scratched his forehead and tapped his foot against the tile floor. "Yeah, okay, let's call it a wrap for tonight. I'll see you two in the morning."

Chapter 4

Dime paced back and forth in that special room set up downstairs. The scent of musty basement filled the air and stung his nostrils as he descended the staircase, but he didn't care. He was used to it. The dark wood paneling glued to the cinder block walls buckled in some spots due to moisture. He didn't think to run the dehumidifier as often as he should. The basement served only one purpose these days, and company didn't stop by as they did back then—when life was good and his marriage was strong. Even if he did have company, they wouldn't be allowed in that room anymore—it was his private place. A small refrigerator and bar were all that remained of the happier days, nearly ten years ago. Friends and family used to spend time in that typical Wisconsin rec room during holiday gatherings. Music played, and guys sat around the green felt–covered poker table, each with a beer in their cup holder, playing cards. Women cooked the meals and danced together with a glass of wine in hand. Laughter resonated in that room years ago. After the wife left, things changed. The friends and family didn't come around anymore. Today the room stood quiet and had a different purpose. It had fallen into disrepair, looking much as it had when he was just a kid.

His focus had shifted, and his mind went dark long ago. The psychiatrist prescribed medication for his dangerous, psychotic mood swings, but pills were the enemy, and so was she. Women weren't to be trusted, especially somebody like a female shrink. He canceled all his future appointments with her. She was sneaky and conniving—they all were. He had to keep his thoughts and focus sharp—just like his knife.

Dime stood in front of the corkboard wall and stared at years of saved newspaper clippings and photographs. He poured a Stella Artois into a glass as he studied the face in most of the newspaper articles. She was just another woman that he hated, yet in his own disturbed way, he wanted her. Her flawless alabaster skin was like fine china. Her eyes were a brilliant green, and her hair was the color of raven feathers. She was tall and slender yet had sexy curves. Well-defined arms gave her a toned, strong appearance.

He walked to the side table ten feet away. His lips curled, forming an evil grin as he reached in the drawer and pulled out the knife. With a quick flick of his wrist, he threw it at the wall, stabbing through her face in one of the photos.

I'll make that bitch sit up and take notice, one way or another. She'll learn soon enough that I demand respect.

He was ready to plan his next kill, but he'd have to follow her first to learn more. Her routine needed to be ingrained in his mind. He needed to study her habits, what she did every night after work, where she went, who she visited. The next one would be more personal. She'd pay attention to him whether she wanted to or not.

The bag containing Morris King's cell phone and wallet, along with Dime's own bloody clothes, still sat on the floor where he'd tossed it last night. With a grunt and a shove, he pushed the bookcase to the side and deposited the bag behind it in the large cutaway area of the paneling. He pushed the bookcase back into place, making sure it was centered perfectly between the pictures of his mother on the wall, and took a seat on the edge of the wooden chair that had always been downstairs. His legs bounced in agitation as he scribbled notes in the spiral notebook he kept close at hand. He glanced at the bottle of prescription medication next to him on the side table. It mocked him. *Partake of me and you'll be all right*, it seemed to say. The voices echoing in his head caused his temples to pound and his eyes to blur, but he was having none of it. With an outburst of rage, he threw the bottle, and it smashed violently against the basement wall. He didn't need those drugs to be okay. In his mind, he was fine the way he was. When he needed to, he could control the impulsive, aggressive behavior he had been diagnosed with. The pills would cause him to lose his focus—his mission. He hadn't taken them for months, and right now he had another job to do.

Chapter 5

I arrived home just after seven o'clock and felt spent. The deli dinner I'd picked up—two slices of baked ham and a pint of German potato salad—would be fine, and I had no ambition to cook anyway.

A few minutes every night, I gave Polly and Porky some attention. I opened the cage and placed my finger under Polly's feet. She hopped on, and I lifted her out. Polly was my first lovebird, but after six months of watching her in the cage alone, I realized she needed a mate. That was where Porky came in. Today they thrived as a couple, and my guilt had passed. I cooed, petted her pretty aqua feathers, and gave her a little kiss on the head. I did the same with Porky. Lovebirds were easy pets and didn't require much maintenance. Plus they were far snugglier than goldfish. I filled the clear plastic water dish with fresh water and poured more birdseed in their cup.

My deli take-out dinner was wolfed down in no time as I sat at the antique oak claw-foot table my grandma had left me in her will. I always loved the table as a kid, and she remembered that before she passed away. My favorite TV cop series played in the background.

I put my empty plate in the sink and walked from room to room, looking at everything I could live without. With Lance pressuring me to get the house listed, I knew I had to get rid of a lot of things. He'd already taken what Cassie, his girlfriend, wanted. I was certain her small apartment in Richfield was getting cramped.

Buying a two-bedroom condo was my plan—it was really all I needed anyway. No yard maintenance either; I was looking for a place that had all of the yard work included in the HOA fees. I added that note to my list of requirements. With a little online research a few weeks back, I had found Melissa Mately—a friendly, engaging Realtor who was very ambitious. She had already done a walk-through of the house last week and given me tips on how to stage it for a quick sale. She was ready to list the house whenever I was. I told her I'd get back to her soon. I hadn't scheduled a visit to any condos yet, but procrastinating wasn't getting me anywhere—it had to be done. I pulled the card she had given me out of my wallet and dialed her number.

"Hello, Realty World, this is Melissa Mately speaking. How may I improve your day?"

"Hi, Melissa, it's Jade Monroe. I'm wondering if we can set up sometime Sunday to look at a few condos in North Bend."

"Jade, it's great to talk to you again, and yes, we absolutely can. Let me grab a piece of paper."

I waited for her to return to the phone as I studied my fingernails. I was months overdue for a manicure, but it would have to wait.

"Okay, I'm back. I have eight listings available. All I need are your general likes and dislikes, then we can narrow them down."

We went over what I was looking for and decided to tour four condos on Sunday afternoon. I felt better after hanging up. I was finally starting the process of moving forward.

I snuggled on the couch with two soft pillows, and a glass of red wine sat on the coffee table. I had all intentions of vegging out and relaxing in front of the TV. My buzzing phone woke me. I must have dozed off during a commercial. I looked at my cell phone screen—Amber was calling. My younger sister and I were close and usually talked every night before bed.

"Hey there, Sis." I sat up, rubbed my eyes, and squinted at the clock above the TV. It was already nine thirty.

"You have sleep voice," she said.

"Yeah, you busted me. Guess I dozed off for a bit. What's up?"

"We need to talk."

"Isn't that what we're doing?" I chuckled at my sister's nonsense and walked into the kitchen. I grabbed a glass out of the cabinet above the sink, filled it with water, and sat at the table.

"I can't take Bruce any longer. Mom turns a blind eye to his drinking problem. She says she doesn't want to get into it with him and needs to choose her battles. Meanwhile the creep leers at me, especially when he's had one too many."

"He's so disgusting. You are leer-worthy, though," I teased. Amber was a beautiful young woman with long brown hair and gold flecks in her hazel eyes. She had recently turned twenty-one.

"Jade, I'm serious. Can I move in with you? Lance is gone, so you have plenty of room. I promise I'll pitch in. It will make your life easier if I'm there. Plus I'll cook meals now and then and clean the house. I swear you won't regret it."

"I haven't said yes yet, and you know living here is temporary, even for me. The house is going to be sold soon, I hope. My plan was to buy a condo meant for one, and I'm actually going to start looking with real intent."

"Jade, I *do* have a job. I'll pay you rent, so that way you can afford something a little larger."

"It isn't about affordability. I have to think about it. We'll discuss it more on Saturday, face to face, okay?"

"Yeah, I guess."

"Good. I'm going to bed. Talk to you tomorrow." I hung up, shuffled down the hallway, and climbed into my bed.

Chapter 6

Sleep was hard to come by these last few days, and I woke up earlier than usual. One cup of coffee held me over while I showered and got dressed. My travel mug was filled with what remained in the pot, and I kissed the birds good morning and left.

I entered the bull pen and planted my rear in my chair—it was only seven fifteen. A vending machine bagel with cream cheese would be plenty until lunchtime, unless something distracted me from my noon meal. Jack walked in at quarter to eight. He slapped the doorframe and stuck his head in to say good morning. A jumbo cup of gas station coffee was in his hand—as usual. He said he was headed downstairs to talk to Dan and Kyle and to see if Doug had started Morris's autopsy.

"Let me know when Doug thinks Terrance can come in to ID the body," I said before he disappeared.

"Sure, no problem."

I went to our beverage station and the coffee bag felt suspiciously light, so I gave it a shake—empty.

"Damn it."

I was going to meet up with the guys downstairs anyway. Hopefully, if there was any coffee left in their pot, I could mooch a cup from them. When I entered, Jack, Kyle, and Dan were in the crime lab discussing the lack of forensic evidence at the scene. I got lucky—there was still some coffee. I poured myself a cup, tasted it, and decided it was okay. I'd get by. I tore open two powdered creamers and stirred them in, then joined the guys at the table in the center of the room.

"Trying to find forensic evidence at the site was pretty useless, huh?" I said.

Kyle shook his head and sighed. "That area is nothing but weeds and farm fields. Our only chance would have been tire tracks or something dropped from a pocket, but that was a bust. We found nothing other than deer crap and fox scat. No human tracks, gum wrappers, cigarette butts, or anything of the like."

"I doubt if this investigation is going to reveal anything in Washburn County. As far as what we actually have, it looks like the lake just happened to be the unfortunate dump spot," Dan said.

"Has anyone checked in with Doug yet?"

Jack answered, "Sorry, I forgot to tell you."

"Yeah, Doug is well under way with the autopsy. He should be able to give you an initial update before the end of the day. It isn't like we don't already know the cause of death, though," Dan said.

Jack and I headed back upstairs. I sat at my desk, again

paging through the jackets that Lindstrom had given us yesterday and thinking about what he had said. We didn't have much to work with, only hunches that came to light during the conversation with him. The killer, in his opinion, wasn't someone from their area. The MO was wrong. Thugs in the inner city would just shoot the victim and leave the body, not try to hide it at a lake in another county. The local gang members didn't fit the profile of someone who would go to the trouble of doing that. They liked to take credit for their actions and have rival gangs fear them. The perp was someone, and something, different, according to Lindstrom.

"Monroe, Steele, in my office, now, please."

Lieutenant Clark called us in and closed the door at our back.

"Have a seat."

We each sat in a blue guest chair facing his desk, waiting for the lecture to begin. His face scrunched into a frown, his forehead furrowed with deep lines as he looked over the file we had started on Morris King. Over the last two days, we hadn't accumulated much.

"Where's this case going? No leads at all?"

I spoke up first. "The dump site is clean. Clayton and four deputies scoured every inch of land in the general area and found nothing of value. Kyle and Dan didn't find any trace near the body, and Jack and I interviewed a number of the residents around the lake. Nobody saw anything unusual."

Jack added, "Billy pulled the cell phone records. We

matched Morris's most recent calls to a number of boys he runs with, but there was nothing out of place there. It looks like they talk all the time. The only call that stood out was an incoming he took at 1:05 a.m. Wednesday that lasted just a few seconds."

That appeared to pique the lieutenant's attention. "And?"

"And it came in from a burner phone. We can't track it."

"Damn it. Anything else?"

"The plan is to spend the day in Milwaukee trying to track down the four boys that were supposedly Morris's closest associates. We'll get their statements, establish alibis, find out if any of them were with Morris two nights ago, and see what shakes loose. I doubt if we're dealing with reputable people," I said. "Everything they tell us—if they talk to us at all—could be total fabrication. We have no idea who we're dealing with yet."

Jack told the lieutenant about the conversation we'd had with Detective Lindstrom and how he didn't think the killer was one of their locals.

"Okay, keep me posted throughout the day. Even though the media doesn't know the cause of death, they're still looking for information and calling here every few hours."

Doug caught up with Jack before we headed out. According to his initial exam, Morris appeared to be a relatively healthy young man, considering his lifestyle. He had suffered a broken wrist and several cracked ribs during his lifetime, but his organs looked normal and healthy. His last meal was fried chicken. The cause of death was the more than obvious gaping slit that extended from ear to ear across his neck. He bled out in a matter of minutes. Doug estimated the murder weapon to be a thin, long, and extremely sharp blade, strong enough to slice open Morris's throat in one pass and nearly sever his spinal cord. He guessed it to be a knife with at least an eight-inch blade. The man must have been taller, strong, and very quick to overtake Morris so easily, Doug had said.

"That's all I have for now. The tox report is going to take a few more days. Mr. King can come in and make the ID anytime today."

"Okay, thanks," I said, "I'll let him know."

I called Terrance King just before we left for Milwaukee and told him to come in. He'd have to check in first at the reception counter and ask for our county ME, Doug Irvin.

Jack and I headed out and climbed into the Crown Vic at ten o'clock. Thankfully there was nothing pressing we needed to address in our own county right now.

Jack merged onto the freeway heading south and set the cruise control.

"Amber asked if she could move in with me." I turned my head to catch Jack's expression as he drove.

"No shit? Why would a twenty-one-year-old college student studying behavioral sciences want to live with her older sister, the cop?"

I gave him a dirty look. "Because she loves me, but the real reason is she says Bruce grosses her out."

Jack laughed and gave me a wink. "Or maybe she wants you as her test subject. She can practice her shrinking on you, but in her defense, Bruce grosses me out too. What's he up to now that's giving her the creeps?"

"Who knows? She says he leers at her when he's had too much to drink. Apparently, Mom doesn't want to admit her choice of a third husband was her worst so far."

"Do you want me to rough him up?"

I laughed and knuckled Jack's arm. "Thanks for the offer. It would have been better if my parents had never divorced. Dad is such a great guy. I hope you'll have a chance to meet him someday. I just wish he didn't live so far away. He's due for a visit, though, and Amber could use some Dad time."

"Yep, I was at the family cottage in Hudson the last time your old man was in town. Well, if your dad is anything like the stories I've heard, he'd probably take Bruce out with one swipe. Tom Monroe—the living legend."

I grinned. "He is a tough one, that's for sure."

"What is he now… a captain?"

"Oh yeah."

"The San Bernardino Sheriff's Department, right?"

"That's right, and I'm really proud of my old man. He's one of the good guys. He taught me everything I know. My mom really screwed up when she let him go."

Chapter 7

I pulled up the addresses on my phone's GPS as Jack drove. We arrived at the first house, which was the residence of Kevin Bryant, at ten a.m. Not one house on the block looked any better than the next. They were all in shambles.

I patted Jack's shoulder. "I'm not looking forward to this. Glad we're here together, partner." We took the wooden steps up to the porch of the brown brick two story and rapped on the door. Several dogs barked from farther inside. "What's with the damn dogs around here?"

The door creaked, and a woman looking to be in her early forties peered out at us from the six-inch opening the chain lock allowed. From what we could see, she wore a threadbare green chenille bathrobe, and her hair was in disarray. She held a cigarette in her left hand. She leaned against the doorframe and looked us up and down.

"What do you want?" she asked. A sneer lifted the right side of her mouth.

We showed her our badges and introduced ourselves, saying we needed to speak with Kevin.

"I'm his mama, and Kev's not here."

"Ma'am, it's important that we speak to him. It's in reference to a friend of his, Morris King," I said.

"Haven't seen him."

She blew a puff of smoke in my face.

"Ma'am, Kevin isn't in trouble, but we do need to speak with him. Do you have any idea where he might be?" Jack asked.

"Look at the park by the hoops. Kev and his boys hang out there." She pointed down the street and slammed the door in our faces.

I placed our cards in her mailbox before we left.

Jack smirked as we headed back to the car. "Guess she has issues with the law. Let's check the park and see who we come up with. How lucky could we get if they're all together? We wouldn't have to hunt them down one by one."

"Yeah, don't hold your breath. I'm picturing a group of tight-lipped punks or a bunch of runners. Good thing I wore flats."

Jack parked the car in the lot and killed the engine. We exited and walked toward the basketball hoops while I scanned the surroundings. A large grassy area with picnic tables was directly to our right. Beyond that was a playground. Half a dozen kids were enjoying the warm day on the swings and monkey bars. Garbage cans were plentiful, but it appeared that the trash never made it quite that far. Four guys were shooting hoops, and four more were seated on the pavement off to the side of the court.

They smoked cigarettes and drank malt liquor from forty-ounce bottles even though it was barely after ten o'clock. All eyes were on us as we approached.

"Gentlemen," I said.

They snickered and hooted but stayed seated.

Jack took over, looking a touch more threatening than I did. He explained that nobody was in trouble and we were only looking for four guys to speak with. He called out Devon, Kev, Marshon, and James. Two of the boys shooting hoops turned toward us. The one with the ball bounced it continuously while sizing us up. The other pressed his hands deep into the front pockets of his baggy pants. I kept my eye on him.

"I'm Kev, and he's Marshon," the one with the basketball said as he pointed to the guy with his hands in his pockets, "but we don't talk to pigs unless we're under arrest. Are you arresting us all?"

The group laughed. Kev was posturing for his boys and trying to act tough. We weren't fazed and actually expected that type of behavior.

I approached Kev and stared him down. "I'm sure you're well acquainted with being arrested, but that isn't why we're here. We need information regarding Morris King. We've been told he hangs with you."

"Haven't seen him," Kev said. He lit a cigarette and glared at us. "Why should we help you? Why are you talking about Morris?"

"Because Morris is dead, and we need to find his killer. If you really are his friends, you'll help us."

Chatter erupted from everyone around the hoops.

"No way, man. Morris can't be dead," Marshon said. He shook his head and paced the court. Anger and frustration lit up his face.

"I'm afraid it's true. Now can we just have a few minutes of your time? Anything you say could be helpful in finding his killer. We need to know the last time any of you saw Morris and where. Who are his friends and did he have any enemies? We only need a few minutes," I said.

Marshon, Kev, and two other young men followed us to a picnic table and reluctantly sat down on the other side. I had my notepad ready, and Jack began asking the questions.

Marshon said that Morris's friends were all there and accounted for. They were the bunch at the basketball court.

"He didn't run with anyone but us. We keep each other safe. We're tight, ya know? And enemies, yeah, we got them, but this doesn't sound right to me. Anybody killing anybody around here would be mouthing off. I haven't heard anything."

"Do you have a few people in mind? Maybe somebody we can talk to?" Jack asked.

Kev looked at Marshon and waited for a nod. "Bobby James and LeJon Clyde come to mind. That's all we know. They live down by Center Street."

After we spent thirty-five minutes more of getting questions and answers, it appeared that Morris was dealing oxy and had a meeting set up late Tuesday night with someone named Dime. According to Marshon, Morris had dealt with him once in the past, but he didn't like him.

Apparently the Dime guy freaked Morris out, according to Marshon, but Morris met with him because the money was good.

"Freaked him out in what way?" Jack asked.

"Don't know—just sketchy because he wasn't one of us. Morris didn't know what to expect."

"Do you have any idea what time and where they were going to meet?" I asked. "Do any of you know Dime? Is he from the area?"

"Nah—don't know him, never laid eyes on the dude. I went home after midnight. Morris was still waiting, over there by the hoops." Kev pointed over his shoulder toward the basketball court. "But he did tell me he was packing a blade—just in case."

"He had a knife?" Jack stole a glance in my direction. "Was the park where they were going to meet?"

"Nah, don't think so. Some abandoned house, he said. That's all I know. Dime told Morris to come alone—didn't want to be seen by anybody."

"There's a lot of vacant houses in the area, aren't there?" I asked.

"Yep, sure is," Marshon said. "Man, he shouldn't have gone alone."

I nodded. "Okay, I guess that will do it." I looked over my notes. I didn't need anyone's addresses or phone numbers. I had everything already in their police record jackets. I passed out a handful of cards and thanked them for the information. I knew exactly where to go.

"Jack, do you think Morris was killed with his own

knife? He didn't have a knife or a sheath on his body. The killer may have seen it and thought Morris was going to double-cross him. He could have killed him right there to keep from being killed himself. And if he was there to buy oxy, then why didn't he take it with him?"

"You're right, the killing could have happened that way, but if this Dime character intended to kill Morris anyway, he would have brought his own weapon. The oxy—I have no idea. What we need to do is find the house they met at. It's very possible that could be our crime scene."

I stepped up my pace and reached the passenger side door before Jack got to the car. "What kind of name is Dime anyway? Is that some type of nickname referencing a dime bag of weed, him being into drugs and all? I mean, the guy *was* there to buy oxy, yet it doesn't make sense that he left it behind." I climbed into the passenger seat, pulled the belt across my torso, and clicked it. "Okay, head to the third district precinct again. We need to update the guys and find out what was discovered at the King residence. I bet you ten bucks they have jackets on these two guys"—I glanced at my notes—"Bobby James and LeJon Clyde. I think we should plan a search of the abandoned houses in the neighborhood too."

When we arrived at the precinct, Jack and I sat down with Lieutenant Colgate and told him what we'd learned from Morris's boys. I suggested searching the abandoned houses in the area. Some had to be well known as drug houses. The murder could have taken place in one of them. He agreed and said he would contact the Vacant Building

Registration Department. They held records of all the abandoned buildings within the city limits.

Lieutenant Colgate excused himself to make the call while we spoke to Aaron Davis from their forensic team. According to him, they had retrieved quite a bit of opiates and marijuana from the King residence. Five deputies and two forensic officers cleared the house. They hadn't found anything that would lead to a potential suspect—it was a dead end.

Lieutenant Colgate returned. "Okay, they can get us a list of every vacant residence in a ten-block grid, but they can't get to it until tomorrow. Let's reconvene then and decide how to proceed. Come on back after lunch. They said they'd have what we need by then."

"Okay, thanks, Lieutenant. See you tomorrow."

Jack and I got back in our car and headed to North Bend. We discussed the case the entire way. Working together as a joint effort, I was sure that between the Milwaukee PD and ourselves, we could solve the case and wrap it up. Morris King's killer would be brought to justice soon.

We hit the city limits, and Jack slowed the car down. "Got plans for tonight?" he asked.

"Of course, it's my yoga night. Wanna join me? There's plenty of time. It doesn't start until seven forty-five."

Jack smirked. "Could you see me in yoga pants doing those stupid moves?"

"Hey, they aren't stupid. Yoga gives me a little peace in this messed-up world, plus it keeps me limber. And yeah, I could see you in those tight little spandex pants, I'm guessing pink ones."

He laughed. "I think I'll stick to being a gym rat. I have a manly image to uphold, you know."

Chapter 8

Dime turned onto her street and parked a half block from her house. She lived in a decent residential neighborhood filled with ten-year-old cookie-cutter subdivision houses. Hers was a tan ranch-style home with dark green shutters. The lower part of the facade was styled with a stacked-stone veneer.

From where he had positioned his Jeep under a maple tree along the curb, he had a perfect view of the driveway. The tree kept his identity and most of the vehicle hidden from view. He waited for her to arrive home. Tonight would be his first night of surveillance. He'd study her every move and the times she came and went. The thought made him rub his hands together in anticipation. She annoyed him, and his anger toward her was increasing. The spiral notebook sat on the console beside him. He picked it up and jotted down the date and her name, then waited some more.

Headlights approached, and a car slowed—it was her. She pulled into the driveway, stopped without parking in the garage, and exited. A double beep and flashing headlights seemed to assure her the car was secure as she walked up the sidewalk. She unlocked the dead bolt and entered the house through the front door.

I guess you aren't staying in tonight, are you, bitch? Let's find out where you're off to. He pressed the button on the side of his watch to check the time. The face became illuminated in a light aqua color so he could read the hour and minute hands. He wrote down the time she had arrived home and waited for another thirty minutes while he drank a can of beer.

The porch light flashed on and caught his attention. She walked out and climbed into her car. He jotted down seven thirty in his notebook. Once she backed out of the driveway and was safely a block ahead, he started his vehicle and pulled out slowly from his obscured position. He clicked on his headlights as he followed.

She drove out of her subdivision and headed toward downtown North Bend, only a few minutes away. At the intersection of Main and Washington Street, she sat at a red light, apparently waiting for the green turn arrow. After the light changed, she turned west on Washington. He was back several car lengths. With his Jeep raised higher due to the big tires and suspension, he was able to see her car ahead of him, and it was first in line to turn.

Go, go, go, damn it. I have to catch the turn signal, or I'll lose her. He beeped his horn at the car directly in front of him. The driver, a young woman, appeared to be talking to somebody in the backseat, ignoring the green arrow. She looked at Dime through her back window, flipped him the bird, and then continued on. The object of his obsession had already turned left, but he made it through the light just as it went from yellow to red. He caught a glimpse of her Mustang again when her brake lights lit up and the blinker flickered. She turned right into the strip mall two blocks up. He drove by slowly and turned in at the second driveway to watch from a distance. The twenty-year-old strip mall held eight businesses. The majority were nine-to-five establishments, but three of them were still open. Pegasus Greek Diner, Yoga by Elise, and a discount store were brightly lit. He counted over twenty cars in the parking lot. He didn't stand out as he inched his Jeep closer to her vehicle. She seemed to be preoccupied, staring down at her cell phone. He had the perfect view of her through the windows of the parked cars between them. Parked two rows back and three vehicles to her left, he watched as she exited the car and pulled several items out of the backseat. She entered the yoga studio.

The sign above the row of windows flickered in pink neon outlined in purple. To him it looked cheap and hideous. *Yoga by Elise, huh? I know one thing about you, Elise, you have no taste. Let's find out more.* He Googled the studio and read her biography. Elise had opened the business in 2005. She held three daytime classes and three evening classes every week. A longtime resident of North Bend, she was happily married with two kids under ten. Her favorite pastimes, other than teaching yoga, were gardening and bicycling. *You sound as boring as hell. We need to liven things up. I'll see what I can do about that.*

He had a perfect view of everyone inside the studio, getting ready for their class. Young moms chatted among themselves as they placed their yoga mats on the floor and got into position. The teacher stood in front, facing the class and the floor-to-ceiling windows that spanned the length of the studio. The instructor was definitely Elise. She looked just like her biography photo. A blond, bubbly looking thirtysomething, she had a topknot ponytail that flopped around her head as she led the class through its yoga maneuvers. She already annoyed him. He checked the time and wrote it down. Yoga class—seven forty-five, Thursday night.

The class appeared to wrap up at nine p.m. when everyone gathered their mats and headed toward the door.

He slinked down in his seat as the group of women exited. Laughter and chatter surrounded him as they made their way to their cars, some right next to his. He remained behind as the lot emptied, and the interior lights finally went out inside the studio. He watched Elise exit the building, lock the door, and head to a white Malibu sedan near the entrance at nine fifteen.

That night, she would skate by. He only wanted to follow her home and pick out the darkest spot along the route to end her life soon.

Chapter 9

"Did Mr. King come in yesterday and ID Morris's body?" Lieutenant Clark asked as he leaned against his office door.

I looked up from my desk and answered, "Yes, sir. Doug said he came in, made the ID, and signed off on the paperwork."

"Good. What time are you two heading back to Milwaukee?"

"Lieutenant Colgate asked us to come back this afternoon. I guess the Vacant Building Registration Department won't have the paperwork ready until then. The PD is going to pull the jackets for Bobby James and LeJon Clyde too."

"That's good. Hopefully this case can be solved, and the sooner the better. Even though Morris was a criminal himself, he certainly didn't deserve that brutality. Where's Jack?"

"He had a dentist appointment this morning. Guess it's hard to get in these days. He didn't want to change his appointment again."

"That's fine. Keep me posted throughout the day."

Jack got in at ten thirty. The left side of his face was frozen so he drank his vending machine soda through a straw to avoid drooling.

"How am I going to eat lunch?" he asked, complaining.

"You'll be fine in an hour or so. We'll hit a drive-through before we get to the precinct in Milwaukee. By then, your mouth won't be numb anymore."

Jack's Novocain wore off by noon. He grabbed a burger at a fast-food joint right off the freeway. I ordered a large Coke.

We arrived at the third district precinct just after one p.m. and were escorted to Lieutenant Colgate's desk. He stood and shook our hands. According to the lieutenant, the home listings and addresses had been faxed over just minutes earlier. He called a deputy in the records department to bring them up.

"We should have the listings in a few minutes," he said.

He excused himself to pull the jackets for Bobby James and LeJon Clyde. He returned five minutes later with the folders in hand. He slid them across his desk for us to page through.

"Wow, these guys are no joke. Why aren't they in prison?" I asked.

"They've both done time, but eventually they get out and go about committing more crimes. It isn't long before they're back in again. It's like a revolving door with them."

"Do you think they're good for a murder like this?" Jack asked. He ran his hand through his hair as we both waited for a response.

"Murder, yes, but dumping a body an hour away, not so much. Neither of those boys have probably left Milwaukee county in their life, unless it was because they were incarcerated somewhere else."

"Okay, thanks for the insight. We'll check out their alibis anyway just to be sure."

A female deputy entered the bull pen and handed the faxed vacant-house listings to the lieutenant.

"Come on. Follow me," he said. "There's more room in the cafeteria."

He led the way, and over a table in the lunchroom, he laid out the paperwork and circled all the vacant houses within a ten-block radius.

"Sergeant Monroe, just as a heads-up, these are the houses that have been reported as vacant by owners who walked away due to foreclosures and the like. There's probably a good twenty-five percent more that haven't been reported. They're the ones that have just been abandoned with everything left behind. They're the perfect place for homeless, drug dealers, and so on. You need to be careful. This search can be a daunting task for the two of you, and you could run into trouble at any of these places. Criminal activity is ongoing and brisk in this area."

"Apparently so," I agreed. "How many houses did you circle?"

"Twenty-seven, and there are likely ten more that weren't recorded. As a professional courtesy and safety measure from department to department, I can spare four officers for the afternoon. I'd prefer it if each of you went with one of our fellas rather than together or alone. We know how crime works around here and how these criminals think. They're fast and sketchy, and many of them are armed and on drugs."

I looked at Jack and nodded. "Let's do it. We're ready whenever your officers are. We'll track down the boys later."

"Okay, let's section these streets off on this list and divide up the properties," Lieutenant Colgate said. He called in the officers that would assist us, introduced us, and explained the situation.

I added, "We're looking for blood and any obvious trace evidence for now, nothing more. If this gruesome murder took place in any of these houses on the ten-block grid, it will definitely stand out. The victim's throat was slashed to the point of almost severing his spinal cord. There will be a mess. Let's partner up and roll."

We divided up, joined the officers in their squad cars, and headed out. With the support we now had and the number of houses we had to search, we could feasibly be done with the ten-block quadrant in a few hours. If we didn't find what we were looking for, we'd have to regroup and come up with a different plan.

The officer I was searching with was John Tyler, in his fifth year at the police department. He was an ex-Marine and had served two tours in Afghanistan. He seemed friendly and had mentioned he was newly married with a six-month-old daughter named Lilly.

We cleared the first house. Aside from it being a dilapidated mess, nothing else stood out. A few blocks later, we entered the second. The house stunk and was littered with drug paraphernalia, soiled blankets, rotting food, cigarette butts, and empty beer cans and bottles.

"This place is hot—looks like the druggies are still using it," John said. "We should take our time and see if there's anything relevant to the case here."

I nodded.

We searched through clothes and garbage and found nothing besides the obvious and an infestation of cockroaches scurrying about. I wrote down the address and the contents of the building in case we needed to return. We carried on. John radioed to the other officers—nothing yet.

I checked the time after hearing my stomach growl. I hadn't eaten since before I left my house that morning. My watch showed it was closing in on two thirty, but we continued on.

We entered a two-story brick house with a blue plastic tarp covering part of the roof. Most likely a large hole was under that tarp. I'd been told that even in the city, raccoons could get in through openings and cause a lot of damage. All the upstairs windows had been boarded. We entered through the front door. The scent of moldy walls and carpet hit me as soon as we walked in, and it stung my nostrils. I covered my nose with the back of my left hand as we walked through the front rooms. Voices coming from the back of the house caused me to draw my service weapon from my shoulder holster. John drew his too. He nodded ahead to the room that was probably the kitchen. I acknowledged him and walked slowly in that direction. A closed wooden swinging door separated us from the voices on the other side. John took the lead as we approached. He leaned against the wall, his gun pointed at the doorway, and nodded. I readied myself, and with a sharp kick to the door, it flew open and smacked the wall behind it. Two black males stood at the kitchen counter, one counting money, the other with what looked like several ounces of weed.

John blocked their exit to the back door, and I covered the door we had just broken through. We ordered them to the floor and hooked them up. John called it in, and another squad picked them up. We had more pressing things to do.

We cleared the house and headed out. As we walked back to his cruiser, John's radio squawked, and the officer Jack had paired up with said they had found something. They gave us the address, only seven blocks away, and we took off, red and blues lit and the siren singing.

Police tape was already going up to cordon off the property's perimeter when we arrived. The last squad car that was out with us pulled up to the curb behind our cruiser.

"What have we got?" I asked as I stepped out of the car.

Jack's brow furrowed when he looked at me. "Over here, Jade. We found a bloody mess inside."

I stepped into the doorway at the back of the house and took in the sight. "This could be our scene," I said. I ran my fingers through my hair. The sight in front of us told a violent, vicious story. Someone had met their death in that run-down room. We stayed near the door we entered, so as not to destroy possible evidence, and took in the scene. We stared at the massive amounts of dried blood that had sprayed forward and hit the cabinets, then continued down to pool at the counter. A five-foot wide area of blood stained the floor. I mentally tried to recreate how the murder took place. I snapped a few pictures with my cell phone, using the flash. We needed more light in the room, and the forensic team, immediately. With no electricity in the house, we might miss out on collecting some precious evidence. Even in the afternoon hours, the room was dimly lit.

"Everyone, glove up. Let's get these doors and windows open to get more light in here," John said. He called out for an officer to radio the station. We needed a generator, lights, and the forensic team, ASAP. "How do you want to handle this, Sergeant?" he asked me. "Washburn County has the body, and we have the possible crime scene."

I stepped outside to think and John followed close behind. "Okay, John, let's call your lieutenant and see what he wants to do. Jack, call Lieutenant Clark and give him the news. We don't know yet if this blood belongs to Morris King. Only a DNA match is going to tell us that. Get Doug on the horn. Have him fax over everything he has on Morris so far to the third district's crime lab. I'm pretty sure Morris's blood profile is already done. To confirm this as our actual crime scene, we'll need a definite match from a test sample here at the house."

A black car pulled up to the curb. Lieutenant Colgate and Detective Lindstrom stepped out. They approached us as we waited outside on the driveway for the forensic team to arrive.

"Sergeant Monroe, Detective Steele." Lindstrom nodded at us and shook our hands. "Guess we should take a peek. Forensics should be here in a few minutes. They had to load up a generator and lights in the van."

Bill Lindstrom and the lieutenant excused themselves and walked up several steps to look into the kitchen. I heard muffled cursing coming from one of them. They came back out a few minutes later, both shaking their heads.

Lieutenant Colgate addressed us after he hung up from a call. "Sorry for the interruption. Gruesome scene, that's for sure. I just spoke to the power company. They're going to try to work with us to get electricity up and running again if they can. This house has been in shambles and vacant for over two years. We're not quite sure if the wiring is still safe and viable. Animals often take over vacant houses and chew on things. The power company will check, and hopefully they can restore electricity, even if it's temporary, while we work on this investigation."

We turned to hear another vehicle pull up and stop. The forensics van parked, and the team got out with their gear. Lieutenant Colgate addressed a few officers, asking them to lend a hand getting the generator out of the back and setting up with the portable lights.

Detective Lindstrom spoke up. "I guess we should clear the area and let the team do what they do best. Let's head back to the precinct and figure out how to go forward if the blood evidence does indeed belong to Morris King."

We followed Lieutenant Colgate and Detective Lindstrom back to the police station and gathered in the lieutenant's office. With the door closed behind us, we pulled up the guest chairs and discussed what the next step would be.

"The city of Milwaukee has a lot of resources, Sergeant Monroe," Lieutenant Colgate said. "We don't want to spread your local department too thin. The drive to Milwaukee every day to work this case would take you away from your own duties in Washburn County." He pulled the coffee carafe from the brew station and filled our cups.

"I appreciate the concern." I crossed my right leg over my left knee and reached for my coffee cup. "What do you have in mind?"

"If the blood in the house on Meinike Avenue comes up as a match to Morris's, well, it's a pretty good guess that we've found our crime scene. We can work it from there. He lived in Milwaukee. The crime, if the blood is a match, happened in Milwaukee. The only thing we're missing is Morris's body. His uncle intends to handle the funeral arrangements?"

"Yes, he said he would," Jack responded.

"I'll agree to release Morris's body to you if the blood is a match. Of course, we'll need approval from higher up. If your forensic team finds any trace evidence that might help us in our own county, we'll need it. Also, as a professional courtesy, we'd like a phone call if you solve the case and actually apprehend Morris's killer," I said.

"You got it, Sergeant. Our boys in the crime lab should

be able to tell us if it's a definitive match first thing in the morning, especially with Morris's DNA already on file."

"Then I guess that should wrap it up on our end for now. Are your guys going to conduct the interviews with Bobby James and LeJon Clyde?"

"Yep, I'll get a couple of detectives on it right away," Lieutenant Colgate said.

Detective Lindstrom spoke up again. "I'll do it. I'm familiar with them already. I'll let you know how the interview goes."

"Thanks. Let's catch up tomorrow," I said.

Jack and I stood, shook hands, and left. I looked at the clock in the car—six o'clock. I suggested stopping on our way back to grab a bite to eat.

Jack found a decent restaurant right off the freeway, and he pulled in. We exited the car and seated ourselves in a booth. We ordered our much-needed meals and sat back, both of us exhaling a deep sigh. It had been a long day. The waitress brought over a carafe of coffee and placed it on our table, smiled, and told us our orders should be up in just a few minutes.

"So how do you feel about handing off Morris's case?" Jack poured creamer in his coffee, stirred it, and passed the small stainless steel container over to me.

"It's the sensible thing to do if the blood in the house is actually his. If they do find relevant trace, we're already working the case as a joint effort anyway."

"Yeah, I guess. I just hope this perp is caught quickly. Someone that vicious needs to be taken off the streets as soon as possible."

Chapter 10

He sat in the basement, going over his notes from yesterday, a beer on the side table. Following Elise Adams home last night took him through town for several miles, then three miles of country roads before ending in a rural subdivision. He needed to avoid cameras and traffic if he was going to be successful. The best place to take her out would be after she turned left on Country-Aire Road. There was nothing but darkness on that two-mile stretch. He remembered seeing the sign for Glacier Hills County Park about a mile down that quiet road, void of houses. It would work out perfectly. Elise had a yoga class until nine, and he would be waiting for her afterward. The fun would happen on her drive home.

It looks like we're going to get to know each other up close and personal tonight, Elise. I'm looking forward to it. He chuckled, went upstairs, and clicked off the basement light, then made himself dinner. He had three hours to kill before showtime.

Later as he drove to North Bend, he decided to watch

for her from the Country Inn parking lot several blocks from the yoga studio. She had to pass the hotel to go home, and he knew the strip mall had camera surveillance. Her white Malibu would be easy to see, even at night. The city streetlights continued on for a mile beyond the hotel before rural darkness took over. The hotel had cameras too, but he'd already decided where to park. The cameras faced the main parking lot and hotel lobby. He'd park along the driveway at the back exit. The spot was perfect. He'd have access to the street and a good view of Elise when she drove by. His vehicle wouldn't be on camera either.

At 9:27, she appeared. She waited third in line at the red light in front of the hotel. He quickly jotted down the time, pulled the black hoodie up to conceal his face, then started his car and pulled out. He didn't have to follow so closely this time—he knew her route. He'd pull her over on Country-Aire Road.

The black gloves and his kill bag sat on the passenger seat. He would use his own tools only if absolutely necessary. He'd prefer to use her yoga gear—a fitting end, in a way—and nothing to tie him to the crime.

He saw her left blinker flash—the time was near, and his heart was racing. He'd wait until he was close to the park entrance to make his move, about halfway down that eerily dark road. She was about four car lengths ahead of him when it was time to act. He sped up, swerved around her Malibu, and slammed on his brakes in the center of the road, forcing her to stop. His plan was in motion, and within a split second, he was at the driver's side window.

"Ma'am, help me, help me. Please, I need a cell phone. My wife is having a seizure in the car. I'm lost."

She stared, wide eyed and hesitant, before lowering her window.

Wrong move, Elise. Hasn't anyone ever told you not to stop on dark, deserted roads for a stranger? You fool.

With his leather-gloved hand balled in a tight fist, he reached through the window, punched her face as hard as he could, and knocked her out. He looked down the road both ways—no headlights. This task needed to be completed quickly and efficiently. With the driver's door open, he shoved her across the console to the passenger seat and slid in. He adjusted the driver's seat and drove the Malibu in through the park entrance, past the empty guard shack, and to the farthest end of the parking lot. He looked across the seat—she was still out. The dim interior light illuminated the shifter settings. He jerked the knob to Park, turned off the car, and got out. The night was quiet and dark with nobody around. He had Elise all to himself. Dime walked around to the passenger side and opened the door. In an instant, she coiled her legs and kicked him in the face. Dime staggered back.

"Now you're going to pay, you bitch."

He grabbed her ankles as she screamed and kicked, but another hard punch to the face silenced her. He checked the contents of her yoga bag and found exactly what he needed. Stretch cords, a mat, and a pair of black tights would do the trick. He pulled the headlamp out of his pocket and secured it around his head, then grasped each of her ankles and yanked her out of the car. Her head hit the doorsill with a loud thump, then he pulled her into the darkness. Dime trudged through a swampy area loaded with cattails, over the top of a ridge, and back down into a gully before releasing her legs and letting them drop to the ground. He unrolled the mat that was jammed into the front of his zipped jacket and spread it out, then took in his surroundings. A thick stand of trees and a lot of underbrush covered the ground in this secluded area. The location was perfect.

He flopped her unconscious body onto the mat facedown and hog-tied her hands and feet behind her back with the stretch cords, then moved on to the tights. With the tights wrapped twice around her neck and his knee on her back for leverage, he pulled them toward him. Gurgles sounded from deep within her throat, and her body jerked in protest until the life was choked out of her, and she was dead. He released his grip, and her body fell forward with a thud. Dime covered her corpse with twigs, leaves, and branches he scoured from the area. He checked the time— 9:55. Taking a different route back to her car would be smart, and there wouldn't be noticeable disturbances in the ground cover. He didn't want to make the cops' job too easy for them.

At her car, he pulled her cell phone and wallet from the yoga bag, removed the battery from the phone, and left her keys in the ignition. A token clue was placed on the hood of her car.

The short jog to his Jeep took only three minutes. He

started the engine, made a U-turn in the park entrance, and headed to his house twenty minutes away. He looked forward to morning and hoped there would be something on the local news about a missing yoga instructor.

Dime checked his face in the bathroom mirror when he got home and saw a noticeable knot on his forehead from her kick. Luckily she was wearing only tennis shoes. He applied ice and went downstairs to drink a beer. Elise's phone and wallet went behind the bookcase with Morris's belongings. Dime climbed the stairs, turned off the basement light, and got ready for bed.

As he reached to turn out the bedroom table lamp, the voices spoke to him again. *See what she made you do. It's all her fault, as usual, the bitch.*

Chapter 11

I entered the bull pen with a cup of coffee from Pit-Stop. I figured it wouldn't hurt to try it. Jack was a fan. A bag of a dozen assorted doughnuts would offer a good start to the morning too. I'd be generous and share.

I'd planned to work for a few hours, considering it was Saturday. Half days were meant for catching up if there was something pressing and clearing paperwork off my desk if there wasn't. I planned to follow up with the guys from the third district precinct and see if they got a blood match. Maybe soon we'd be able to release Morris's body to his uncle so he could arrange a proper burial. If the DNA from the crime scene matched, and there was no other usable forensic evidence for us, we could wrap everything up on our end and have Morris's body transported to Milwaukee. Detective Lindstrom might have some information about his interview with LeJon and Bobby too, if he found them.

I'd work until noon then go home and begin sorting through things I wanted to get rid of. I'd promised Amber we'd talk about living arrangements. I hadn't given it any thought at all since she mentioned it. I wrote myself a note to call Melissa Mately again to confirm our appointment to look at condos tomorrow. It would be fun, and Amber would love to tag along. I was tired of Lance's calls and was ready to get on with my life. He wasn't coming back. I'd start going through things seriously—no more procrastinating.

Jack walked in with coffee from Pit-Stop too.

"You must have just missed me," I said. "This cup of mud isn't too bad."

"You like?" He lifted his jumbo cup and slurped it from the opening in the plastic lid.

"Yeah, I think it might grow on me, but I could never drink as much as you do. I'd have serious heartburn. Here, check out the doughnuts I bought. Help yourself." I laughed when he dove for the unopened bag. He would get first dibs. The lieutenant, Clayton, anybody else that happened by, and I would enjoy whatever was left.

The phone rang on Jack's desk. "Washburn County Sheriff's Department, Detective Jack Steele speaking. Yes, uh-huh. Okay, sir, that's correct. Just turn left on Schmidt Road. We're right behind the courthouse. Two-story tan building, you can't miss it. Yep, see you in a half hour."

"Now what's going on?" I asked as I leaned my chair back and stretched. I had hoped for a quiet morning.

Jack grabbed the notes he had just scribbled down and took a seat on one of my guest chairs. "Isn't this the name of your yoga instructor?"

"What?" I sat up quickly, and my body involuntarily stiffened. "Let me see." I grabbed his notepad and read the name, *Elise Adams*. "Oh no. Her husband says she didn't come home last night?"

"Yeah, he's on his way in, should be here in a half hour. He's dropping their kids off at the grandparents' house first."

"I'll give the lieutenant a heads-up. We can't file a missing person's report yet, though. It's too early."

Jack nodded.

The loud buzz of the security door between the bull pen and the reception counter made me look up from my desk. Perry Adams was escorted in at nine fifteen by Jan Seymore, one of the desk deputies that rotated between dispatch and the reception counter. Mr. Adams's eyes were visibly red and swollen. Jack and I stood and introduced ourselves when he walked in.

I pointed to a guest chair at my desk. "Mr. Adams, please take a seat. How do you take your coffee?"

"Black, please."

"May we call you Perry?"

"Sure, that's fine."

"Okay, start from the beginning. I want to tell you up front that I attend your wife's evening yoga classes. Elise is a wonderful woman."

"Then you were there last night?" he asked, hope filling his eyes.

"No, sorry, I went to Thursday night's class. What can you tell us, Perry?"

"Nothing out of the ordinary. She called at nine fifteen. Class just ended, and she was packing up. She wanted to know if we had enough milk for the kids' breakfast cereal. I checked and said we had plenty. That was it." He paused to compose himself and wipe a tear that rolled down his cheek. "Our kids were already tucked into bed and sleeping. I went to bed myself and clicked on the TV. I intended to wait up for her to get home, but I must have fallen asleep."

"How long does it usually take Elise to get home from the yoga studio if she doesn't stop anywhere?" Jack asked as he flipped the page in his notepad.

Perry rubbed his forehead as he thought. "I don't know, twenty minutes, I guess."

"So what happened when you woke up earlier?" I asked.

"The kids ran into our bedroom, wondering where breakfast was, around seven o'clock. I looked to Elise's side of the bed, and it hadn't been slept in. I knew right away something was wrong."

Clayton was thoughtful enough to grab the carafe and fill our coffee cups. I nodded a thank-you. "Go ahead," I said.

"I ran downstairs and searched the house. I called out her name, but she didn't answer. That's when I opened the garage door and saw her side of the garage was empty. I started calling her cell phone right away, but it went straight to voice mail like it was turned off."

"What time was that?"

"Um… I don't know… around seven fifteen, I guess."

"How many times did you try her phone?"

"Six or ten… I don't remember. A lot."

Jack glanced at his notes. "You called here and spoke to me at 8:05."

"Yeah, that sounds right. Now what? We have to find her. You'll start searching, right? Elise doesn't do this type of thing. She's a responsible woman and a good mom."

Jack flipped the page in his notepad again. "We need to know the make and model of your wife's car and the route she takes home. A person has to be gone for twenty-four hours before we can file an official missing person's report, but we can do some looking around. We'll have a few deputies check her usual route home. Would you mind drawing us a map from the yoga studio to your house with the street names she takes? Maybe she just broke down somewhere."

"Sure, but that wouldn't explain why she didn't call home or answer her cell."

I handed Perry a sheet of printer paper so he could get started. I sensed Elise was in some kind of trouble, but saying she could have had car problems and keeping him busy might relieve his anxiety for the time being.

"Clayton."

"Yeah, Sergeant."

"Head to the strip mall and check every business that has camera surveillance facing the parking lot. I want to see Elise get into her car and leave. We may be able to get other footage along her route home, if that's indeed where she was heading."

"What is that supposed to mean?" Perry asked indignantly.

I put my hand up as if to pump the brakes. "Give me just a second, Perry. Clayton, get video copies back here from every angle of the parking lot. Round up Billy and Todd on your way and get them in here to go over the footage. If we're going to do this by her last known whereabouts, then the strip mall belongs to the city. They may want to take the lead. We'll take the city limits out into the county jurisdiction, where their residence is, if we have to. I'm fine with that. Either way, call the police department and give them a heads-up. We aren't going to make this an active case yet unless something looks suspicious on the video feed."

"Got it, boss."

"Okay, Perry, what year, make, model, and color is Elise's car?"

"It's a white 2014 Chevy Malibu sedan. I can't think of the plate number right now, I'm too frazzled."

"Jack, can you pull up her DMV records and get the tag number?"

"Yep, no problem." He had his pen ready to write it down.

"How's the marriage, Perry? Anything hinky going on, like affairs, dishonesty, or financial problems? Have you fought recently?"

He buried his face in his hands. "No, of course not! Our marriage is perfect. We have two great kids. I love my wife, Sergeant Monroe. We love each other."

I glanced at Jack and gave him a concerned look. Perry finished the map of the route Elise usually took home and handed it to me. I excused myself and went out front to talk to dispatch.

"Jan, I need you to get this out." I handed her the sheet of paper.

She put on her reading glasses and looked it over.

"I want you to have a few deputies check out this route. Call North Bend Police Department and have someone meet Clayton at the strip mall. We're looking for a white 2014 Malibu sedan. Get the tag number from Jack. He's checking on it right now. The car could be broken down along the road or possibly in a parking lot at a hotel, restaurant, or business. Run the gamut. Get some eyes out there and keep me posted. It isn't officially a missing person's case yet, but with the crap that went down earlier in the week, I'd rather be safe than sorry."

Chapter 12

By ten o'clock, Clayton had checked back in. He and Detective Don Miller from the police department looked over several tapes from Pegasus Greek Diner next door to the yoga studio. Nothing appeared unusual or suspicious. The video time stamp showed Elise climbing into her car at 9:17. By the time she exited the parking lot, six empty cars were in front of the restaurant, and another had just driven away. Clayton said the videos showed her pulling out of the parking lot in the direction she would take to go home. No other car followed hers. They viewed several tapes from different angles of the parking lot, including the back lot where the Dumpsters were located, but nothing seemed amiss.

"The business owners made us several video copies, Jade. They gave me and the police department a stick to review the footage on our own. I'm going to take it down to tech. If anyone can catch something we didn't see, it's Todd and Billy. They're the best when it comes to fine details."

"Okay, go ahead and get them downstairs. Get me a list

of all the businesses along her route home that have camera surveillance. I want to see her car pass by every one of them until there aren't any more businesses. Let the city boys know that too," I said.

"I'm on it, boss."

I entered the small cafeteria where Perry sat alone. I took a seat next to him.

"Can I get you something from the vending machine?"

"No, thanks. Sergeant Monroe, I saw the article in the newspaper a few days ago about the man who was found at Cedar Lake. He was murdered, wasn't he?"

"Perry, it's an ongoing investigation. I'm not at liberty to discuss it with you. You read what the media wrote just like everyone else."

"What if—"

"Let's hold on for a bit," I interrupted. "When was the last time you tried calling Elise?"

"Five minutes ago. Still goes directly to voice mail."

I felt the phone vibrate in my pocket. "Excuse me for a second." I walked over to the row of vending machines at the end of the cafeteria and checked the text. Lieutenant Clark wanted me in his office immediately.

"Perry, I'll be right back. Why don't you make a call to your folks? Talk to your kids, reassure them. Sit tight."

"Yeah, okay."

I headed back through the bull pen. Jack got up and was right on my heels.

"The lieutenant texted you too?"

"Yep."

I rapped on the door, and he waved us in.

"Close the door, Jade. Sit down."

"What's up, Lieutenant?"

"I just got a call from the park patrol out at Glacier Hills. He recognized the white Malibu he heard about on his police scanner. It's sitting vacant at the farthest end of the parking lot. He felt the hood—the engine was cold. He said a lone dime sat on the hood. Round up everyone and get out there now."

"Shit. Morris King had a dime in his pocket, nothing else. Boss, that sounds like a calling card to me. The person Morris met up with that night calls himself Dime."

"I know, Jade. We'll go over all of that again after we see what's going on in the park. Right now, we have to move."

"What do you want me to do with Perry?"

"Have Billings sit on him while we check the area. If we find Elise's body, the husband stays for interrogation, even if he isn't our main suspect. Right now, we don't have anyone else. Get Kyle and Dan out there right away. Have somebody call Doug and Jason. If we find a body, they're going to be working today too. It's not sounding good. Let's go."

My cell phone buzzed as Jack and I headed to one of the cruisers. Amber was texting me, wanting to know if she could come over. She wasn't scheduled to work until six o'clock. We could have a girl's day, do lunch, and discuss the living arrangements. I sent a quick message to her.

Sorry, Sis, I have an emergency. I'll get back to you as soon as I can.

I jammed the phone into my pocket and zipped it up. Jack flipped on the red and blues as he squealed out of the parking lot and headed west.

We arrived at Glacier Hills County Park in less than ten minutes. Four patrol cruisers, Clayton, and the forensic team arrived ahead of us and were already in the parking lot.

"Hear or see anything?" I asked as we approached.

"We were waiting for you, Sergeant," one of the patrol officers said.

"Did anyone talk to the guy from park security?"

Clayton responded, "I got his statement. He said he only touched the hood of the car with the back of his hand, nothing else."

"Okay, let's spread out. This is a big park. I want to take a quick look at the vehicle first." I pointed ahead at the expanse in front of us. "You guys start searching that meadow. We're looking for a thirtyish blond woman, shorter than me. She'll likely be wearing workout clothes. Let's move."

Kyle and Dan were already at the Malibu, doing a quick once-over to see if anything looked suspicious. Goose bumps rose on my arms. I felt certain we were looking at a crime scene. I didn't view Elise as somebody that would wander off for an overnight hike in the park, plus there was that damn dime. Jack and I walked over and joined Kyle and Dan. I leaned over the hood and felt it with my gloved hand—stone cold. The dime sat about a foot back, dead center where it wouldn't be overlooked. Kyle snapped a few pictures.

"Anyone take a peek inside?"

"We've only looked through the windows—haven't tried the doors yet. The yoga bag in the backseat looks like it's been rifled through. The doors are unlocked, and the keys are still in the ignition."

"Damn… that isn't a good sign. Who would wander off and leave their keys in the ignition with the doors unlocked? Kyle, did you take any pictures through the windows?"

"Yep, all done. Let's open her up."

When Dan opened the driver's side door, I immediately noticed that something was off. I only had a minute to process what I was thinking. The search was more important right now. We had people spread out in the meadow to our west, and Jack and I were heading into the woods in a few minutes.

"Hang on a second here. Jack, how tall are you?"

"Just over six foot."

We both looked at the seat position. I knew Elise was shorter than me. I climbed in and sat. My feet didn't reach the gas or brake.

"Jack, have a seat."

He climbed in after I stepped out. His feet reached the pedals perfectly.

"Okay, we know she didn't drive this car back here herself. How tall did Perry look to you?"

Jack rubbed his chin. "Probably your height, five foot eight or so. He isn't a tall man."

"Yeah, I thought the same thing. Okay, let's head out. Guys, get pictures of that seat position and do your usual onsite routine. Photograph the surroundings before the car is moved, then get the flatbed out here. This vehicle is going back to the evidence garage with us. Has Doug been called?"

"He's on call and waiting for us to notify him if necessary," Kyle said.

I saw the lieutenant pull in and park his Crown Vic.

"Clayton, update the boss. Tell him we're heading into the woods."

Chapter 13

"How do you want to proceed?" Jack asked as we stared at the expanse of heavy woods ahead.

I'd been to Glacier Hills many times. Lance and I used to hike quite a bit, and I knew the park was well over one hundred acres. There looked to be at least fifty acres of dense forest with hiking and snowmobile trails in front of us. People used the meadow to run their dogs, and it was a beautiful habitat for wildlife, primarily deer. That was also a good fifty acres.

"Shit, I don't know. First off, our perp is at least your height and likely big and strong. Elise is shorter than me and slender. I bet she doesn't weigh much more than a hundred pounds. Heck, Morris was a lightweight. This guy could probably carry or drag a body for a while without losing steam." I looked at the trails—hard-packed from plenty of use, no shoe prints or evidence of someone being dragged. "Do you think the city boys would lend a hand? I don't want every weekend warrior out here along with the media hounds, especially when we don't know what we have yet. For all we know, Elise could have had a boyfriend drive her car back here and park it. They could have taken off together."

"Doubt it. That doesn't explain the dime on the hood," Jack said.

"I know, just wishful thinking. Now I know why Morris only had a dime in his pocket and no other change. It was deliberate." I looked around and thought of the magnitude of the searching we had in store. "I think we're going to need the dogs. It will make finding Elise go a lot faster." I radioed Clayton. "Hey, call the police department. Tell them we need the dogs and any available bodies who are free and willing to help out here, ASAP. I'll owe them a beer at Joey's when this mess is over with. Have the dogs get Elise's scent off the yoga bag. Hurry, Clayton. We need help. Keep everyone else out. Shut this park down after they arrive and tell Clark the plan."

"I'm on it, boss."

Jack and I walked down to where the trees met the meadow. We needed a definite starting point instead of just entering the woods in the center. We decided to walk in a back-and-forth grid about twenty feet from each other. We began the search and called out to Elise every few minutes. The forest was relatively quiet other than our own voices, birds chirping, and squirrels skittering about, chasing each other from tree to tree. From the meadow, the voices of the guys calling Elise's name echoed back to us. With the heavy leaf cover from the oaks, maples, and basswoods in our search area, the canopy was dark, making any body hidden there easy to miss.

Thirty minutes into our search, we heard voices and dogs barking from back at the parking lot. I took a deep breath of relief, hoping the K-9 unit could speed up the search. So far we had nothing.

I made a quick call to Billings to ask how Perry was holding up. Billings was the best person to sit with Perry. He had a calming personality that worked well in this type of situation. Having a seventeen-year-old daughter had taught him a lot about being patient. Billings was forty-four, wore his head clean shaved, and had a perfectly groomed goatee. He was the typical teddy bear, which our department needed, and I knew I could trust him with handling Perry for as long as he had to.

The problem with sending Perry home was that he'd have to pass the park on his way. He'd see the squad cars sitting alongside the road at the park entrance. For now, I didn't want him to interrupt our search. He might have been involved in some way too. He had to stay put. Finding Elise was of the utmost importance right now, and when we did find her, I wasn't expecting anything good.

Billings said Perry was okay for now and was sitting tight. He also told me that Lieutenant Colgate from Milwaukee had called and said the blood evidence found at the abandoned house matched Morris's that we had on file. That house was indeed the crime scene. I had to process how we'd go forward with that bit of information. It looked as though we had a killer with a calling card and some type of agenda. This could be someone who was just getting started. Billings also mentioned that Detective Lindstrom had cleared Bobby and LeJon. They were in Detroit together most of last week, as confirmed by people in Milwaukee and Detroit. They were dead ends.

I pressed my fist into my eyes and gave them a thorough rub. Allergies affected me every year at this time. "Billings, call Lieutenant Colgate back and tell him what's going on with Elise. Have his detectives talk to Morris's boys and Terrance again. We need a list of names. I don't care if it was Morris's doctor, dentist, grandma, friend, or enemy. We need names of everyone they can think of that Morris had contact with. We'll get the same type of list from Perry and see if there are any names that crossed both lists. Tell Colgate I'll follow up with him after we find Elise. We've got to nip this nutcase in the bud and quick."

"Got it, Sergeant."

Jack and I had covered only a small part of the woods when he suggested I head back to the parking lot and group up with the guys that had just arrived. I agreed and left.

"Jade, good to see you again but not under these circumstances." Lieutenant Brian Colbert held out his hand and shook mine. Detective Don Miller stood at his side along with two patrol officers, the K-9 unit, and their handler. The two German shepherds sat at attention, their ears perked and ready to go on command.

I wiped my brow and took a deep breath. "Guys, thanks for assisting and bringing out the dogs. We really need them. This park is too big for the few of us. I have three officers in that meadow to our right, and Detective Steele and I were working on the wooded area to our left. We haven't gotten far."

Lieutenant Clark hung up from a call and joined us. "So, how do you want to proceed with the K-9s?"

The handler spoke up. "We'll need the woman's scent, and then we'll split the dogs up. One can go with the officers in the field, the other in the woods."

"Okay, over here," I said as I led them to the car. "Her yoga bag is in the backseat with some articles of clothing inside."

The handler nodded. "That should do it."

Once the dogs had Elise's scent, we split up and headed back out, the German shepherds leading the way. We entered the woods again and met up with Jack about a quarter of the way in. We followed thirty feet behind the German shepherd that was assigned to us. Within twenty minutes, Odie, the K-9 we were with, seemed to be on to something. He caught a scent and ran ahead with his nose glued to the ground. He barked, skirted around a marshy area, and picked up speed. As the five of us reached the hill Odie had just crested, we saw him waiting below. He barked his alert and sat in a wooded gully next to an unusual mound dead center on the canopy floor.

My heart sank when we reached the spot and I saw a piece of lime-green cloth and the blue yoga mat sticking out from below the brush and twigs. We knew it was Elise. We cordoned off the area and radioed Dan and Kyle, who were still going over the Malibu. We needed them at our location now. We had another DB on our hands. I told them to call Doug and Jason. We needed them too.

Chapter 14

"She's in full rigor," Doug said as he glanced at his wristwatch. He turned to look at us over his shoulder. "I'd say she's been deceased twelve to fifteen hours, possibly more."

Dan and Kyle searched the scene for telltale signs and trace evidence. The killer seemed to have made sure his victims were left outdoors in remote areas. Animals, the temperature, and weather conditions could affect our scenes and remove any signs that a human had passed by. I was sure he'd counted on that.

Elise had no defensive wounds, no trace under her nails, just dirt and weeds covering her body, along with black ants that had recently gathered. She did have dried blood in her nose, her face was black and blue, and her mouth jammed full of leaves.

"What do you make of her facial injuries, and why would she have leaves in her mouth?"

I could barely look at her. Her face was badly bruised, and the sight of her body stiffened in that unnatural, hog-tied position disgusted me.

"It looks like she was beaten about the face before she was killed. I'll go out on a limb right now and say her nose was broken. I'll know more once she's on the table, though. The leaves? I'm guessing he wanted to shut her up," Doug said.

I stared at Elise again. Just two nights ago, she led my yoga class. She was vibrant, happy, and full of life. She was an innocent woman and someone I viewed as more than an acquaintance—she was a friend. Nobody deserved her fate. The very things that made her happy had been used to take her life. I was more than pissed, and the sick killer still roamed free. He'd left no evidence, and just as with Morris, we had nothing to go on. We were left shaking our heads. The only thing certain was that we were dealing with the same killer in both cases—the man that called himself Dime.

With the sound of a zipper being fastened, Elise was sealed in the body bag, and the guys loaded her onto a backboard, secured her with straps, and carried her out of the woods. With her body in the van, Doug and Jason left for the Medical Examiner's office. We'd need her clothing gone over carefully when Kyle and Dan got back to the forensics lab. We had to find some clue to catch this killer.

We thanked everyone that had helped us search for Elise and parted ways. Our deputies pulled down the yellow police tape and opened up the driveway that led into the park. The officers from the police station left with the dogs. Jack, Clayton, Lieutenant Clark, and I stood in the parking lot discussing this new turn of events. Kyle and Dan waited until the Malibu was loaded onto the flatbed before leaving. The car would be taken to the evidence garage, where they would go over it more thoroughly. They had to piece the puzzle together and see if there was anything of value we could use.

Lieutenant Clark spoke up. "You know we're going to have to search Perry's house. I highly doubt if he's involved in any way, shape, or form, but we'll get our chops busted if we don't do it. I'm calling it in. We should have a warrant within the hour. We're going to have to sit on him until the search is over."

Perry had been detained at the station for hours. Billings had kept him calm and well caffeinated for most of the day. Now came the hard part—telling him that his wife was dead and we had no idea why.

"I know one thing for sure," Jack said.

I wiped my dirty hands on my pants. "Yeah, what's that?"

"We don't know any more now than we did before, and I'm going to need a stiff drink at some point before the day is over."

Back at the sheriff's department, I took Perry into one of the interrogation rooms to tell him the devastating news. My least favorite part of the job was informing family members of their loved one's untimely death, and today would be particularly hard. No way on earth would I tell Perry how Elise was found. She was dead, and nothing would bring her back. He didn't need to know the horrific details. I told him we found her in the park, and only an autopsy could definitively tell us how she died. It could take a few days.

He sobbed openly as he leaned over the table with his head in his hands. "Was she murdered? Was it the same guy that killed the boy at Cedar Lake? What am I going to tell my kids? Why Elise?"

I shook my head and looked at the floor. "Perry, I don't have those answers. I need to tell you, though, that your house is being searched as we speak. That doesn't mean we're pointing fingers at you, but we do need to clear you of this crime so you can take care of your family. Would you mind giving us a DNA sample too? Everything we're asking is to help eliminate you as a suspect."

"Sure, go ahead. I have nothing to hide."

I motioned for Kyle to come in. He swabbed the inside of Perry's mouth and took the sample downstairs.

"I'm sorry for your loss, Perry. Elise's car is in our evidence garage. I thought you should know. It may be a while before we can release it to you."

"What about Elise? Where is she?"

"She's downstairs in the ME's office."

"I want to see her. Don't I need to identify her?"

I couldn't let Perry see Elise yet. Rigor had her body stiffened in a horribly contorted position. We'd wait another day or so for the rigor to relax before having him ID her.

"Yes, you do, but not just yet. I knew Elise, Perry. It's her. We'll call you in a couple of days to come in for an official ID. Right now you need to call your parents and tell them what happened. They have the kids, don't they? We can't let you leave yet, but you should make that call."

"Sergeant, please find the person that did this to Elise. I don't have a wife anymore, and my kids just lost their mother. I don't know how to go forward from here."

I squeezed his hand. "You have my word. We'll find this monster and bring him to justice."

I watched as Perry was led to a phone. We had to confiscate his cell phone—it was protocol. I said a silent prayer for him and his family. He was a broken man, and my heart ached for his loss, but we had to stay focused on catching this madman. I went back to the bull pen where Jack, Clayton, and Billings sat. The lieutenant came out of his office and joined us at a corner table.

"How's Perry doing?" Lieutenant Clark asked.

"Not good. How are we going to find this killer, Lieutenant? We don't have a damn shred of evidence. Forensics has pictures, Doug has a body, and us? We have nothing. No leads, no suspect, no motive, no eyewitnesses, and no evidence."

"Okay, then, what do we have?"

Jack spoke up. "We think the perp is at least my height, and he must be strong and fit. He's likely from around here because he knows the area well. He may be someone that deals and takes drugs, hence his nickname, Dime. There isn't a connection between Morris and Elise as far as we know. Perry didn't seem to recognize Morris's name other than from what he read in the paper."

"We have to follow up on that anyway to make sure

there's no connection whatsoever between the two. Maybe Elise knew someone Morris knew."

"We're already on that, Lieutenant," I said. "Billings told Lieutenant Colgate that they need more names on Morris's end. We can cross-reference the list I intend to get from Perry. We'll see if anything shakes out. I'll ask him to start on it while he's waiting here anyway."

"Good. Just think of every angle you can. We need Perry to give us a list of his own acquaintances too. What does he do for a living?"

Jack checked his notes. "He's a CPA."

Lieutenant Clark slapped his hand on the table. "Okay, follow that too. Maybe somebody didn't like the way Perry prepared their taxes. I don't care how stupid it sounds, check everything. Talk to the North Bend PD and see if they want to lend a hand. They can dig in deeper with the business owners from the strip mall. Maybe somebody there had a beef with Elise. I'll have a few deputies pull extra shifts. We need videos from businesses along her route home. Just because nobody followed her out of the strip mall doesn't mean they weren't waiting somewhere else. Get some deputies out there collecting video feed from every business that has surveillance cameras. Get the tech guys on it. I don't care if they have to pull double shifts. Let's move."

"Got it, boss," Billings said as he scratched his goatee. "I'll get more deputies in here."

"Okay, get a plan under way. We need something solid. We have to apprehend this maniac before he becomes a serial killer." Lieutenant Clark cracked his knuckles. "I'll call downtown and see how much the city can pitch in. If this gets worse, we may have to call in help from the state patrol too."

Chapter 15

Clayton and Billings went through Morris's file again. They searched for hours for any clue that would connect him and Elise. It didn't make sense. We needed to gather names and find a common thread.

I looked at the clock—four thirty. What had started out as a half day of work had turned into another murder with no leads.

"I'm ordering a couple of pizzas. We can't live on vending machine candy bars forever."

I called Dick's Pizzeria and placed the order. They said to expect the pizzas in thirty minutes. Jack and I went downstairs to talk to Kyle and Dan.

We entered the forensics lab. I wanted to ask if there was anything new, but their blank looks told me all I needed to know. They didn't have anything to offer. There wasn't any trace evidence on Elise's clothing, the stretch cord, tights, or mat. They hadn't found any fingerprints other than Elise's on the car's door handles or steering wheel. The only evidence on her clothing was from the park—dirt, leaves, and twigs.

Jack and I sat at the table with Dan and Kyle and brainstormed. I was sure they needed a break anyway.

"I'm thinking this guy knows how to play the game. It may be his first rodeo or not, but he knows how to avoid being detected. He doesn't use the same kill method twice, and we have no idea where he's going to pop up next, or who his target will be. He leaves nothing behind and no trace of his actions. What are we missing?" I asked.

I looked from face to face, hoping for an epiphany, an aha moment from anyone, but nobody said a word.

"You guys didn't find anything at either scene, such as a murder weapon, fingerprints, or tire tracks. Morris had a knife according to his boys, and he was killed with a knife, but none was found. Elise was killed with her own yoga gear. It can't be a coincidence that this killer doesn't have to bring his own weapon to commit the crime. Even though there isn't a connection between the two of them that we know of, the killer has chosen Morris and Elise deliberately. These aren't random murders. He knows who he's going to target and how he's going to kill them. There had to be something that connected Elise to Morris."

"Or someone," Kyle said.

Jack spoke up. "Maybe that's it. It's possible that the connection isn't actually between Morris and Elise at all. It could be someone the killer knows that connects them."

I squeezed my temples. "That's awesome. How in the world are we going to figure that one out?" I breathed a deep sigh. "Okay, guys, we need a mental break. I took the liberty of ordering a couple of pizzas." I glanced at the clock. "They should be here in about twenty minutes. Come on up and join us in the lunchroom. I'll tell Doug and Jason."

I entered the autopsy room and found Doug sitting at his computer. He glanced up when I approached him. "Sergeant, what can I do for you?"

"We have a few pizzas on the way. They should be here in fifteen minutes or so. Come on up and join us. Where's Jason?"

I noticed Doug had just finished filling out the online paperwork for Morris's transport to Milwaukee. He got up and turned on the printer.

"I sent him home. There's nothing more to do tonight. We're okay to release Mr. King's body, right?" he asked.

"Yeah, that should be fine. There's no forensic evidence on him. The tox report showed traces of THC, nothing else, right?"

"That's right."

"Okay, then, we have all the photos and documentation we need. Lieutenant Clark said I could sign off on it. Go ahead and shut it down. There's nothing you can do for Elise until the rigor relaxes anyway."

Doug muttered something under his breath.

"Did you say something?"

"Yeah, I said I'll be up in a few minutes."

We gathered in the lunchroom, each of us scarfing down slices of pizza like hungry animals. With everything going on today, it was likely that nobody had thought much about eating until now. My phone buzzed in my pocket, and I excused myself when I saw the call was from Amber.

I stood by the beverage station and answered. "Hi, Sis."

"What has you so busy on a Saturday?" she asked. "Are you still at the station?"

"Yeah, sorry, today has been a total nightmare."

"Can you talk about it?"

"Nope, not yet. I have a feeling work is going to take center stage for a while. You know, I just thought of something you could do that would help us both out."

"Really? I'll do whatever I can."

"How about taking the lead on looking at condos for me? I have an appointment with Melissa Mately at Realty World tomorrow to look at four places. She has a good reputation and is a buyer's agent. She knows what I'm looking for and seems like a perfect fit for us. I was going to compare Realtors but why bother?"

"So are you saying I can move in with you?"

I heard her excitement through the phone line. I loved my little sister, and just hearing somebody that actually sounded happy warmed my heart.

"Maybe, but I *do* have conditions."

"Anything."

I looked back at the table. I wanted to keep my conversation with Amber private, but our lunchroom wasn't that big. I tried to whisper. "You can't shrink me, and I mean about anything. No relationship shrinking, no work shrinking. If I feel like sharing, I'll let you know."

"Done. I promise you won't be my test subject, but we can talk about sisterly things, right?"

"Sure, as long as my private life and work cases don't

end up as one of your school essays. Also, you can only move yourself and your clothes for now. Once we actually move into a condo, you can bring the rest of your stuff from Mom's house. We aren't moving it twice. Deal?"

"Deal."

"Okay, then, can you do me a favor before you head to work?"

"Yep, shoot."

"Call Melissa and tell her she can expand her search parameters to include three-bedroom condos. Introduce yourself and tell her you're going out with her tomorrow on my behalf."

"Got it. Give me her number."

I rattled off Melissa's phone number and told Amber that some of us from the department might stop in for a drink later when we left work. I was pretty certain we'd all need one.

After the lieutenant called the North Bend PD, they collected videos from a handful of businesses on Washington Street. Between their tech team and ours, they would start going through the videos later when the evening shift began.

We said good night to the deputies in the bull pen. We left them with a to-do list and promised to be back first thing in the morning. I told them that a call should be coming in soon from the deputies searching Perry's house. If they got the "all's clear" on the house, they could release Perry.

"Make sure he eats something too and try to keep him

comfortable," I said. "Call me if he's let go tonight."

"Yes, Mom," Mitch Bryant, one of our evening deputies, said.

"Smart-ass. Okay, we're out of here."

A couple of drinks to wind down and a soft pillow would do it for me. Tomorrow would be another day at the station. I got into my car and led the way.

We entered Joey's Sports Bar and Grille at seven o'clock. Jack, Dan, Kyle, Clayton, and Billings joined me. We needed a mental break from these cases even if it was just for a few drinks together on a Saturday night. The place was crowded and loud, the perfect distraction.

Amber had worked part-time at Joey's since she turned twenty-one. Our family had known Joey Spaulding and his wife, Emily, for years, and when I was a college kid myself, I used to frequent the place often. Amber was the perfect bartender. As beautiful and outgoing as she was, people flocked to the bar to sit up close and personal with her. She had a magnetic personality and drew people in. Amber was fun loving and engaging but also sympathetic, and she listened to the late-night woes of the sad sack whose relationship or dead-end job was taking them nowhere. Her behavioral science classes served her well.

"Bless her heart," I said as we made our way through the crowd, "she saved us a table."

Amber grinned and waved from behind the bar and pointed to the table that had a "reserved" place card sitting on top.

Classic rock music blasted from the jukebox to our right,

and the long horseshoe-shaped bar with the deep red vinyl diamond-tufted front was to our left. A row of matching barstools held twenty-five or more people, mostly college kids. Ten bar tables filled with people enjoying the weekend were scattered throughout the large establishment, and TVs were perched on every corner shelf near the ceiling. Pine paneling and old-time beer signs gave the place an "up north" vibe even though it was located on West Lincoln Street and had been there for the past thirty years.

"Okay, I've got the first round," Jack said. "I'll grab a couple of pitchers of beer."

I got up and headed to the bar with Jack. "I'll go with you. We need a few bowls of pretzels too."

Amber leaned over the bar and gave us each a kiss on the cheek while the pitchers were filling at the tap.

"We need pretzels too, Sis," I said.

Jack teased Amber while we waited for the beer. "So, I hear a change for the better is coming. Anytime you need me to straighten Bruce out, just say the word."

Amber laughed. "I can't wait to move in with Jade. That guy is sick, and I don't mean it in a good way."

She lifted the heavy pitchers and placed them on the bar. Jack handed her a twenty and told her to keep the change. She gave him another kiss on the cheek and filled two snack bowls for me. One had pretzels, the other popcorn, but it would take a lot more than pretzels and popcorn to help me forget those images of Elise that were playing in my mind. For now, knocking back a few beers with friends would have to do it.

Chapter 16

Dime stood near the entrance; he blended in with everyone else at the crowded establishment. He intended to stay by the door. The view was better from that vantage point anyway, and he could make a quick exit if needed. He pulled his hoodie up and covered his head as he watched Amber from a distance. What a beauty she was. Good family genes. He licked his lips. He'd have to get to know her better, on a much more personal level. The voices in his head spoke up. *In time—everything has to be at the right time.* He smiled and answered, "Yeah, I know."

Dime overheard Amber talking to a customer at the end of the bar. He inched closer so he could hear the conversation. With all the patrons in the bar, enjoying their Saturday night, he was invisible to everyone anyway.

When he'd heard enough, he slipped out of the door. Dime climbed into his Jeep, checked the time on his watch, and wrote it down. The page contained everything related to Amber Monroe. The name of Joey's Sports Bar and Grille, along with the time and date, were listed under her name. He pulled out of the parking lot and drove the twenty minutes to his house in Jackson City.

The basement sanctuary, his place for solitude and clarity, awaited his arrival. Classical music played in the background as he got comfortable on the wooden chair. He pulled the usual Stella Artois out of the refrigerator and placed a cardboard coaster beneath it so a water ring wouldn't form on the side table. His notebook rested on his lap. With his reading glasses perched on the bridge of his nose, he reviewed everything he had written down. He'd overheard Amber telling that customer at the bar how excited she was to be looking at condos with Melissa Mately tomorrow. According to her sister, Jade, Melissa was the best Realtor in town. Melissa would list Jade's house for sale and find them a great condo. Dime decided he'd pay Melissa a visit tomorrow before Amber showed up. Realty World might have to hire a new agent soon.

I'll act like I'm new in town and plan to buy a house. She'll happily give me all her contact information, as ambitious as she sounds. Melissa and I are going to have a private showing real soon.

Killing Melissa would fit into his plan perfectly. Nobody would expect that. She wasn't on anybody's radar. With her occupation, she could easily meet up with foul play. Being a hot-looking female Realtor was stupid on so many levels. Any nutcase could call and lure her away to a remote location and have their way with her. He stared at her picture and profile on the Realty World website. Melissa Mately was single, thirty-two, and ambitious. She was one of their top earners. He'd have a great time alone with her before she would die. He thought about the best way to kill her. It had to be relevant to her job. That seemed to be his new MO.

I could jam the house-listing sheet down her throat and choke her with it. Maybe I could impale her with the stake from the For Sale sign. He chuckled at his options. *I have to find a very remote home to have her show me, something secluded and very expensive. It has to be a home that isn't shown often because of the high asking price, and preferably with acreage. I don't want nosy neighbors seeing me.*

He took a sip of his beer as he scanned his tablet for listings with acreage. *Hmm... this one looks interesting.* An aerial photo showed this private enclave on Oriole Lane as the ultimate gentleman's farm. A four-thousand-square-foot home with a five-car garage and several outbuildings was their most expensive listing. It was being offered with seventeen acres, ten in open field, perfect for raising horses. The house sat in the middle of seven beautifully wooded acres located at the end of a meandering paved driveway. This was a prestigious sanctuary for the most discriminating buyer wanting privacy.

Yes, this one will definitely do. I'm all about privacy. I'll check out the area tomorrow.

Chapter 17

Lieutenant Colgate had several detectives working the Morris King end of the case. They paid Terrance a visit and had him write down every person's name he could think of that Morris had known, no matter how insignificant the relationship might have been. Terrance came up with fourteen names. They rounded up Morris's boys too at the park. Another twenty-six names were added to the list. Detective Lindstrom called my desk at noon.

"Washburn County Sheriff's Department, Sergeant Monroe speaking. How may I help you?"

"Sergeant, Detective Lindstrom here."

"Hi, Bill, what have you got?"

"Well, first I wanted to extend my sympathy. I heard about the second victim from the lieutenant. I hear you knew the deceased."

"Yeah, it's such a shame. She was actually my yoga instructor and a casual friend. We're expecting her husband soon. He said he was getting together every name he could think of for us, including his own acquaintances. How's it going on your end?"

Jack held up the coffeepot. I nodded. He poured me a fresh cup.

"We have forty names between his little gang boys and the uncle. I can email or fax you the list."

I took a sip and responded. "That would be great. Fax is fine. I'm not optimistic that we'll find a match, but at least we can rule out a connection if none of the names cross-reference. Oh, by the way, we're releasing Morris's body back to his uncle on Monday. A transport will deliver Morris's body to… hang on"—I checked my notes—"shoot, all I have is Calvary Baptist Church. That isn't going to work. I'll have to call Terrance King and find out what funeral home he plans to use."

"Don't worry about it, Sergeant. I'll handle it. You have enough on your plate."

"Are you sure?"

"No problem. Okay, you should be getting the fax any minute now. Keep us posted if you get a match. Better yet, keep us posted anyway. Enjoy your Sunday if you can."

"Same to you. Goodbye." I hung up the phone and pulled the sheet with the list of names out of the fax machine. Now all I needed was for Perry to finish his list. He was released late last night and apparently spent the night at his folks' house. He called in a half hour ago and said he needed to stop at home to pick up his own tax client list.

"Is Doug here?" Jack asked.

"I haven't seen him. Maybe he's taking today off. Elise's autopsy will probably go better tomorrow anyway, but he's going to have to make that decision. Perry will have to come back again for the ID. Maybe a picture of her face is all that's necessary for now. We could probably show Perry that much."

The door between the reception counter and the bull pen buzzed open, and Perry was escorted in. He looked a mess. Bags hung under his still red, puffy eyes. His hair looked as though it hadn't been washed or combed. He walked in with a manila folder in his hand.

We stood and greeted him, then I offered him something to drink. Jack pointed to the small table near the wall.

"Let's sit over here, Perry. Jade, do you have the list from Detective Lindstrom?"

"Yep, sure do." I carried two cups of coffee and the sheet of paper to the table and took a seat. Jack was on one side of Perry, and I was on the other. "So, this list contains your and Elise's friends, family, and casual acquaintances?"

"Yes, it's all I could come up with. Here's the list of all of my clients' names too."

"Thank you. This shouldn't take long. Would you like something from the vending machine? Chips, cookies, anything?"

"No, I'm fine."

I knew he wasn't fine, and I'd heard he didn't eat anything last night when the deputies offered him food.

"Are the kids at your parents' house?"

"Yeah. Can we cut the small talk and just get this done? I'd like to be with my children."

I replied, "Sure thing."

I made a copy of the list Detective Lindstrom sent so Jack could compare names to Perry's client list, and I could compare the names to Perry's personal list. I ran down both sheets side by side with my index finger, hoping for a match—nothing. Perry had ninety tax clients, and Jack checked them all—no names matched.

Normally the husband was the primary suspect, at least in the beginning. We checked everything in Perry's house, and it was clean. Todd, Billy, Luke, and Lee went through his phone records, credit card receipts, and bank statements. He hadn't purchased or added to Elise's life insurance policy. We knew Perry wasn't involved.

"Okay, that should do it for today."

"When do I get to see Elise? What's the holdup with the ID?"

"The ME isn't here right now, Perry. It will most likely be tomorrow. I'll call you when the time is right." I thanked him and sent him on his way.

Jack sighed and plopped down at his desk. "Looks like we're back to square one."

"Do you think we'll solve this case? Some murderers are never caught, you know. Look at Dennis Rader. He probably would never have been caught if he hadn't been sending letters and taunting the cops himself. That was still fifteen years after the fact. I know we're good cops."

Jack agreed. "Of course we are, but this guy is smart. He knows how to avoid detection, and he's careful. When was the last time you talked to your old man?"

"A couple of weeks ago. Do you think I should call him?"

"Maybe an opinion from someone that isn't involved could shed some light."

"Maybe." I stood just when my cell phone buzzed. Amber was calling. I assumed she was going to tell me all about the condos she'd toured with Melissa. "Hi, Sis, are you guys done?"

"Not yet. We have one more place to look at today. This is *so* much fun. Melissa is a pretty cool lady. I could see you two hitting it off as friends. You have similar personalities."

I chuckled and had actually thought the same thing myself when I met Melissa. "Well, do you have any favorite condos yet? You have to let her know your favorites so I can go back and look at them too."

"Oh, for sure. I don't think we should even bother her with the two-bedroom units anymore. Don't forget, I'm going to help with the rent and bills. Three-bedroom units are where it's at."

I laughed again. "Okay, just keep the listing sheets of the ones you like. Come over tonight and have dinner with me. We'll catch up, and bring the sheets with you. I'm excited to see them."

"Will do. I'll be over by five."

"Sounds like you guys are going to be roomies soon," Jack said as I hung up. He leaned back in his heavy leather office chair and entwined his fingers behind his head. "Man, this is a comfortable chair."

"It should be, you paid a fortune for it."

"I had to. My ass is glued to this thing more hours than I care to admit."

I agreed with a nod. "Anyway the house has to be sold first, so I don't want to get ahead of myself. I did tell Amber she could move in for now, but only herself and her clothes. The bedroom set and the rest of her junk has to stay at Mom's until I buy a condo. That will give her time to get rid of some of the stuff she doesn't need."

I went downstairs to talk to Billy and Todd in the tech department before I headed home. Billy had just hung up from a call with the tech guys at the police station downtown. They were discussing a tape they'd both reviewed, and they'd come to the same conclusion: it led nowhere. Originally they thought somebody could have been following Elise, but after looking at another tape from farther down the block, they saw the vehicle in question pull into a gas station. So far, according to Todd, nothing looked promising.

I stopped at Chin's Chinese Restaurant on my way home and picked up dinner. Chin's had the best take-out food in town. I figured I owed Amber some extra face time. We'd have more quality time to discuss the condos and look at the listing sheets if I wasn't slaving over a hot stove. I was never the best cook anyway, and cooking wasn't one of my favorite pastimes, so Chinese would do it for dinner. I knew Amber would talk my head off, describing the condos she'd viewed. She was probably more excited than I was since she had never lived anywhere other than with Mom.

I checked the time as I set the table—four forty-five. She

should arrive any minute. I set out a small plate and put both fortune cookies on it. She could take her pick of the fun treat after dinner. We'd both read our fortunes out loud. A heads-up knock sounded ten minutes later, then Amber let herself in.

"I'm here, and I'm bearing gifts."

I peeked around the corner from the dinette into the foyer, where she sat on the bench, removing her shoes. It was nice that I didn't have to remind her. I was sure Amber would be a great roommate—she was neat and respectful.

"I bought Chinese."

"Oh, yum. I hope you got Chicken Almond Ding, pot stickers, and fried rice."

"Is there anything else?" I smiled.

"Yeah, I brought two bottles of wine, one for you and one for me. We can hang out, talk trash, and get tipsy."

"Sounds good. Let's eat."

By five thirty, the table had been cleared and the dishwasher loaded with the few plates we'd used. We sat on the sofa and got comfortable, each with a glass of wine, as we looked over the condo listings. The plate with the fortune cookies sat on the coffee table in front of us.

"Can I pick which fortune cookie I want?"

"Sure, go ahead. You have to read it out loud, though."

"Okay, here goes."

Amber tore the cellophane wrapper open with her teeth and pulled out the cookie. She cracked it in half and slid out the small white strip of paper.

She cleared her throat. "Okay, here goes. It says, '*A secret admirer will soon be revealed.*' Wow…mysterious, huh?" Amber laughed. "There *is* Sean from school. I think he's had a thing for me for a while. Okay, now it's your turn."

I cracked open my cookie and stared at the message.

"You have to read it out loud. It's the rules."

"It's just a stupid saying."

Amber pulled the note from my fingers. "I'll read it. '*A stranger will present you with a gift.*' That's a nice fortune. I like yours better."

"Well, whatever, you can have my cookie too. Let's plan next weekend to view a few more three-bedroom condos, and I want to take a look at the ones you liked already. I have to get Melissa to list the house right away too."

"Jade, I'm really excited about moving in with you. I promise you won't regret it. Mom is already talking about making my old bedroom into a craft room. That means there's no turning back."

I squeezed her hand. "I know, hon, and I won't change my mind. We're in this together, and here's your own set of keys." I laughed. "These are Lance's old ones. He definitely has no need for them anymore."

Chapter 18

Dime relived the encounter he'd had with Melissa Mately yesterday. He sat at the table, enjoying his Monday morning breakfast with a sly grin on his face. Suckering the ditzy bleached blonde into believing anything he said was as easy as taking candy from a baby. He had entered Realty World around eleven forty-five and saw her sitting at her desk. The bell above the glass door clinked when he passed through. She looked up and smiled. He checked the parking lot before he walked in. Only one car sat outside, and he assumed it belonged to her.

"Good morning." She chuckled when she looked at the clock. "Oops, I guess it's almost noon. Hi, I'm Melissa Mately."

She stood to shake his hand.

"Hi, I'm David Ingles. Is that your car outside? I love that model. I was actually looking at the new Infinity sedan myself."

"Yes, I just bought it a few months ago. I'll admit, I love that car and gold—well"—she laughed—"it's the color of success."

He looked her over slowly. "It sure is."

"Well, Mr. Ingles, is there something I can help you with?" She glanced at the clock again. "Actually I'm waiting for a client to arrive. I'll be locking up in a few minutes."

"No problem, just checking out the Realtors in the area to see who really wants my business. You see, I'm new in town and was hoping to tour some of the more upscale, private properties you have listed, like the one on Oriole Lane, but if you're too busy—"

She hushed away his comment. "I'd love to work as your Realtor, Mr. Ingles. Oriole Lane is quite the property. I'd be happy to show you that home and any others in that general price range if you like, maybe later this afternoon?"

"How about giving me your card and I'll think about it? I'm not sure if later would work for me. How does your schedule look during the week?"

"Let me take a peek here and see."

Dime listened as she mumbled to herself while clicking through her computer's calendar.

"Hmm… I guess I didn't realize how busy I was, clear through the weekend. I have an all-day showing for condos on Saturday. I could probably fit you in after my last appointment on Tuesday. That's at five o'clock."

He deliberately paced as if he were losing interest. "Maybe."

"It's no problem, really. I aim to keep my clients happy." She smiled and waited for him to make eye contact with her, but he didn't.

He stared at her business card as if he had to think about

it. "I'll get back to you if it works for me. Thanks." Dime headed for the door.

"Are you sure? I'd love to show you our executive properties at your convenience if Tuesday doesn't work. Please call me if you change your mind."

The bell above Realty World's glass door clinked, and he was gone.

He laughed at the memory from yesterday and looked at his watch—eight a.m. Dime wiped his mouth with the paper napkin, balled it up, and tossed it into the stainless steel trash can next to the stove. His plate and cup went into the sink, and he left the house.

He thought of the right approach to connect with Melissa tomorrow evening while he drove. He didn't want his fake name or the property she was going to show him to come up on her appointment calendar. He would wait and call her at the last minute, probably around five thirty. He'd make sure to remind her that if she couldn't accommodate his needs, he would work with a different Realtor. He knew she didn't get to the position of being a top earner by slacking off. Dime was sure she would agree to show him the property on Oriole Lane.

He pulled into the lot and parked his Jeep. As long as she was on his mind, he went ahead and set the alarm on his watch for five thirty tomorrow afternoon. Melissa Mately would get a phone call. Her ambition, or lack of it, would determine her fate.

The voices came to life and told him to make a quick call to the florist before going inside. He obeyed.

Chapter 19

A mixed floral arrangement was delivered to the sheriff's department by a driver from Lilly's Garden at nine o'clock. The delivery man told Jan at the reception counter that the flowers were for Jade Monroe. Jan signed for them.

The arrangement was huge, colorful, and filled with purple and yellow lilies, tulips, carnations, baby's breath, and roses. Jan sniffed the flowers before buzzing herself through to the bull pen.

"I'm jealous," she said, as she entered the room. "Sure wish someone would send me flowers once in a blue moon."

"Check that out," Jack said. He whistled as he watched Jan to see where she was taking the vase.

I looked up from my computer when Jan zeroed in and locked eyes with me.

"These are for you, Jade."

"From who?" I cleared a space on my desk for the beautiful, expensive-looking vase of flowers.

"No clue, and there wasn't any card. The driver just said they were for you, and here they are. I wish I had a secret admirer that would send me flowers."

My mind flashed back for a second to the fortune cookie note. I shook it off. I didn't believe in that nonsense. "What florist delivered it?"

"Lilly's Garden. Anyway, I'm jealous."

"Me too," Jack joked.

"Knock it off. I'll get to the bottom of this. I'll call the florist and find out who bought them. Somebody had to pay the bill. Thanks, Jan."

"Yep, no problem."

Jan exited the bull pen while I stared at the flowers. They *were* beautiful.

"So what do you think it means? Your birthday isn't for another week, your house hasn't sold yet, Lance hasn't reconsidered… has he?"

"Heck no. I am impressed, though."

"Really? About what?"

"You. You're a guy. Guys don't remember birthdays."

"Ouch. My name isn't Lance."

"Thank God." I breathed a sigh of relief. "Now I know who they're from." I smiled widely.

"Who?"

"Amber. Who else would do something so sweet?" I chuckled and remembered that she'd read my fortune cookie too. "I'm letting her move in, and she looked at condos for me yesterday. We went over the listings last night at my place while we had a Chinese dinner together."

"And you didn't think to invite me? Damn it, girl. I sat alone watching a Lifetime movie and with a TV dinner on my lap."

I chuckled. "You know I don't believe a word you said. Anyway, it was our way overdue girl's night." I looked at the clock. Amber was in class; I couldn't call right now, so I texted her instead. *"Thanks for the flowers, Sis. They're beautiful, and you're a sweetheart."*

My mind drifted back to Elise. The autopsy would be complete soon, and Perry could finally ID her. I was certain Doug had started it.

"Could you do me a favor, partner?"

"Sure, name it."

"I'll make a fresh pot of coffee if you go downstairs and check on Doug's progress. I'd like to call Perry and tell him when he can come in. Ask Jason if he set up the time for the transport company to pick up Morris's body too. I want to call Terrance and let him know."

"Yep, on it. Get that coffee started."

I poured water into the pot and lined the basket with a paper filter. I knew we'd go through an entire pot, so I made twelve cups, scooping six heaping tablespoons of Colombian Roast into the basket. I hit the start button and knocked on Lieutenant Clark's door. He glanced up through the window and waved me in.

"Jade, what can I do for you?"

"We're stuck, boss. None of the names from Morris's list of associates cross-referenced with Elise's names. Plus, we know Perry isn't good for this crime."

He ran his palms over his eyes and exhaled a groan. "Yeah, I know. I'll admit I haven't slept much this last week." He rubbed the belly that his starched shirt was stretched across and leaned back in his chair.

I nodded. "I just don't know where to go with this. Even with a profile on this killer, we still have nothing. He's a ghost. The media can't help us. We already know who our victims are. Plastering their photos across the TV screen isn't going to do anything except agonize Perry even more. We can't even put together a composite of the killer for the media. No eyewitnesses."

"Have all of the people in Elise's yoga class from Friday night been interviewed?"

"Yep. They all left before she did, and she never mentioned plans other than going home after the class."

"So that's a dead end too. And her car? Did the guys get anywhere with the seat being pushed back, any trace?"

"Nothing. The perp must be gloved at all times. We're not doing our victims justice." I smacked the doorframe with my open hand and walked out, irritated.

Jack entered the bull pen just as I got back to my desk.

"Doug has about an hour left with Elise. Jason said the transport company is on their way."

"Good, I'll call Terrance and give him a heads-up."

Jack sat down and rapped his knuckles on the desk. "I'd tell Perry to come at noon to be on the safe side. Of course the autopsy is just for protocol, right? Elise was a healthy, fit woman, wasn't she?"

"Yeah, the only thing off might be the toxicology report if she was slipped a drug. Highly unlikely, though. We saw the time stamp on the video of her leaving right after class, and it didn't sound like she intended to stop anywhere.

Anyway, the tox report should be back in a few days. I know Doug is busy right now, but Clark wants the rest of us in the lunchroom to touch base on everything we've done so far. I'll call Perry first and tell him to be here at noon."

I picked up my desk phone and made two calls. The first was to tell Perry to come in at noon for Elise's official ID and the other call was to Terrance. Morris's body would arrive at Phillips Funeral Home in a few hours. Terrance said he would let me know what day the funeral would be scheduled for. Jack and I planned to attend.

We went through everything again with the lieutenant. This time our group included Kyle, Dan, Todd, and Bill. We had several officers from North Bend PD, John and Lucas from their tech department, and Detective Miller on speakerphone with us.

Over the course of an hour and with each person sharing their bit of information, we still came up blank. We agreed it would take a miracle and a lot of luck to catch this killer.

Perry was a mess, and it was difficult dealing with him when he came in to ID Elise, but it had to be done. He was an emotional wreck, and I could feel his pain. He asked if I would accompany him to the viewing window, and I agreed. I didn't think he was strong enough to handle seeing her alone. He seemed as though he was ready to collapse any second. Perry squeezed my hand tightly when Jason opened the blinds and rolled the gurney to the window. He lowered the white sheet covering Elise's face. Perry's entire body shook as he sobbed and nodded. I motioned for Jason to close the blinds.

The visitor's lounge was a peaceful shade of biscuit and peach colored blinds covered the windows facing south. Two couches and two side chairs lined the walls and a few magazines and a Bible were spread across the coffee table. Soft music played so quietly it was barely audible. I sat there with Perry, feeling awful for him, and stayed until he was composed enough to drive home. Just watching Perry made me wonder how Terrance was dealing with Morris's death, so I called him back and talked for a bit, just person to person. Even though it didn't seem as though Terrance and Morris were as close as they could have been, I knew the man was grieving nonetheless. I offered my condolences again and told him Jack and I would be at the funeral on Friday.

I busied myself with monotonous paperwork for the rest of the day. I didn't have anything else to work on, and I felt hopeless.

"Jack, I'm heading out unless you need help with anything."

"Nah—go ahead. I'm right behind you. Unless new leads come in, we're at a standstill anyway. Let's see what the lieutenant thinks about releasing Elise's body soon. I'm sure Perry wants to give his wife a decent burial."

I noticed the flashing light on my phone just as I was ready to drop it into my purse.

A text had come in hours earlier from Amber. *"Don't know what you're talking about, Sis. No flowers from me. Sorry I didn't think of it. Remember the fortune cookie? Sounds like you're getting some good karma."*

I seriously had my doubts.

Chapter 20

His load was beginning to lighten.

It's time to get this party started again. As usual, I've gone unnoticed. I think it's the perfect day for Melissa and me to get better acquainted. Dime had checked out the weather forecast for the entire week. A slow-moving warm front was coming in from the southwest. It ensured dry weather and plenty of sunshine going into next weekend. No tire tread marks or footprints would be found at the home on Oriole Lane.

He headed out in his Jeep and drove east on Decorah Road, a two-lane state highway that would take him away from North Bend. He could have set up the appointment with Melissa any time during the week, but he knew she had a five o'clock appointment, and he wanted to catch her off guard. He headed in the general direction of the home for sale on Oriole Lane and checked the time, even though the alarm was set on his phone.

A small bar with a worn-out facade came into view on the south side of the highway. Two cars sat in the gravel parking lot facing the front door of Eddy's Tap. Dime assumed one of the cars belonged to the bartender.

What's the harm? I still have a half hour before I need to call Melissa.

He clicked the right-turn blinker and slowed down. The Jeep's oversized tires kicked up gravel from the unpaved parking lot as he pulled in and parked. Dime exited his vehicle and walked the ten steps to the front door. He reached back and pulled up the hood on his black sweatshirt and put on the dark green aviator glasses he kept in his pocket. The old saloon-style swinging doors squeaked when he pushed through them. The bar had a strange western and biker bar theme going on. Motorcycle forks and handlebars were bolted to old barn-beam support pillars as wall art, and the barstools were saddles on posts. The bartender wore a black leather vest and a cowboy hat. He waxed the ends of his mustache so the tips curled up and held their twisted, thin shape. The walls were lined with Harley posters of nearly naked women posed provocatively on motorcycles.

Dime grumbled as he took a seat, careful to avoid the saddle horn between his legs. He shrugged and cracked his neck from side to side. Having to get the bartender's attention annoyed him since the place was nearly empty.

He called out, "I'll have a Stella Artois."

Mr. Mustache walked over. "A what? Never heard of that before. Is that some kind of fancy-ass beer?"

"Fine… how about a Guinness?"

The bartender stared at him.

"I'll have a Bud Light."

"That I can do, pal. Can or bottle?"

"Can, and pour it into a glass."

Dime sat at the bar, mindlessly watching the evening news on TV. An old-timer sat alone near the door, plugging quarters into a video poker machine. Dime took a gulp of beer and continued staring at the screen. He still had time to kill. He chuckled at the thought, clever man that he was. The world news segment had just ended, and the local news had begun. A mention of the two recent murders in the North Bend area perked him up. The old-timer stopped playing video poker momentarily and turned to watch the news report. According to the anchorman, there were no suspects in custody, and the sheriff's department had no leads. It was a mystery to everyone in this normally safe, family-oriented community, and people were fearful. Parents were advised to watch their children closely and to keep their doors locked even during the day. The anchorman reminded TV viewers that if anyone had information that could help the North Bend Sheriff's Department or local police department apprehend this killer, they could call the number at the bottom of the screen and remain anonymous.

Dime laughed, muttered something, and then laughed again.

The bartender gave him a scowl. "Man, why is that so funny to you? Some sick SOB is out there killing people."

Dime slid off the saddle stool, tossed a five on the bar, and walked out. The alarm on his watch sounded just as he climbed into his Jeep. He grinned and pulled out his burner phone to call Melissa.

It rang four times before she finally answered. "Hello, Realty World, Melissa Mately speaking. One moment, please."

Melissa apparently had another caller she found more important, which made Dime mad. He was tired of women like her treating him with no respect. Dime heard the phone click back over to him several minutes later.

"I'm so sorry to keep you waiting. This is Melissa again. How may I improve your day?"

His anger subsided momentarily. "Hello, Melissa, David Ingles here. Remember me from Sunday?"

"Of course I do, and I'm delighted you called."

Me too.

"So have you decided to take a look at Oriole Lane after all?"

"I certainly have. How about right now?"

Silence filled her end of the phone line.

"Hello?"

"Sorry, I had to think for a second. Um… I just finished my last showing and was headed back to the office. I have to write up a listing description for a client that wants to sell her home. I hadn't heard from you so I made other plans. Can we schedule it for tomorrow instead? I'd kind of like to get this listing done tonight."

"You know, never mind. I have to go back to Philly tomorrow for a while. Maybe I'll check out some other Realtors when I come back to North Bend. Thanks anyway."

"No, wait. I guess I can turn around. I don't want you

to leave town unhappy with my professional services. I aim to please. I'll meet you at the residence if you don't mind doing it that way. How about six fifteen?" Melissa's voice began to cut in and out. "Hello, Mr. Ingles? My battery is going. Did you hear me?"

"Yes… I said six fifteen is perfect. See you soon. I'm looking forward to it." *I can't believe some women are that naive dealing with strangers. First, Elise opens her window on a dark, deserted road, and now Melissa is going to meet me by herself at a remote home for sale. Anyone that stupid deserves to die. Hmm… and then there was Morris.*

Dime pulled away from Eddy's Tap. Gravel crunched under his tires until he hit the blacktop of the highway and headed east.

From the bar, the drive would take ten more minutes. He had a bit of an advantage being able to arrive before Melissa did. He'd take a few minutes to scope out the surroundings. From the aerial view on the listing, the driveway looked long and private with a heavy pine forest leading in. Nobody would see their vehicles from the road. With the house vacant, he'd have plenty of quality time alone with the foolish Realtor.

Dime hit his left blinker and turned off the highway onto Oriole Lane. His head swiveled left and right as he drove slowly. The secluded street was perfect for his needs. He passed only one house a half mile back, and who knew what lay ahead. He didn't see any other homes nearby when he slowed at the driveway with the For Sale sign hammered into the ground next to the road. The sign displayed the

Realty World logo, her contact info, and Melissa's smiling face.

You won't be smiling for long. The voices in Dime's head smirked as they encouraged him to turn in, and he did.

The paved driveway made enough of an *S* curve to obstruct the view of the house. Beds of multicolored flowers and shrubbery flanked the sides of the driveway, telling Dime that groundskeepers were retained to keep appearances up while the house stood vacant. He parked, got out, took off his sweatshirt, and left it in the Jeep. He looked back toward the driveway to make sure he couldn't see the road.

"Nice digs," he said as he took in the front of the house. Before him stood an enormous, sprawling Arts and Crafts–style two-story home. The covered porch filled the length of the house and was large and inviting. Two flagstone columns stood on either side of the matching flagstone steps leading up to the porch. Every window on the front of the home was accented with leaded glass, including the arched window over the thick oak double doors. The home's clapboard siding was painted a soft celery green, and the accent trim around the windows was a pale yellow. Each door of the five-car garage had arched windows on the oak doors, matching the house's front door. More flower beds lined the flagstone walkway that led from the driveway to the porch steps. A smile lit his face, and he whistled at the sight before him, then headed down the path to check the outbuildings. The one to the right could be the perfect place for Melissa to meet her maker. The latex gloves jammed in his pocket were ready when he needed them. He put them on temporarily to push open the double doors of what looked to be a horse barn. Six gated stalls stood on either side of a wide center walkway. Remnants of scattered straw still covered the floor. When he walked in, he saw harnesses and bridles that had been left behind hanging in the tack room. He reached out and touched the old, worn leather-and-steel accessories. *These will come in handy.*

A noise sounded behind him. He turned and slipped off the gloves when he saw Melissa entering through the creaky barn doors. The evening sun hung lower in the sky and pierced the opening as she walked through. He could only see her as a silhouette walking toward him.

"Hello, David. I see you've begun without me."

He held out his hand and shook hers. "Good to see you, Melissa, and thanks for adjusting your schedule to accommodate my short notice. What a great property. Shall we check out the house first?"

"Well, as long as we're out here anyway."

"Humor me, please. I'd rather end our tour outside. I'm anxious to see the house."

"Oh… okay, then, right this way."

Melissa entered the code on the lockbox attached to the heavy wooden front doors. She opened the box and removed the key, then slid the key into the dead bolt and turned it to the right. The lock clicked, and they entered the enormous foyer. Dime had no interest in touring the house, but he didn't want to create suspicion on her end. He'd play the game for a while until the voices gave him the command. A blind side at the end of the tour would be worth waiting for.

"So, Mr. Ingles, why a house this large? Do you have a family?" Melissa carried several listing sheets as they walked.

"Oh, I guess we didn't discuss much on Sunday, did we? If I remember correctly, you were heading out."

She apologized. "That's right, but late spring into summer is our busiest season. So, the family?"

"Yes, they're in Philly. They'll arrive once I pick out a home. My children are still in school for a few more weeks. They told me they want horses, hence this type of property."

"That's wonderful. How many kids do you have?"

"Two—a boy and a girl."

"And the missus, does she like to cook? The kitchen is to die for."

Dime chuckled under his breath.

Melissa smiled at him. "Let me show you what I mean. Right this way."

Dime followed her through the large foyer. Saltillo tiles glistened on the floor. Down the oak-paneled hallway heading toward the back of the house was the living room with floor-to-ceiling windows. Heavy roughhewn beams accented the cathedral ceiling. The living room faced the back pasture where his nonexistent horses would graze. The kitchen was to their right, beyond the butler's pantry and dining room.

He whistled, playing it up for all it was worth. "Nice kitchen. Anna's going to love it."

"I bet she will. The center island's butcher-block top is three-inch-thick oak." She glanced down at the listing sheet and read off the brand names. "The stove is Wolf, and the refrigerator is Sub-Zero. I'm sure your wife will appreciate those high-quality appliances. The subway tile backsplash is a recent addition. Everyone seems to love subway tiles these days."

"Uh-huh. Let's check out the bedrooms."

"Of course. They're all on the second floor. Right this way."

Melissa led Dime through several more tiled hallways before they reached the staircase, which was just off the family room. She stopped for a few seconds to let him appreciate the enormous stacked-stone fireplace whose facade reached the ceiling.

"Here's an interesting fact. The listing says that mantel"—she pointed to it—"was hewn from an oak tree that grew right on this property."

Dime glanced at the mantel, then followed the stonework to the ceiling with his eyes. "It's amazing."

The house tour took another thirty minutes. Four large bedrooms were upstairs besides the master suite. Each bedroom had its own private bath with windows facing the front or back of the property.

"This home is wonderful. I'm sure my family will be more than happy to live here." Dime noticed the twinkle in her eye and the grin that spread across her face when he made that comment.

All she cares about is making a sale. It's only about the

commission. They're all the same—you're nobody to her. Kill the bitch and get it over with.

Dime rubbed his temples. The time was near, and the voices were calling the shots.

"Are you okay? You just grimaced like a headache was coming on," Melissa said.

"What? Oh, sorry, I'm fine. I get seasonal allergy headaches now and then. Shall we move on to the garage and the outbuildings?" he asked. He reached into his front pocket and felt for the gloves.

"Sure, right this way." She led Dime back downstairs and through the mudroom into the five-car garage. "This is the ultimate garage. It's perfect for three cars, a few toys and bicycles, and it's heated."

"That's a plus. So we have the horse barn and the other building. What was that one used for?"

"I believe it's a tractor shed. There's a ten-acre pasture, you know."

"Of course. Let's spend some time in the horse barn. I had just walked in when you arrived earlier. My kids will be excited to hear more about it."

Melissa read the outbuilding descriptions from the listing sheet. "Apparently, there are twelve stalls in total. Have you ever owned horses?" As she talked, she entered through the double barn doors for the second time.

"Not yet."

"Well, it's an ambitious enterprise, I'm sure. I hate to say it, but this beautiful residence has been for sale for eight months, and you're only the second person I've shown it to.

I imagine it's out of most people's price range."

Dime smiled as he reached into his pocket and slipped on the gloves while he followed behind her. "That's what I'm counting on."

Melissa continued walking. "I guess this is the tack room, whatever that means." She giggled coquettishly as she entered the area. "I'll admit, I don't know a thing about horses."

"Or about taking safety measures when you're alone with a stranger."

"I'm sorry, what?"

She turned toward him and stared. Terror spread across her face as she acknowledged the predicament in which she found herself. Her eyes darted left and right for a way to escape. He blocked the only exit from the room with his large body. She didn't have time to duck before he swung a bridle that caught her in the face. She stumbled backward and hit the rough wooden wall. He swung the bridle again and again, connecting with her face each time, until she was unconscious. Blood ran down her forehead and dripped off her chin, soaking her white blouse.

He smirked and cocked his head while he stared at her. *You aren't that hot anymore, are you?* He gathered the gear he needed. *That was so easy. I love blind sides. If only I had a picture of their faces at the moment of realization.*

Dime wadded up the two listing sheets and grabbed the bridle and a length of leather strap.

"This should do it. Oh yeah, I can't forget the dime."

He started with the prep work by opening the small

bottle of hand sanitizer he kept in his other front pocket. He poured some in her hands and rubbed them together. He'd shaken her hand earlier and didn't want to take any chances. He was careful not to touch anything in the house while his hands were ungloved. Her car keys were in her blazer pocket. He pulled them out.

The balled-up listing sheets were jammed deep down her throat. He cleaned the dime with the hand sanitizer and placed it under her tongue while humming a little ditty that was stuck in his head. He closed her mouth and pinched her nose. Her body jerked involuntarily while it was being starved of oxygen. Dime glanced at his watch and held his position another three minutes before releasing her and checking for a pulse. There wasn't any. He placed the bridle in her mouth, wrapped the leather strap around her neck, and carried her to a stall. With the strap, he secured her in a sitting position to the stall gate from the inside. It would be more difficult to see her that way. He wanted the cops to earn their living, and he wasn't going to make finding her too easy on them.

He walked to the fifth stall on the left and opened the bag he had placed there earlier. A clean change of clothes and another pair of latex gloves were inside. He rolled up the bloody gloves and removed the clothing he had on, then tossed them into the bag. After putting on the clean pair of gloves, he flipped the toggle switch for the barn lights and pulled the doors closed. Back inside the house, he walked through to the garage and hit the button to open one of the overhead doors. He drove her car in, then opened the briefcase that sat on the passenger seat. Inside were her purse, cell phone, and a calendar listing all of her appointments for the month. He pulled the battery out of her phone and threw it back in, then closed the briefcase. He grabbed it by the leather handle—it would go along with him. Dime got out, adjusted the seat back to the position Melissa had had it in, and closed the car door. He wouldn't make that mistake twice. A scan across the garage told him it looked fine. He lowered the overhead door and entered the house. A slow, methodical walk from room to room would guarantee him the house looked the way it did when they entered. He turned off the lights and exited out the front.

He put the key back into the lockbox and clicked it closed.

Dime checked the time—seven thirty. He climbed into his Jeep and drove away. The voices in his head laughed with him as he headed toward home.

He wondered how to keep Melissa's coworkers from missing her. He wasn't quite ready for her to be found yet. He'd have to think about that, maybe while lounging in the basement, enjoying a beer. A thought popped into his mind as he passed North Bend. He pulled over and turned around.

I'll text one of her coworkers from her phone and make something up. I have to do it at Realty World's office, though.

Dime headed in that direction—it was nearly eight o'clock now. He drove by the office slowly, making sure the lights were off and the parking lot was empty. He pulled in behind the building, parked, and retrieved her cell phone and battery from the briefcase. With his own phone, he pulled up Realty World's website and clicked on the list of agents. Each name popped up on the screen. He put the battery back in her phone, turned it on, and noticed it was almost dead. He'd only need a minute. A quick look around confirmed he was still alone. There were no headlights approaching or people walking the area. Dime scrolled through her contact list and found a name that would do just fine—Adriana Cruz. She was another top earner at their agency. He pressed the yellow envelope icon and tapped out a short text.

Adriana, I had to leave town abruptly—family emergency. I may be gone for a few days. I'll be in touch. Thanks.

Dime smiled. He knew if it got that far and the cops pinged her phone, the last message would show it came right from Realty World's own parking lot.

Sounds legit to me. He removed the battery again and drove home.

Chapter 21

I changed the bird's water and filled up the seed bowl as I talked on the phone. Multitasking seemed necessary every time I spoke to my mom. She was the only person I knew that could talk on the phone for two hours at a time. My Bluetooth was a godsend.

"Yes, I'm sure, Mom. Amber isn't going to be an inconvenience. Actually, now that I've given it some thought, I'm looking forward to having her as a roommate. She's a breath of fresh air. You know she's moving because of Bruce, don't you? Maybe you should talk to your husband about keeping his distance until she's out of the house. Bruce is strange, and you know it."

"Jade, please don't start with me. I'm doing my best to keep the peace."

I filled my wineglass and set it down, then clicked the remote and turned on the TV. I muted the sound.

"Whatever. Amber is moving in this weekend, but her junk is staying there until I'm out of the house. She said you wanted to make her bedroom into a craft room?"

"Yes, I've taken up scrapbooking and knitting."

"Cool. Anyway, we're going to check out a few more condos on Saturday. I'm definitely ready for a mental health break. Maybe looking at a few potential places to live will be a fun distraction."

"Do you want to talk about it, honey?"

"Sorry, Mom, it's work related. Read the paper. You'll get some idea of what I've been doing lately. Right now I just want to veg out and drink my wine."

"You know, your birthday is Saturday. Let's all go out to dinner after you girls look at the condos and Amber moves her things in."

"Okay, I can do that as long as no shit hits the fan before Saturday night. You make the plans, and Amber and I will meet you wherever you decide."

"Promise me you'll work on your cursing, honey."

"Sure thing, Mom. Good night."

I looked through my closet for something appropriate to wear to Morris King's funeral. Terrance told me during a phone call earlier that the funeral was scheduled for Friday at eleven a.m. with a luncheon to follow. As far as I knew, Detective Lindstrom and Lieutenant Colgate would be there too.

I slid the wooden hangers from right to left along the pole and found a navy-blue pantsuit that would work fine. A floral scarf wrapped around the collar of a simple white blouse would accent it nicely.

My thoughts returned to what had been on my mind before the phone call from my mom. I knew the flowers I received yesterday hadn't come from Amber. The florist said she couldn't remember what the person looked like that bought them, but they paid in cash. According to her, it had been a hectic day with a huge wedding flower order.

I didn't pursue it. Lance always told me I was good at that—avoidance. I was a great cop—according to him—but even better at avoiding life issues, like the lack of communication between us. The only issue I was aware of was that my husband was having an affair with another salesperson at the Toyota dealership where he worked. I was pretty sure he didn't want to communicate with me about that. Fast forward ten months—she was in and I was out. I'd been replaced, and life went on.

After the ten o'clock news, I went to bed, hoping for a decent night's sleep but not expecting it.

The alarm sounded at six a.m. I was awake anyway and waiting for its loud beep to go off. I got up, stumbled to the window, and turned the wand on the blinds. The sun poured in—it felt good. I started the coffeepot, said good morning to Polly and Porky, fed them, and hit the shower. I appreciated the fact that my hair was normally my friend. If the weather was dry and the humidity was low, my thick, straight hair behaved with very little effort on my part. A quick comb-through, a touch of mascara, and a little blush were all I needed to look presentable on most workdays.

I ate a piece of toast with raspberry preserves, drank a cup of coffee, filled my travel mug, and headed to the station. Within minutes, I had arrived.

"Morning, Jade."

I looked up from my desk and nodded. "Billings."

"You're in early. Need help with anything?" Billings plunked down in one of my guest chairs and set his cup on a sheet of paper. He looked at his watch. "It's seven o'clock."

"Yeah, I know, but I couldn't sleep anymore. Thought I'd clean up my desk and file away some of these closed cases from last month. We also have a few criminals being transferred to Waupun today. I want to talk to them before they leave our jurisdiction. Maybe they'll do a little singing before their lives get a whole lot worse." I took a sip from my travel mug. "Once Jack gets in, I want to pay a visit to some of our local informants too. There has to be word on the street about our murder cases. Somebody has to know something. We've got to get out and pound the pavement. Sitting here doing busywork will drive me nuts."

"I hear you, Sergeant. Just say the word. Clayton and I will pitch in wherever you need us. The more sets of eyes, the better. We can go through all of the interview logs again, hit the streets, go back out to the crime scenes, and scour the areas one more time—whatever you need."

"Thanks, Billings. I'll let you know."

Jack walked in at eight o'clock alongside the lieutenant. They parted ways at the bull pen, Jack to his desk, the lieutenant to his office.

"Well, partner, what's on the agenda for today?"

"We should hit the streets, see if there's any new chatter. The local lowlifes should have heard something by now."

"You'd think. I'm up for it. Anything else?" Jack filled

two coffee cups from the fresh pot Billings made when he got there.

"Thanks. Yeah, I've got to go upstairs and talk to a few of our guests before they leave our five-star accommodations." I smiled.

Jack laughed. "You mean the local pharmacists?"

"The very ones. They're being transferred to Waupun today. Guess their attorneys couldn't get the charges reduced. They're each looking at substantial time for intent to sell, not just possession."

"More than three grams each?"

"That's right. See ya—wouldn't want to be ya. I thought they might want to make a final goodwill gesture before they leave town. Maybe I can set them up with nicer roommates or something if they give me a few names."

"Okay. Well, whenever you want to hit the streets, let me know. Hand me those folders. I'll file them away."

"Thanks, I appreciate it. Billings, call a florist in Milwaukee and order an arrangement to be delivered to Phillips Funeral Home for Morris King's funeral on Friday."

"Got it, boss."

I checked the time—eight thirty. "Billings, hold down the fort. I'm going upstairs." I signed in at the reception counter and took the stairs to our jail. "Hey, John, I'd like to have a chat with Manny Gomez and Frank Luis before they head out. I'll only need thirty minutes of their time."

"You got it, Sergeant Monroe. Would you like them linked up?"

"Yeah, if you don't mind."

"Give me ten minutes."

"No problem. I see one of my favorite magazines." I took a seat and waited.

John returned a few minutes later and told me the inmates were ready for me. I nodded and walked into the cafeteria. At this time of day, nobody had visitors, and meals weren't being served. The two men sat at the table nearest the door. A deputy watched through the window separating the cafeteria from the guard station.

"Gentlemen," I said as I sat down across from them, "I hear you're moving into the big house today. It must be an exciting time for both of you. Something different, right? New faces, new friends, new enemies." I looked at their sheets in front of me. "Hmm… you're both getting ten years? That sucks. Guess your state-appointed attorney doesn't care much for meth pushers."

"What do you want, lady? We've got packing to do," Manny said, spewing the words at me.

I laughed. "Cute. Everything you need for the next ten years will be provided for you by us—the taxpayers. As far as I know, a couple of orange jumpsuits and a pair of rubber sandals should do it." I gave them both the once-over. "Pink looks more like your color, though. Anyway, I might be able to help you out with your accommodations. You know, maybe a down feather pillow, something of that nature." I grinned at both of them and cocked my head to the right.

They huffed.

"No? Not appealing enough? What would you boys

think of bunking together? That in itself is like winning the lottery. You'll sleep better at night not worrying that your roommate has a shiv under his mattress, or worse. You could be bunked with a three-hundred-pound guy named Bubba. All you have to do is give me some names. I want big names, not the punks you run with." I looked at the analog clock above the door. "See the time?"

They both turned around and looked at the wall.

"Man, I'd hate to be you right now. Your lives are going to change substantially in a few short hours. It's nine o'clock, and your transport bus leaves at noon. If I don't hear anything from you by eleven, the offer is off the table. Have a nice life, boys."

I got up and walked out. A thought popped into my head as I took the stairs down to the bull pen.

"Jack, Clayton, Billings, come with me."

They looked up from their desks, pushed their chairs back, and followed. I rapped on the lieutenant's door. He waved us in.

"What's with the expression, Jade? You look like you just had an epiphany." The lieutenant set his paperwork down and gave me the floor.

"I might have. What if we're looking at this murderer the wrong way?"

Jack spoke up. "Meaning?"

"Maybe the name Dime doesn't have anything to do with drugs. What if his nickname means he did a ten year stint in prison?"

"You could be on to something, but even that would be

tough to track down. We don't have a real name, age, or description," Clayton said.

"True, but it gives us a little more to work with. We could start with state correctional institutions and the inmates that served ten-year sentences. Maybe even the guards would know if someone had that nickname. We could ask on the street too. We have to do something, Lieutenant. Wishful thinking isn't going to catch this monster."

"You're right, Jade. Okay, divide up the thirty or so facilities in the state and get the lists of all inmates that served ten years and have been released within the last year. We have to start small. This task could eat up all of our time otherwise. Talk to people on the street. Tell the North Bend PD what we're doing. We don't want to step on any toes. I'll give you a few weeks to pursue this avenue and see if it goes anywhere. We'll reconvene before the end of the month and see what we have. If nothing shakes out, we'll try something else. Let's move. Nice work, Jade."

"Thanks, boss. Okay, Clayton, print out a list of all the state prisons and meet us in the lunchroom in ten minutes. Billings, did you take care of the flowers for the funeral?"

"Yep, all done."

"Jack, could you get Todd and Billy up here?"

"Sure thing."

Chapter 22

Six of us sat in the lunchroom, going over the list of thirty-five state correctional facilities in Wisconsin. Billy and Todd brought along their laptops from the tech department and worked their magic. With the software they had access to and the parameters we told them to use, they were able to pull up all the criminals in the state who'd served ten-year sentences and been released in the last year.

"Okay, Todd, you take half of them and Billy the other half. Now narrow those names down to people who served their sentences for violent crimes. I'm not interested in white-collar criminals." I looked at their screens. "Only forty names? Maybe we should go back further. See how many names fit that criteria going back five years."

Billy hit a few keys and pulled up almost one hundred fifty names.

"That's doable. Is there any way to get their photos and descriptions too? How about by age? I don't think we're looking for anyone over seventy, do you, Jack?"

"Doubt it. Let's go by age first, then description."

I nodded. "Yeah, sure."

We waited while Billy punched that information into the search parameters.

"Okay, that dropped it down to one hundred fifteen inmates under seventy. What's next?" Billy asked.

Jack spoke up. "Let's go with everyone five foot ten and taller. Weight can vary too much. After that, let's see if any of them are from southeast Wisconsin, preferably Washburn County. Maybe even if they have family in the area too."

"Sure, hold on." Todd pulled up a list of sixty-two inmates that had been released in the last five years that were five foot ten or taller and less that seventy years old.

"That's it—sixty-two? That's a good start and not at all overwhelming. Print out all of their names, photos, addresses, and parole officers' contact info. We'll start making calls after lunch. I've got to run upstairs and see if my boys have anything they want to discuss before they leave our fair county in an hour. Everyone be back here at one o'clock."

I was hopeful and felt as though we were doing something that might give us leads. I took the stairs two at a time. I asked John if Manny and Frank had any information they wanted to share with me before they were sent up the river.

"They only said your name and a few choice curse words in Spanish. They're being processed out of the county right now into the state system. Do you want to give them one more opportunity to talk to you?"

"Nah—they had their chance. They can enjoy the next ten years in a real prison. Tell them I said to enjoy their new digs."

"Yes, ma'am, with pleasure."

I headed back downstairs. Those two punks weren't going to upset me. I was sure we'd find the main players in their meth-making organization soon enough. For now, it felt good to get two of them off the street.

"Wanna go out for lunch?" Jack asked. "My treat."

"Why are you offering to pay?" I gave him a suspicious grin.

"You deserve it, that's all. I know this case is keeping you awake at night. Hell, it's definitely wearing me down. You need a little break, Jade, plus your birthday is Saturday. I haven't heard mention of a party, so this is the least I can do. Come on. Let's go to the Washington House. It will be a nice change from vending machine sandwiches."

"Okay, you got a deal. It will be nice to relax over lunch for once. No talk of work until we get back to the station, though."

Jack pulled the invisible zipper across his lips. "No talk of work. I promise."

We grabbed an unmarked cruiser from the lot, and within five minutes, we were parked on Main Street. Seven brick steps led up to the entrance of the Washington House restaurant. The three-story building stood taller than the rest in the historic center of Main Street. A brass plaque was bolted on the outer wall next to the front door. The limestone building had been erected in 1861 as an upscale hotel in the heart of North Bend. Over the years, it had gone through many changes, but the building currently housed apartments on the upper levels and a nice restaurant and bar on the first floor. Live music played every Wednesday and Saturday night.

The hostess stand was just beyond the foyer, and a long, ornate oak bar was beyond that. Our eyes had to adjust from bright sunshine to the dimly lit bar area in front of us. Beautiful stained glass pendant lights hung every five feet above the bar.

Gabi was written across the hostess's plastic name badge pinned to her burgundy long-sleeved blouse. The name itself made me grin.

"A table for lunch or just a drink at the bar?" she asked, wearing a wide smile.

Jack spoke up. "A table for two, please."

"Certainly, right this way."

Gabi seated us next to the fireplace. Since it was close to summer, a fire wasn't lit, but it was a pretty place to sit anyway. White linen tablecloths covered the tables, and a rose in a bud vase sat in the center of each one. I had a sudden flashback to the vase of flowers on my desk. I quickly dismissed it as Gabi went over today's lunch specials with us.

"May I get you started with something to drink?"

"Sure, I'll have a raspberry iced tea," I said.

Jack placed the napkin on his lap. "I'll take the same."

I looked around the dining room. As many years as I'd lived in North Bend, I had never been in the Washington

House. "This is kind of fancy for lunch."

"Yeah, so what? You're worth it as long as the bill stays under ten bucks." Jack chuckled.

I pinched his arm. "You're terrible."

He winced and rubbed the red mark harder than necessary. "So is Amber excited about moving this weekend?"

"Absolutely. I'll admit, I wasn't too keen on the idea at first, but now I'm kind of looking forward to it too."

"That's great for both of you, and I get it. Look how close I am to my brothers, and we're closer in age than you and Amber are. You'll really get to know each other a lot better this way."

"Yeah, and getting her away from Bruce, the perv, isn't such a bad idea either."

Jack laughed. "You know, my offer is still on the table. Just say the word."

I grinned and opened my menu. "Everything looks good. I think I'll have the caprese sandwich on toasted ciabatta bread. That sounds delicious."

"It does, but you're over ten bucks already with your iced tea."

"Jerk."

The waitress appeared with our beverages. "Have you decided yet?"

"Sure have. The lady will have the caprese sandwich, and I'll have the sirloin burger with home fries. Jade, do you want something on the side?"

"Um… okay, I'll have a fruit cup with my sandwich."

The waitress took our orders and our menus, thanked us, and left.

"So what did Amber think of the condos she looked at last weekend?"

"There were a few she really liked that I want to take a look at myself. We have an appointment set up for Saturday with Melissa Mately again to look at three-bedroom units. I hope the house doesn't take too long to sell."

"You've got a nice place, Jade. It should go quickly, especially with summer coming. Kids will be out of school in a few weeks, and families will be moving."

"Yeah, I'm kind of looking forward to living somewhere that doesn't have Lance memories."

Jack nodded. "It looks like our lunch is coming."

The waitress carried a tray to our table. It held the best looking lunch I had seen in a long time, and nothing was wrapped in cellophane.

Chapter 23

We reconvened in the lunchroom just after one o'clock. Billy had placed a pitcher of water and cups on the table. I thanked him for thinking of it.

Sixty-two photos and profiles of recently released inmates lay spread out across the long lunch table.

"We should divide these up by counties. Some might share the same parole officers. That could speed things up. Let's do that first and see what we have."

It took only fifteen minutes, and the sixty-two sheets of paper were stacked into five counties. Milwaukee County held twenty-seven names.

"Why doesn't that surprise me?" Jack said. "What else do we have?"

Billy spoke up. "Washburn County has six names, Marinette County has four names, Racine County has fourteen, and Kenosha County has eleven."

"All right, Billy, you and Todd work on Milwaukee. I'll take Washburn. Jack, you can have Racine. Clayton, you take Kenosha, and Billings, you take Marinette. Let's call the parole officers and get some idea of these guys. It will probably take the rest of today, maybe even tomorrow if we don't get through to all of the parole officers this afternoon. Let's get started. Write down everything they tell you. Don't leave anything out."

At three o'clock, Lieutenant Clark came into the bull pen to check our progress. We each sat at our desks. Todd and Billy sat at the empty desks that Detectives Jamison and Horbeck used at night. Clark said he was impressed with our determination.

"Okay, take ten and tell me what you have," he said.

"In Milwaukee County, we've gone through eight names with the parole officers so far. Of those eight, five of them hold down steady daytime jobs and haven't missed a day of work in six months. One guy has severe back problems, and two live at halfway houses with a ten o'clock curfew. Nobody goes by the nickname Dime," Todd said.

"Jade, what do you have for Washburn County?"

"So far, boss, not much. I'm going to dig in with Barry Nicolaus a little deeper on two guys he mentioned. I'll pay him a visit tomorrow. He said both of these guys have past issues with domestic violence and animal cruelty."

"Anyone else, anything that stands out yet?" the lieutenant asked.

Jack, Clayton, and Billings looked at each other and shrugged.

"Okay, keep it up. Good work, everyone. Oh, by the way, Jade, call Perry and tell him Elise's body will be released tomorrow." The lieutenant stepped into his office and closed the door behind him.

I sighed. "That's good news. Perry can start making funeral arrangements. I hope the craziness is over for a while."

I called Perry's house, but nobody answered. I left myself a note to try again in the morning.

By the time we wrapped up our calls to the parole officers, it was after five o'clock. We realized these people held regular work hours, and we were beginning to get more voice mails than real people on the phone.

"Let's call it a day. There's no need to leave messages and then call back tomorrow anyway. We'll start fresh in the morning. Thanks, guys."

Jack rubbed his eyes and stood up. "I'll walk out with you, Jade. I'm beat."

We exited together and walked to our cars parked side by side.

"See you in the morning, partner. Thanks for lunch," I said.

He got in his car, waved, and drove away.

I realized now that a few things would have to change with Amber moving in. The shoulder holster with my service weapon couldn't just lie on the breakfast bar as it normally did anymore. I gave it some thought as I drove home. *I should keep it in my bedroom from now on. I don't want to freak her out with it just lying around.* I thought about my dad too. *I'll call him tonight after he gets home from work. We need to catch up, and I'd like his take on this killer.*

I arrived home and pressed the garage door remote. I

waited as the overhead door opened. The door from the garage led into the laundry room with the kitchen just beyond that. Polly and Porky's cage stood in the dinette and faced the bay window looking out to the side yard. They enjoyed the morning sunshine pouring in from the east. Their birdseed messes were easier to sweep up from the tile floor rather than the carpet. I walked in, removed my shoulder holster, and set it on the breakfast bar. I went to the birdcage and greeted them, just as always. Tonight, Porky hopped on my outstretched finger. I petted him and gave him a kiss. With fresh water and more birdseed, they were content for the night.

I knew there wouldn't be much of a dinner choice in the refrigerator, but I could get creative if I had to. I pulled open the door and groaned. Other than condiments and a half quart of suspicious-looking milk, the refrigerator stood nearly empty. I ordered Chinese again and told them I'd pass on the fortune cookies. This time, I opted for delivery. I didn't have the energy to go out again and pick up dinner. With a glass of wine in my hand, I plopped down on the couch and let out a sigh. I checked the time—another hour before Dad would be home from work. I reached for the remote sitting on the coffee table when a sound startled me. A definite thump sounded from one of the bedrooms down the hall.

I didn't really hear anything, did I? My mind tried to rationalize the sound. I could talk myself out of thinking I heard something. *I'm a brave and reasonable woman—it had to be a noise coming from the furnace or the air conditioner or the refrigerator, didn't it? What the hell was that?*

I heard my heart pounding in my chest and waited—certain it was my imagination. The horrific images of Morris and Elise popped into my head. I listened again—my ears perked. Another thump sounded. Now I had to do something. I had to act. Luckily my shoes were off, and I could move about without making noise. I crept to my service weapon and pulled it out of the holster. Moments like this made me hate living alone. The hallway light needed to stay off or whoever was on the other side of the bedroom door would see me when I opened it. They'd have the advantage. My years of police training kicked in within seconds. I racked the slide of my pistol and chambered a live bullet. My back was pressed against the wall as I moved silently down the hall with my weapon drawn, trying to determine which room the sound came from. With each step I took, I stopped and listened, then moved on. The last room was the one Amber would use. I pressed my ear against the door. The sound came from inside. I stood against the wall, knowing I'd have to swing the door open and hit the light all in one movement. I took a deep breath and reached for the knob.

"Son of a gun. I don't believe this crap." I stopped and listened to the familiar cry of Spaz, pawing and whining on the other side of the door. I lowered my weapon and opened the door. Amber's cat ran down the hall in a flurry of hissing fur.

"What in the heck are you doing here?" I grabbed my cell phone and called Amber.

"Hi, Sis," she said.

"What in the hell is Spaz doing here? I almost shot him."

"What? Don't you dare shoot my cat."

"Why didn't you tell me you were bringing him over already?"

"Jade, have you read any of the texts I sent you today?"

"I was busy making calls all day. I didn't look at them."

"I texted you that Spaz was in my new room, and the door was closed. I wasn't sure how it would work with him and the birds. Better safe than sorry—right?"

"Yeah… smart thinking. I guess I'm just tense lately. I heard a couple of thumps and thought the worst. Spaz must have jumped off the bed or something like that. We'll figure it out, Sis. I can always put the birdcage in my bedroom until we move."

"Do you want me to come over, Jade? It sounds like you need some company."

"Sure, that sounds good. I'm going to call Dad later too. We'll talk to him together on speakerphone."

Chapter 24

Amber talked on the phone to our dad while I ate dinner. I never grew tired of Chinese food, but like a generous sister, I gave Amber the pot stickers.

She explained to Dad that she was moving in with me and that we were going out to look at condos again on Saturday. I added my two cents every few minutes and told him about the scare Spaz had given me earlier.

"Amber, honey, don't forget your big sis is a cop with a big gun." He laughed when I described how I slinked down the hall, ready to shoot whatever was on the other side of that door.

"All I can say is Amber is lucky I recognized Spaz's voice and put two and two together. That cat wouldn't have made it to nine lives with a hole from my gun through him."

Dad let out a full belly laugh. We chuckled. On a more serious note, I went on to explain to my dad the situation we were dealing with in North Bend.

Amber curled up on the couch and watched TV, leaving the cop talk to us.

"We don't have any leads to go on, Dad. It's really

frustrating. We find the bodies after the fact, with no idea who he's after. The bodies are found outside, and there's no forensic evidence anywhere."

"No defensive wounds or DNA?"

"Nope, nothing."

"Sounds like he may have blindsided them, especially if they didn't put up a fight."

"I think Elise did initially. Her face was beaten pretty badly, like he punched her. It's likely Morris didn't know anything since his throat was slit. The guy obviously approached him from behind and overpowered him easily."

"So, what do you have, honey?"

"Only our suspicions. The guy must be six foot or taller and strong. That's it, Dad, nothing else." I lowered my voice to continue. "He's left a dime at each location, though. He wants us to know it's him. I guess the dime is his calling card since he goes by that name."

Tom sighed. "Not a lot to work with, honey. He isn't ready to be caught yet, but he likes the game."

"That's what it sounds like. We don't want to find another dead body, but without more clues, this guy is always one step ahead of us."

"Keep me posted and stay safe. That goes for your sister too. Watch over her, Jade. Call me anytime you want if you feel like talking about the case."

"I will, Dad. Love you."

"Love you too, honey. Tell your sister good night."

"Will do." I hung up and sat next to Amber on the couch.

She paused the TV and turned to me. "Jade, I've been doing some serious thinking."

"Really, about what?" I got up and grabbed the wine bottle off the kitchen table. I brought it to the living room and filled both our glasses.

"I want to change my major to a criminal justice degree. I've given it a lot of thought, and I want to follow in your and Dad's footsteps. Having a minor in behavioral sciences will come in handy too. I think someday I'd like to be an FBI profiler."

"Wow, I'm speechless. I had no idea, Amber. I'm so proud of you, honey, and Dad will be too. Are you sure this is what you want to do?"

"I'm positive. I can start with criminal justice as my major in the fall. I'll figure out what additional courses I'll need to take. To be honest, I was never that keen on being a shrink in the normal sense of the word, but I do like the idea of figuring out how people think. Being a profiler, somewhere down the line, sounds exactly like what I want to do with my life. I know I have to go through the ranks and proper channels. Once I graduate, I intend to enroll in the police academy." Amber chuckled. "I looked at the requirements to be a cop. I have to pass a psychological exam by a licensed psychiatrist. Maybe I can shrink the shrink."

"Knowing you, you'd probably try."

"So, would you be willing to tell me about the murder case you're working on?"

"Honey, I can't tell you any more than what we've told

the press. Those details are already in the newspaper. You aren't a cop yet, and we can't let certain things get out. I'm sorry. If there was anything I thought was a danger to you, of course I'd let you know. I promised Dad I'd keep you safe." I caught a glimpse of Spaz crouched low, slinking toward the birdcage and ready to pounce. "Yeah, that isn't going to work. Want to help me carry the cage into my bedroom? There's no way in hell Polly and Porky are going to be Spaz's evening meal."

"Sure. Sorry Spaz had to come early. Mom said he was already getting into her yarn."

Amber finally left at ten o'clock. She had early classes, and I was usually up by six thirty anyway.

"Sorry about tonight, Jade. Just think how fun it will be to look at condos together on Saturday, though. Cool, right?"

"Very cool. Oh, I don't know if Mom mentioned it, but we're all going out for dinner together Saturday night for my birthday. Don't know where yet—she's picking the place. Anyway, bring over your clothes and a few things you can't live without Saturday morning. Melissa said she'd check in with us before we meet up."

Amber grabbed her purse and keys. "Thanks for the pot stickers and not shooting Spaz." She grinned. "Night, Jade."

I hugged her. "Thanks for stopping over, Sis. I don't seem to sleep well lately, so I'm hitting the sack now. Good night."

Chapter 25

I was thankful for the six hours of sleep I got—most nights, four seemed to be my best, if I was lucky. Every night, I'd toss, turn, and punch my pillow until I was exhausted enough to fall asleep. Ideas bounced back and forth like ping-pong balls in my brain until I started writing them down so I could dismiss them. A full day lay ahead of us once we all got to the office. We would finish up our phone calls and hit the streets, hoping to talk to anyone that knew of someone named Dime or had heard of anything suspicious related to the killings.

A stop at the gas station for a jumbo coffee encouraged me to indulge in a box of two dozen doughnuts to share throughout the bull pen and with the tech boys. They were more than helpful, and I truly appreciated everything they had done for me. I never pictured myself drinking a jumbo gas station coffee, but my life was changing, and I'd get by just fine.

I placed the large box of doughnuts on the table at the back of the bull pen. Hopefully they'd last longer if they weren't on Jack's desk. I chuckled at the thought. I'd never known anyone who was as unhealthy an eater as Jack, yet he was muscular and never got sick. He was strong, had endurance, and could outrun most eighteen-year-olds.

I looked at the clock above the door. Todd and Billy should be downstairs by now. It was after eight. I'd invite them upstairs for doughnuts since they were so helpful yesterday. My heart told me to invite everyone. We were all involved in this case, like it or not. I stopped by Doug's office. He wasn't there but Jason was. Kyle and Dan were just getting in. I told all of them that plenty of doughnuts were upstairs, and if they wanted any, they'd better go now. Jack, Clayton, and Billings should be arriving any minute, and Lieutenant Clark had already grabbed his pick of the bunch.

Back upstairs, the guys were gathered in the bull pen around the table. Somebody had brought napkins in from the lunchroom, a great idea since some of these were sticky, filled doughnuts. By the time Kyle, Dan, and Jason made it upstairs, the first dozen were gone.

"Okay, guys, as soon as we finish our breakfast treat and wash our grubby little fingers"—I grinned—"we can get back to where we left off on the phones yesterday. After that, we'll hit Settler's Square and a few of the parks."

"Sounds good," Clayton said. "Billings and I will walk through Regency and Riverside Parks."

"Yep, those are the parks I would have suggested anyway. Jack and I will take Settler's Square and all of downtown. Let's make calls until eleven, then hit the streets."

We picked up where we'd left off yesterday. Talking to parole officers seemed to be the most logical and reliable way to get information. They would have an extensive file on each person we asked about, plus they could tell us anything that seemed off about them. They'd have had face time, one-on-one experience with each person they were assigned to. That in itself would be valuable information for us.

I checked the notes I had left on my desk. One was to follow up on two guys with the Washburn County parole officer I spoke to yesterday. Both could be persons of interest. I also had written myself a note to call Perry. We would release Elise's body today to any funeral home he chose. I'd contact him first before I got too involved with the other calls. My mind drifted back to last Thursday night and how I'd enjoyed the yoga class with Elise. That was the last time I saw her alive. I remembered her larger-than-life personality and the happy smile she wore when she conducted those classes. I shook my head.

"Jade, is everything okay?"

I hadn't noticed Jack staring at me.

"We'll get this sicko. I promise you and the residents of North Bend. They need to feel safe in their own community," Jack said.

"Sorry, I was just thinking back to last Thursday. I teased you about joining me at my yoga class. That was the last night I saw Elise alive."

"Do you need a minute? We can get started on our own. I know you need to call Perry."

"Yeah, sure. I'll be right back."

I found a quiet interrogation room and closed the door behind me. I sat down, took a deep breath, and dialed Perry's number.

"Hello, Perry Adams, CPA."

"Perry, it's Jade Monroe."

"Hello, Sergeant. I just got the kids off to school."

"How are you holding up?" I regretted asking the question once the words left my mouth. I knew he wasn't doing well, but I didn't know what else to say.

"Well, you know. The kids are having a tough time." He began to cry.

I rubbed my forehead and dug my fingertips into my temples. "Perry, have you decided on a funeral home yet? Elise's body can be released today if you've picked one."

I heard Perry clear his throat.

"I've already talked to the funeral director at Myram & Frank Funeral Home on Forest Street. They just need you to contact them. They said anytime is fine, then I'll go in after that and make arrangements with them."

"Okay, not a problem. I'll call them as soon as we hang up."

"Have you made any progress, Sergeant Monroe?"

"Not yet, but we're working hard on it. We'll catch him, I just can't say when."

He paused, and silence filled the phone line. "Okay, Sergeant. I guess that's it, then. I'll call the funeral home in about an hour and set up a time to go in."

"Thanks, Perry. I'm going to call them right now. Goodbye."

I headed back to the bull pen with even more determination, sat down at my desk, and called the funeral home. After that, I called Barry Nicolaus, the parole officer I spoke with yesterday, to make an appointment to see him. He told me I could come in immediately if I had time.

"Guys, I'll be back in a bit. I'm going over to the courthouse to follow up with Barry about these guys I flagged yesterday." I grabbed the sheets on the two guys and left.

With the courthouse right next to the sheriff's department, I took the sidewalk and entered through the east corridor hallway. The parole officer's office was on the second floor. I entered and told the receptionist, Nancy, I had an appointment with Barry.

"Sure, Jade, give me a second. Barry, Jade is here."

Barry came out of his office and greeted me. He reached out and shook my hand. "Good to see you again. Come on in."

Barry Nicolaus had been a parole officer in Washburn County for the past fourteen years. He and his wife, Lorraine, were casual friends of mine. A few years back, she and I were in the same bowling league.

I always teased Barry about his tie selection. I stared at his tie with box turtles on it and grinned.

"What?"

I laughed. "You never fail to surprise me. That tie is uglier than the one you wore last month when I was here."

"I forgot which one that was," he said, chuckling.

"I didn't. It had motocross bikes on it." I sat down and

opened the two folders I'd brought with me. "I need to know more about these guys. You're aware of the murders we've been dealing with, right?"

"Who wouldn't be? The news isn't spreading the best light on the sheriff's department. They're making it sound like you guys are incompetent."

"Yeah, I really appreciate all their praise—jerks. This guy leaves no evidence, Barry. He's like a ghost." I pushed the folders toward him. "Look at these pictures. I'm thinking these photos are pretty old. I need to know what these two are like now. Our profile is leading us to believe the perp is pretty strong and over six feet tall. We can't pinpoint an age range, but do your two guys still look like these photos?"

He studied the pictures. "Yeah, I see what you mean. These photos are likely from when they were put in the system. Let's see, Adam Ross was released in 2013 after ten years in Waupun. So, that makes him thirty-seven right now. He looked a lot tougher then. Prison can age a guy quickly unless they're always working out and watching their back. Adam has asthma pretty bad, smokes a lot, and probably goes a buck fifty now."

"That doesn't sound like our guy. How about Chuck Banta?"

Barry studied Chuck's picture. "Yeah, he looks about the same. He's a tough one and not to be trusted. He lives at the halfway house on Cedar Street. He does hold down a full-time job at Millsteel, though. The halfway house has a pretty strict curfew. Everyone has to be inside and accounted for by ten p.m. The first killing happened in the middle of the night, didn't it?"

"Yeah, and in Milwaukee. Does Chuck have a vehicle?"

"Nope. The guys that live at the halfway house and have jobs take the shuttle to work every day. They get picked up after work too."

"Crap. It sounds like both of them are dead ends. Can you print out their most current information for me?"

"Sure can, Jade." He called Nancy into his office. "Nancy, pull Chuck Banta and Adam Ross's files and print out everything for Jade, please."

"Sure thing. It will take about ten minutes. So no leads yet?"

"Unfortunately not. We're following up with anyone released in the last few years that served ten. Never heard of anyone nicknamed Dime?"

"Sorry, but no. That's what this guy is going by?"

"Just a hunch that doesn't seem to be panning out so far." I drummed my fingers while I continued to wait for the files.

"I'll ask around. I see quite a few guys every month. I could tell the other parole officers to ask if anyone knows somebody by that nickname. I have no idea if anyone will talk or not, but it doesn't hurt to ask."

Nancy brought in the files and handed them to me.

"Thanks, Nancy, appreciate it. I guess I better go and start hitting the streets. So far we haven't had any luck on the phones. Thanks, Barry."

Chapter 26

Jack and I started at the far south end of Main Street. We knew every little nook and cranny where the loners hung out, some unemployed, some a little sketchy. We planned to talk to everyone that would give us the time of day along the route and end at Settler's Square at the north end of Main Street. On Saturdays during the summer, a large farmers' market was held downtown. Main Street was blocked off to vehicles between seven a.m. and one p.m., and only foot traffic was allowed. Bands usually played at Settler's Square, and it was a fun, family-oriented environment. During the week, Settler's Square was usually inhabited by truant teenagers, people that milled around waiting to meet up with someone, or old people who were just lonely. Usually the city police tried to keep anyone that looked up to no good moving along, but today, we needed to speak to as many of them as possible.

North Bend was a decent town for the most part, and not one that saw many serious crimes. Even the petty criminals had seemed to look over their shoulders lately.

Our town was growing, though, and more people were moving in from larger cities. Many of those people we hadn't met yet, had no idea where they came from, or what they were capable of.

The folks that hung out downtown knew Jack and me. Some of them had had an encounter or two with us in the past and scattered when we approached, while others waved hello.

Johnny Davis was a regular that hung out at the triangle, a small parklike greenspace in front of Cheryl's Bar and Grill. We sat next to him on the bench. Jack always kept two packs of cigarettes with him, menthol and non-menthol. They came in handy when we needed to talk to someone, especially a homeless person. They would sit tight and talk, hoping for more cigarettes as we asked our questions.

"Hey, Johnny, what's new?" Jack asked.

Johnny scooted to the side when we sat and tried to hide the brown paper bag that likely contained a pint of cheap whiskey. Jack offered him a smoke. He happily chose a menthol cigarette.

Jack lit it for him. "So, nothing interesting, huh?"

"No, nope, not a thing." He pinched the cigarette between his lips and inhaled deeply.

"Where are you sleeping these days?" I asked.

He pointed. "Over there, under the bridge. Got myself a nice little camp set up."

"No fires, though, right?" Jack asked.

"Nope, no fires, no sir."

"So, Johnny, have you ever heard of somebody that goes by the name of Dime? I want you to think hard before you answer." I stared at him and waited.

"Yep, sure have. Uh-huh."

I looked at Jack. Doubt was written across his face, and I felt the same way.

"Can I have another cigarette? I want one for later."

"Sure, but first we have to know who Dime is," Jack said.

Johnny pointed at the barbershop in a run-down building on the corner. The small storefront had been a barbershop for as long as I could remember, but these days, I thought it sat vacant. An alley was to the left of it, and the right side was attached to a nearly defunct plumbing store. In all the years I'd lived in North Bend, I'd never seen anyone walk in or out of the place. That entire block of buildings needed updating and new facades. I'd heard the city council's planning committee had that area earmarked for rejuvenation later in the year.

"The barber that runs the place, his name is Dime."

"I thought that place was empty. When was the last time you were in there, Johnny?" Jack asked.

One look at the homeless man told us he hadn't had his hair washed or cut in ages.

"I can't remember. I just know that's his name. Frankie said so."

"Your brother told you that?" I frowned in disbelief.

"Uh-huh. He takes out the trash for him and gets a pack of smokes every week for doing it. Can I have another?" He stuck out his thin, bony fingers and waited for Jack to hand him a second cigarette.

"Okay, thanks, Johnny. We'll go check it out. You aren't lying to us, are you? We know where you live." I gave him a smile.

"Nope, not lying."

"I thought that building was vacant," I said to Jack as we crossed the street.

"So did I." Jack pulled the squeaky screen door open and turned the knob on the wooden interior door.

We entered the old, tired-looking barbershop and saw a middle-aged man trimming another man's hair.

"Hello, folks, be with you in a bit. Just finishing up."

We sat and waited. Jack grabbed a fishing magazine. The cover showed people ice fishing. He frowned and looked at the date. The magazine was from January.

"Help yourself to some coffee if you like," the barber said.

We smiled and declined.

He brushed off the customer's neck and unfastened the cape. The man paid and walked out.

"How can I help you folks? Need a trim, sir?"

We stood and showed him our badges. I asked him to flip the open sign to closed for now. He complied.

"What's this about? I have all my licenses."

"May we see them?" I asked.

"Sure thing." He opened the top drawer in the desk at the back of the shop and pulled out his paperwork. He handed the documents to me.

"Your last name is Sentz?"

"Yep, Joseph Sentz, but everyone calls me Dime."

"Why's that?" Jack asked.

The man laughed. "My old man's kind of humor, I guess. I'm Dime, and my kid brother, Jimmy, is Nickel. I'm the older of the two, and we're five years apart in age. Get it? Our last name is Sentz, like cents. Funny, right? My pop started calling me Dime when I turned ten. He said I was worth ten cents now, a dime. He started calling my brother Nickel then too. I guess the nicknames just stuck."

I glanced at Jack. "Do you live in town, Mr. Sentz?"

"Sure do, across the street from the police station on Walnut Street."

"Your license shows you just opened six months ago. What did you do before that?"

"I was a barber in Atlanta."

"Why move to Wisconsin? It gets pretty cold here in the winter."

"Yeah, I'm not too fond of that. My mom and pop are getting pretty old. They have an assisted living apartment on Meadowbrook, and Jimmy watches over them, but he isn't in the best of health—asthma problems."

"Okay, thanks for the information, Mr. Sentz." I handed back the documents. "Welcome to North Bend."

We walked out with nothing.

"That wasn't what I was expecting." I sighed. "At least Johnny wasn't lying. I don't think that Dime is our man. He doesn't look like he could lift a bag of water softener salt over his shoulder, let alone a person."

"Yeah," Jack said, "I think we can write him off. Let's grab a burger, then check on Clayton and Billings. Maybe they're having some luck at the parks."

We sat on the patio of a hamburger stand, each of us with a cheeseburger and fries, and watched the traffic drive by.

"So tomorrow is Morris's funeral. Do you think it's inappropriate to question people at the luncheon afterward?" I asked as I dipped a fry in the paper cup of ketchup.

"Let's talk to Lindstrom and Colgate. That might be their intention, or maybe they've cleared most everyone already."

"Yeah, okay, good idea. Let's hit Settler's Square after we finish eating." I made a quick call to Clayton as we ate. "How's it going on your end?"

"No luck, Sergeant. We're striking out with everyone, or they're just not in the mood to talk to us."

"All right. We're going to spend an hour or so at Settler's Square, then go back to the station after that. We'll regroup later and see what we do or don't have."

We drove the five blocks back to the downtown area and parked in a public lot. From there, it was only two blocks across a footbridge over the Milwaukee River that meandered through town and back to Main Street. It was already after two o'clock. Only four people sat in the square, each looking off in different directions, watching people go by.

Old man Lewis sat on a bench across from three young

men with skateboards. I approached him and sat down. The others left.

"Hi, Bob, how are you?"

"Okay."

"Getting enough to eat?"

"Yep, the Lutheran church on Sixth Street offers lunch three times a week for us."

"That's nice. Anything new on the streets? Are you staying safe?"

"Got to with that killer out there. That's what I heard anyway."

"Been watching TV, have you?" Jack asked.

"Nope, don't have a TV. That guy told me."

"What guy is that?" I looked around.

"Him." Bob pointed to a man walking down the street a few blocks to our north. "He was sitting here earlier talking to all of us. He said to be careful because there's a killer on the loose."

"He was warning you?" I asked.

"Yep. Nice guy."

"Thanks, Bob. Take care." I motioned to Jack with a nod. "Let's catch up with that guy and see what he has to say."

It didn't take a lot to catch up with the man ahead of us. He looked to be close to seventy.

"Excuse me, sir."

The man turned around. "Are you talking to me?"

"Yes." We showed him our badges. "Do you have a minute? We have a few questions for you."

"Me? What for?"

"Our friend Bob back there"—I pointed to Settler's Square—"said you talked to him about the news broadcast about our local killer."

"Sure did. You can never be too careful. That's why I don't go out after dark. This is my exercise. I come into town, do my errands, and go for walks during the day. I stop, have a beer, play a little video poker, and go home after that. That's my life."

"Where's home?" I asked.

"East of town about five miles. Just past Eddy's Tap. You know the place?"

"I've heard of it. Can't say I've ever been inside."

"It's decent and usually quiet. Strange fella in there Tuesday, though."

Jack frowned. "Strange, how?"

"Mikey, the bartender, and I were in there alone. I was playing video poker when this fella walked in. Never seen the man before. The local news came on about the murders, and the guy started laughing. Strangest thing. Mikey got mad and said something to him. The guy got up and left. Couldn't have been in there more than fifteen minutes."

"Do you remember what this guy looked like?"

"Nah—he had on one of those sweatshirts with the hood pulled up. Just seemed like an odd duck, you know?"

"Could you tell his age or his height?" I asked.

"Sorry, ma'am, I didn't look at him closely. After the news, I went back to my video poker and didn't look up again until I heard the front door slam. That's when I noticed he was gone."

"Do you know what days Mikey works?"

"Hmm… what's today?"

"Thursday," Jack said.

"Yep, he doesn't work again until Saturday."

"Would you happen to know Mikey's last name?"

"Sorry, no."

"Okay, we'll need your name and phone number, please." I pulled my notepad and a pen out of my pocket and flipped to an empty page. He gave me his information. Jack and I handed him our cards and asked him to call either one of us if he remembered anything more about this man.

Chapter 27

We headed back to the station. I asked the boss if we could have a group powwow—he agreed. The four of us gathered in Lieutenant Clark's office.

"Okay, let's hear what you guys have. Clayton, Billings, you two took the parks, right?"

"That's right, boss. We talked to, what"—Clayton looked at Billings, his eyebrows raised—"fifteen people?"

"That's about right."

"And?" The lieutenant scratched at the stubble on his chin.

"And nothing. Nobody had any leads for us. One guy started talking about somebody that went by the name Dime, but his buddy corrected him."

"How so?" the lieutenant asked.

"Well, he said he heard of a poker dealer that went by that name. Apparently, this dealer had his fifteen minutes of fame last year. He dealt the winning hand for somebody who won over a million bucks in a poker tournament in Vegas. The winning hand was a royal flush, all diamonds.

Anyway, the lead went nowhere. His buddy corrected him and told us the dealer went by the name Diamond, not Dime."

We groaned in unison.

"Okay, Jade, Jack, any leads?"

"Go ahead," Jack said.

"We did interview somebody that goes by Dime, but he isn't our guy. He's a barber in town, and his dad had been calling him that name since he was a kid. The family surname is Sentz, pronounced like cents. The dad called the brother Nickel."

I shrugged and listened to more groans. "There is someone I think we should question, though. Apparently, a bartender at Eddy's Tap on the outskirts of town had a strange patron in there two days ago. This patron laughed when the news segment came on TV about the murders."

"That's unusual. So what did the bartender tell you?"

"That's the problem, sir. We talked to an older guy downtown. He told us about the incident, not the bartender. The old man doesn't know the bartender's last name, and he isn't scheduled to work again until Saturday."

"Well, whoever is bartending now should know the guy's last name, right?"

"Yeah, we're going to call there shortly. The bar doesn't open until four o'clock."

"Okay, good work. Jade, make that call at four and find out the guy's last name and his address. You and Jack pay him a visit."

"Will do, Lieutenant. I'll keep you posted."

We headed back to the bull pen, each with a Styrofoam cup of coffee in our hand. I checked the time, and I had thirty minutes before I would make that call. I wrote myself a list of things that needed to be done. I didn't know how much time Jack and I would be at the office tomorrow with Morris's funeral beginning at eleven. We'd check in first, then leave North Bend before ten o'clock. I wanted to follow up with Perry, close out some old cases, and interview more guys that had been arrested earlier. It sounded as though they were part of the same crew cooking meth east of town.

I sat at my desk with a clean sheet of paper and a pen in front of me. I made the call to Eddy's Tap. It wasn't quite four p.m. yet, but most bartenders arrived before they officially opened for business anyway. I wanted to catch whoever opened the bar during a quiet moment before any customers walked in.

The phone rang seven times. I almost hung up when I heard a voice answer.

"Eddy's Tap."

"Hello, I'm Sergeant Jade Monroe with the Washburn County Sheriff's Department. Here's my badge number. Write it down, please, since I'm not there to prove my identity to you. I'm wondering if you could spare a minute of your time."

"Um, yeah, I guess."

"Who am I speaking with, please?"

"This is Terry, Terry Ferring."

"Hi, Terry. Are you a bartender there, or the owner of Eddy's?"

"I'm a part-time bartender."

"Do you know the bartender Mikey?"

"Yeah, sure I do."

I looked at Jack and nodded. "That's great. I'll need Mikey's last name and an address if it's on file there."

"Sure, give me a minute. I have to check in our personnel file. It's in the office."

"No problem, thanks." I waited for a few minutes, giving my fingernails the once-over again. They looked worse than the last time I gave them the time of day.

"Okay, here we are. His legal name is Michael Cole. He lives at 4905 South Merritt, apartment 203, right in North Bend. Do you want his cell number too?"

"Yes, please." I wrote everything down. "That should do it. Thanks, Terry. Goodbye."

"Got what you needed?" Jack asked when I hung up.

"Yep. Let's hope he answers the phone." I pressed the buttons on my desk phone and waited.

Jack, Clayton, and Billings were staring. I swiveled my chair around and saw the lieutenant staring at me too through his office window.

I put my hand over the receiver and chuckled. "You guys are going to jinx this. Stop gawking at me." I sat up straight and faced my desk. Mikey had just answered.

I explained who I was and told him we were investigating the recent murder cases. I asked if Jack and I could stop by. We had a few questions.

"Yeah, that's fine by me."

"Thanks, Mikey. We'll be there in fifteen minutes." I hung up. "Ready, partner?"

"I sure am." Jack reached in the top drawer of his desk and pulled out his notepad. "Let's go."

I told the lieutenant we were heading out.

"Okay, I'm going to stick around until you're back. Brief me when you get in."

We climbed into the unmarked black car we had at our disposal. This vehicle was less conspicuous than a cruiser, especially when parking at a large apartment complex.

The drive took only seven minutes. The one thing I always loved about North Bend was the ease of getting around. No matter whether we were going north to south, or east to west, the drive across town never took longer than fifteen minutes at the most.

We pulled into the parking lot and found a guest spot to park in. The complex looked quiet. I figured most residents were still at work. We walked to the main entrance and entered the vestibule. On the right wall were door buzzers for each apartment, and I pressed the button for apartment 203. The name Mike Cole was written under the plastic plate next to the button.

"Hello."

"Hi, Mike, it's Sergeant Monroe."

"Okay, come upstairs and turn right. I'm the third door on the left."

"Thank you."

He buzzed us through.

Chapter 28

When I knocked on the door, he invited us in. I introduced Jack, and they shook hands.

"Please, have a seat," Mikey said, pointing to the kitchen table.

"Thank you. Would you prefer to be called Mike or Mikey?" I asked as we sat down.

"I guess since this is official business, Mike sounds better. What can I do for you?"

I couldn't help staring at Mike's mustache when I talked to him. "This shouldn't take long. We were told by"—I checked my notes—"Mr. Abe Livingston that you had an odd patron in the bar on Tuesday."

He stared blankly at me. "I guess I need a little more than that. There are a few odd people that come and go."

"Sure, I understand. Abe said the man sat at the bar, wearing a hoodie, and chuckled at the news segment about the murders."

"Ah—yeah, I remember that guy now. What a nut job. Who would laugh at something that horrible, especially when it happens in your own neck of the woods? You know what I mean?"

Jack nodded. "Yes, we do. What can you tell us about him, Mike?"

"Not a lot. I've never seen him before. He was only in the bar for a short while, like he was killing time."

"What about his physical appearance? You know, height, weight, hair color, build?"

"Well, he sat for most of the time. He wore a hoodie and green-tinted glasses. I remember his shirt was nicer, you know, decent. That's why the hoodie seemed odd. That's normally what you'd see a twenty-year-old wear. With the hood pulled up, I mean. This guy looked older. He was kind of stocky, oh, and that's right, he asked for a weird brand of beer. Something I've never heard of. Eddy's is a plain bar, nothing fancy."

I sat upright, my elbows resting on the tabletop. I was interested. "Would you happen to remember the beer's name?"

"Nah—like I said, I'd never heard of it. He did ask for a second choice, though."

"Which was?"

"A Guinness, but we don't carry that brand either. He settled on a can of Bud Light with a glass. Funny how most bartenders remember the drinks more than they remember the customer. After I said something to him about laughing at the news, he threw a five on the bar and walked out. That's all I can tell you. Sorry I'm not much help."

"To be honest, your help is the most we've gotten so far.

You didn't catch a glimpse of what he was driving, did you?"

"Sorry, no. I turned back to the TV when he walked out. I didn't face the window, and the blinds were drawn anyway, with the sun going down and all."

"So, what time would you estimate that to be?" Jack asked.

"Hmm… I'd say close to six. The news was wrapping up when he walked out."

We thanked Mike for the information, handed him our cards, and shook his hand.

"I hope you catch this guy soon," Mike said as he showed us to the door.

"So do we."

Jack and I updated the lieutenant when we got back to the station.

"The bartender didn't have a good description to give us, Lieutenant," Jack said. "He told us the guy was stocky, weird, and wore a hoodie and tinted sunglasses."

"Sounds like somebody who was trying to hide his identity. Who wears hoodies when it's seventy degrees outside?" the lieutenant said.

I agreed. "Good point, boss. Apparently, the guy ordered an unusual brand of beer which the bartender couldn't remember the name of. He ended up drinking a Bud Light, and he wanted a glass with it."

"A bartender that doesn't know the name of a beer?" Lieutenant Clark rubbed his forehead and rolled his eyes.

I shrugged. "In his defense, sir, he said it wasn't a brand they carried. I guess that's why it wasn't familiar to him."

"All right. Let's wrap it up for tonight. You two are coming in before you head out to the funeral, right?"

"Yep, we'll be here for a few hours in the morning. Night, boss."

"Good night."

Chapter 29

I was getting used to having Spaz around. He was good company and seemed to enjoy snuggling up next to me on the couch at night. He'd purr while I scratched behind his ears. I'm sure I was just filler until Amber was here full time. I just needed to remember to keep my bedroom door closed at all times, or Polly and Porky would be toast. Spaz was a seven-year-old Tabby, given to Amber by our dad when she graduated middle school. She loved that cat, and Spaz was part of the package deal. I got Amber—I got Spaz.

Only one more day of living here alone remained. Beginning Saturday, Amber would be my roommate for the foreseeable future. I was pretty sure Melissa would call early, and we'd be out looking at condos for most of the afternoon.

Mom called as I drove home. She said she'd reserved a part of the back room at Stanley's for my birthday dinner. Even though there would be just four of us, she wanted to bring a cake and my birthday gifts along. We'd have that private area for gift opening, picture taking, and cake eating after our meal. I agreed that Amber and I would meet her and Bruce at six thirty.

I started the oven and popped a frozen lasagna dinner on the center rack. It had thirty minutes to go. Meanwhile, I stripped the bed in what used to be the guest room, even though we never had overnight guests. This was Amber's bedroom now, and I wanted a fresh-smelling set of sheets ready for her first night there. Spaz nuzzled up to my legs as I pulled the fitted sheet off, gathered the pillowcases and the sheets, and put them in the washer. I looked through the linen closet, and the set of peach-colored sheets caught my eye. They would be perfect for Amber. Lance had always thought they looked too girlish for a bed a man slept in, and over time, they got pushed farther back in the closet.

The bed was made, and my meal was ready. The timer beeped, and I pulled out the lasagna. I sat on the couch with my meal, a big no-no back in my married days, and enjoyed dinner over my favorite cop show and a glass of red wine. I was hoping a few glasses of wine would help me sleep soundly. I made a quick call to Amber at work, just to check up on her.

"Hey, Sis, how's work?"

"It's all good. We're pretty busy. There's a new guy that's been shining around. I think he's crushing on me. I'm the only person he talks to, but it makes time go faster."

"That sounds nice."

"Yeah, he's okay, but way too old for me. Anyway, I have people waiting for their drinks. Gotta go."

"Okay. Night, Sis."

I took my glass of wine and went to watch TV in bed. After a half hour, I turned off the light. My buzzing phone woke me. I slapped at the light and sat up. The screen on my phone showed Amber was calling, and it was after two in the morning. She had just closed the bar.

"Sis, what's up?" I asked, already concerned. Amber never called this late. She knew I was an early riser.

"I think somebody is following me, Jade."

"What?"

"I'm usually the last one out when I'm on the closing shift. Tommy and Brian left about twenty minutes ago. I locked up and set the alarm. I pulled out of the parking lot a few minutes ago, and suddenly somebody was right on my bumper. The same thing happened when I left your place last night."

"Last night? Why didn't you tell me?"

"I'm telling you now. I wasn't that freaked out last night, but two nights in a row?"

"Amber, drive to the sheriff's department right now. I'll call Detective Jamison and tell him to meet you outside. Pull right up to the door. Don't get out of your vehicle unless he's waiting for you. Do you understand me?"

"Yes, I understand."

"Call me back the second you're with Jamison."

"Okay."

I hung up and called Jamison immediately. I told him what kind of vehicle Amber had and when she should arrive. I calculated that if she'd just left Joey's, she should be at the station in ten minutes, give or take a stoplight or two.

I got up and made myself a cup of tea and paced. The phone buzzed again, startling me to almost drop my cup.

"Sorry, Sis, false alarm. It was Sean following me—the idiot. I asked him why he didn't just call my cell instead of stalking my car like that. He said his phone fell between the seats, and he couldn't get to it. He was trying to pry it out when he noticed me leaving the parking lot. That's why he tore out after me, to get my attention."

"Apparently, he did."

"Then he thought something was wrong when he saw me turn into the sheriff's department parking lot. He pulled in behind me, jumped out, and asked me if I needed help. I guess he just wanted to know if I'd go to George Webb with him for some late night breakfast. Don't worry, Sis, Detective Jamison gave him a talking-to. I thanked the detective for waiting outside for me. Now I'm at George Webb. I'll have a talk with Sean myself too when we get inside. That was totally not cool. Sorry I woke you."

"Don't be sorry, honey. I want you to call anytime you don't feel safe. It's the smart thing to do. Okay, I'm going back to sleep. I'll talk to you tomorrow."

I went back to bed and snuggled under the blanket.

The alarm buzzed loudly at six thirty. My eyes burned. They wanted to close again for another four hours, but that was just wishful thinking. I got up, slipped on my robe, and tapped the green button for the coffeepot. I poured a cup of kibble into Spaz's bowl and hit the shower. After dressing for the funeral, I fed the birds, closed my bedroom door, and left.

Jack arrived at the station at the same time I did. As we walked in, I told him about the near scare Amber had had last night.

He groaned. "Kids."

Jack gave me the once-over when we reached the bull pen.

"What?"

"Nothing. I like the pantsuit, that's all. You look good, and the scarf's a nice touch."

I smiled. "Thanks. You look nice too."

We would spend a few hours doing busywork, then leave. There wasn't enough time to delve deep into anything. I set the alarm on my phone for nine o'clock. I wanted to call Perry and ask if he'd made funeral arrangements for Elise yet. I was hoping hers would be the last funeral I'd attend for some time.

"I'm going to head upstairs to see if our new visitors have anything they want to talk about."

"You mean the Meth Lab Rats?"

I laughed. "The crew has a nickname already?"

"Yeah, and I thought of the name all by myself," Jack said proudly.

"Really? Then maybe you should conduct the interview. Have at it, partner. I'll call Perry."

"Sure, why not? Maybe I can rattle their rat cage." Jack walked out of the bull pen then turned back at the doorframe and grinned. "Wish me luck."

"You'll need it." I chuckled, pushed back my chair, got up, and filled my coffee cup. I looked at the clock and turned off my phone alarm. I'd call Perry now.

He answered on the third ring. "Hello, Perry, it's Sergeant Monroe. I just wanted to touch base with you."

"Hello, Sergeant. I appreciate the call. This is hard, you know."

"I completely understand. Have you made arrangements yet for Elise?"

"I'm about halfway there. I picked out a pearl-white casket. Elise liked white. Do you think that sounds nice?"

"Yes, I do. It's perfect."

"I'm still waiting on the death certificates before we can move forward. I guess they should be ready this afternoon. I'll arrange a funeral date with the director after that."

"Okay, Perry. Please keep in touch, and if you need anything, I'm just a phone call away."

"Thank you, Sergeant. Goodbye."

I hung up and made a note on my desk calendar to check in again with him on Tuesday about the funeral.

Jack was back in the bull pen by nine thirty. We checked in with the lieutenant before we left, and Clayton and Billings said they were going back out to the parks today. Maybe they'd get lucky and talk to someone that knew something.

"We're heading out, boss," I said as I stood against the doorframe of Lieutenant Clark's office. "As far as I know, Lindstrom and Colgate will be at the funeral too. I'm sure we'll exchange new information if either of us has any. We should be back midafternoon."

"Okay, see you both later."

Jack drove our unmarked cruiser while I punched the address into my cell phone's navigation system. "I think this place will be easy enough to find, but just in case."

"Where is it?" Jack asked

I looked at my notes. "Um, it's at the intersection of Capital Avenue and 60th Street. The entrance faces Capital."

"Got it. It's called Phillips Funeral Home?"

"Yep, that's the name. Oh yeah, duh, I forgot to tell you the latest news." I grinned.

"Yeah, don't keep me in suspense." Jack looked over at me. "I'm all ears."

"And then some." I chuckled. "Anyway, Amber said in the fall, she's going to change her major to criminal justice."

"No shit?" Jack merged onto the freeway as we talked.

"Uh-huh."

"What brought that on?"

"She wants to be like us, and my pop. Get this. Eventually, she wants to be an FBI profiler. With two degrees, one in criminal justice and the other in behavioral sciences, she'd probably do really well as a profiler in time."

Jack whistled. "That girl is ambitious. Good for her. I'm impressed. What did your old man say?"

"She hasn't told him yet. I think she's still figuring it out in her own head first. What do you think about me enrolling her in self-defense and gun safety courses over the summer?"

"I think that would be a really good thing to do. She'll need the training eventually anyway."

I agreed. "I can't wait until tomorrow. I'm going to do my best to focus on the day with Amber and Melissa and enjoy looking at condos. I don't want to think about work for at least twenty-four hours."

"And then your birthday dinner is tomorrow night, right?" Jack clicked his blinker to get off on the exit ramp.

"Yeah, we're going to Stanley's."

"That's a decent place. Okay, here we are." Jack turned into the parking lot and killed the motor.

Chapter 30

The parking lot was small and packed with the type of cars one would expect from the group of guys Morris hung with. Lowered, large sedans from the eighties and nineties with limousine-style blackened windows filled the lot.

"Guess this is the right place." Jack smirked.

I elbowed him.

"There's another Crown Vic. Lindstrom and Colgate must be inside."

We entered through the double wooden doors. The vestibule was large, and people were milling around. I saw Terrance in the distance when we passed through the second set of doors. He stood near what looked to be a beverage station. The service wasn't set to begin for another thirty minutes, so we walked over.

"Mr. King," I said, my hand outstretched. "Our condolences go out to your family."

He shook my hand and Jack's too.

He looked around the room. "Well, there isn't much family here. Looks like most folks are Morris's bunch. My cousin is over there"—he pointed across the room—"and Morris's grandma and grandpa on his mom's side are over there." He pointed again, to the left front side of the chapel. He turned and showed us the room behind him.

"Here's where the meal will be after the service."

I nodded. I saw a pulpit set up ahead of the chairs and a curtain closed behind it. I was pretty certain Morris's casket sat behind that. The man Terrance introduced as Minister Johnson shook our hands then excused himself to greet people. The funeral home staff welcomed the visitors too.

I scanned the chapel for Lieutenant Colgate and Detective Lindstrom. I saw them seated about halfway back, talking to several people. I figured they were conducting a few discreet interviews. I decided to let them do their thing for now. We would catch up later.

Jack and I stood back against the wall and sized up the crowd. We recognized Marshon, Kev, James, and a few other boys that we had met in the park a few weeks back. We noticed another group standing off alone and whispering among themselves.

I nudged Jack and tipped my head in their direction. "I hope they aren't a rival gang here to smirk." I kept my eye on them. I was certain Lindstrom and Colgate were familiar with most of the faces in the crowd. A lot of them probably had jackets at the police station.

The minister asked everyone to take a seat. Terrance and whatever relatives were in attendance sat in the front row. Jack and I shook hands with Lindstrom and Colgate and sat next to them near the back. Most everyone else sat in between.

The minister probably didn't know Morris well, but he did know Terrance. He read from a sheet, likely written by Terrance, about Morris's good qualities and how he'd been taken too soon. A short sermon and a few prayers were recited. People walked up to the closed casket to say their final goodbyes. A photo of Morris at a younger age sat on an easel next to the casket. Terrance had mentioned he didn't have any recent photos of his nephew. A few people stayed for the luncheon, but most of Morris's acquaintances left. They didn't have a reason to stay, and it was unlikely they would sit around a table, eat lunch, and visit with the cops.

Jack and I sat across from Colgate and Lindstrom. We each had a plate of food in front of us and a cup of coffee. We talked quietly and exchanged information, which took only five minutes. None of us had any solid leads. We told them how we took to the streets, and the only thing that rang true from talking to people was about the guy at Eddy's Tap. We were told what this man wore and that he laughed at the news broadcast, but other than that, we had nothing. The bar was a small, out-of-the-way place that didn't get a lot of business and didn't have cameras.

We headed back to North Bend at two o'clock and pulled into the station just before three.

We updated Lieutenant Clark and went back to our desks to catch up on our busywork.

"So, did the boys upstairs tell you anything important this morning?" I asked Jack as I shuffled through the paperwork on my desk.

"Nope, their lips are sealed. The DEA shut down the meth lab in that farmhouse off of Decorah in Newburg, but it's likely they just moved the operation somewhere else. We're always chasing the low-level punks. I want the people that are funding these labs and paying the rents. That's who we need to find."

I agreed.

Clayton and Billings walked in, and I gave them a questioning look. Billings shook his head.

"We're dealing with a ghost. No video, no eyewitnesses, no evidence, no description, no word on the street. It's pretty hard to catch someone based on that."

I filed a few cases that had either been solved or dismissed, cataloged evidence that went into our evidence room, and asked Clark if we could release Elise's car. He agreed, and I called Perry to tell him. He was in no hurry to pick it up. I told him it would be parked out back inside the chain-link fence behind the evidence garage. He agreed to come by and pick it up next week.

I wished everyone a quiet weekend and left at four thirty. A hot bath, two birds, and a cat were waiting for me at home.

Chapter 31

I woke to the sounds of dishes and silverware coming out of cabinets in the kitchen. I grabbed my cell and checked the time—eight o'clock. I couldn't believe I slept in that late. I called Amber's phone. It rang in the kitchen, and I grinned. She'd never forgive me if I came out of the bedroom with my gun drawn and ready to fire.

"Hello, Sis, I'm making your birthday breakfast, so get your butt out here."

"Sounds wonderful. I'll be right there." I got up, washed my face, and slipped on a pair of sweats and a T-shirt. I twisted my long hair into a rope and pinched it off with a clip at the top of my head. With my slippers on, I shuffled down the hallway to the kitchen.

Two plates with silverware and napkins, two glasses filled with orange juice, and two cups of steaming coffee sat on the table.

"I could get used to this," I said as I sat and took a sip. "Since when do I have orange juice?"

"You didn't. I bought groceries. I don't know about you,

but I don't intend to starve while I'm living here."

"Cool. What's for breakfast?"

She turned from the stove and grinned. Amber was beautiful. She had perfect hair, perfect teeth, and a perfect shape. Someday she'd fall in love, and I hoped it would last forever.

"I'm making French toast. I know how much you love it, so hand me your plate."

I grinned. "We have bread, eggs, butter, and syrup?"

"Uh-huh, we do now."

"Man, why didn't you move in here a year ago?" I got up and gave her a hug. "I love you, girl."

"I love you too and happy birthday, now sit down and tell me how you like it. I put extra cinnamon in the egg-and-milk batter."

"It's delicious."

I was surprised Melissa hadn't called yet. It was closing in on nine o'clock. I tried her cell, and it went straight to voice mail.

"Melissa didn't call your phone, did she?"

"Nope." Amber looked at the screen. "No texts either."

"That's weird. I'll shower and try her again. Did you bring your clothes with you?"

"Yeah, some, but I'll grab more tomorrow. I thought food for the house was more important."

I ate four pieces of French toast and had two glasses of orange juice, then headed for the shower. "I'll be ready in a half hour. I'll try Melissa again then. Maybe we can just meet her at Realty World and go from there."

"Sure. I'm going to hang up some of my clothes."

I tried Melissa's cell again at ten o'clock. This time the recording said the mailbox was full. I sat on the couch and felt a little disappointed. I was sure Melissa was more responsible than that.

"This is really weird. I'll try the office number." I called Realty World, and a female voice answered. I felt relief until the woman introduced herself as Adriana.

"Hello, Adriana. My name is Jade Monroe. I have the day set aside to look at condos with Melissa. I'm surprised I haven't heard from her yet. We set it up on Tuesday afternoon, and she said she would confirm it with me this morning. We were going to start looking at condos around noon. The odd thing is her cell phone recording says her mailbox is full. Do you have any idea what's going on?"

"Give me one moment, please."

Through the phone line, I heard rustling and drawers opening and closing. Adriana returned to the phone.

"I'm so sorry, Jade, and this is very odd. I got a text from Melissa on Tuesday night saying she had to leave town abruptly. She said she would be in touch, but come to think of it, I haven't heard a peep from her all week. I just checked her desk to see what appointments she had. I assumed she either canceled them or gave them to another Realtor, but her monthly calendar is gone along with her briefcase. I have no idea if she's missed other appointments or not. Give me another second, please."

I heard Adriana talking to someone else, probably another Realtor in the office. She came back to the phone.

"Nobody was asked to cover for her, but now that you said her mailbox is full, I'm assuming she's missed other appointments too. I'm so sorry. I have no idea what places she had lined up, but I would be happy to show you some myself. I'd hate to feel like you wasted your day by keeping it open to look at condos."

I had to give it some thought. Melissa knew exactly what I was looking for. "Um, okay. I'm only interested in three-bedroom units, though, without yard work."

"Sure, give me a second here. I'm pulling some up on my computer as we speak. You want to stay in North Bend?"

"Yes, definitely."

"Okay, I have five vacant condos and two brand-new models I can show you. Would you like to go ahead and take a look at them?"

I breathed a sigh of relief. "Absolutely. My sister and I have been looking forward to this all week."

Adriana laughed. "I know how exciting it is to look for a new home. Would you like to come to the office and leave from here?"

"That sounds perfect, and we'll leave now. Thank you."

"Time to go?" Amber asked as she poured kibble into Spaz's bowl.

"Yep, let's go enjoy the day. How about a beer at Left Field later?"

"That sounds great. I'll even kick your butt at a game of pool."

We met with Adriana, who apologized again. The whole

thought of Melissa bailing on us didn't sit well with me. She didn't seem the type to leave, emergency or not, and not make arrangements with the other Realtors to handle her appointments.

Adriana drove as Amber and I looked over the listing sheets.

"This place sounds awesome," Amber said. "It has a huge clubhouse with a workout room, a library, a business center, and an indoor pool. The split floor plan is cool too."

"Yes, that's a new development on the south side of town. It's called Ashbury Woods. It's very nice, with only fifty-five units. Some are even set back in the woods. Would you like to see that one first?"

Amber looked pleadingly at me. I chuckled.

"Sure, it sounds great."

We toured a three-bedroom unit available at the end of a cul-de-sac. It sat among oak trees and had a private balcony facing the woods behind it. It was large enough for each of us to live comfortably within our own space. The extra bedroom and den were definitely pluses.

"Can we check out the clubhouse too?" Amber asked.

"Of course. The nice thing about this unit is there's a walking path right next to it. The path cuts through the woods and opens up at the clubhouse. It's a fast and beautiful shortcut. Let me show you."

We took the path through the woods, and it was peaceful and serene. I could actually hear birds singing and see squirrels romping. It felt amazing to have something so quiet and relaxing right at our feet when we were still within the city limits.

"This is wonderful," I said. I looked at Amber. She couldn't have wiped the smile off her face even if she'd tried.

The clubhouse was large and inviting. Many residents were inside taking advantage of the workout room. Just beyond the glass doors were a hot tub and a patio with plenty of umbrella tables and grills. The Olympic-size pool was inside, along with saunas and lockers in each restroom. A beverage bar and a large-screen TV were to the left of the pool area.

"Wow." Amber and I spoke the words simultaneously.

We toured five more units scattered throughout town, but my mind kept taking me back to the condo at Ashbury Woods. We returned to Realty World at three o'clock. I pulled the listing sheet out again and checked the square footage and the price for the first condo.

"It looks like you really have your mind set on Ashbury Woods, don't you?" Adriana said.

"It is wonderful, and at two thousand square feet, it's almost as big as the house I have now. You know, Melissa was going to write up a description and get my house listed for sale. Do you know if she did that before she left town?"

"I'll check. All I need is the address."

I gave Adriana my address, and she entered it into her computer.

"Sorry, it hasn't been listed yet. Did she take photos already?"

"Yes, several weeks ago. I was hoping to have the house listed by now. I don't want to step on her toes by having somebody else do it. Did she upload the photos of my house into your database yet?"

"It doesn't appear so. I wish there was a way to get ahold of Melissa and find out when she's coming back. How long do you want to wait?" Adriana asked.

"I'll let it go for a few more days. I'd love to put an offer on the condo, but it would have to be on a contingency basis, I guess."

"We can certainly do that, if you like."

"I think Amber and I need to talk it over before I commit to anything. Are you working tomorrow, Adriana?"

"I sure am, until three o'clock. Here's my card. If you'd like to put in an offer, give me a call. It's been fun working with both of you today."

"Thanks." Amber and I stood, shook her hand, and headed to Left Field. We'd discuss the condo over a beer, then go home to get ready for dinner.

"So, what do you think of the place?" I asked as I slurped the creamy head of my oatmeal stout. I already knew the answer, but I loved seeing her happiness and hearing the excitement in Amber's voice.

"I really love it, Jade. I never knew something that pretty was right in town."

"Me either. What do you think of putting an offer in on it tomorrow before someone else sneaks in and buys it?"

Amber reached across the bar table and hugged me. "I'd be over the moon."

I noticed a thoughtful gaze on her face as she sipped her beer.

"What's going on in that mind of yours?" I asked.

"Nothing important, just wondering."

"About what?"

"Why Mom named us the names she did. I thought all babies were born with steel-gray eyes."

I laughed. "Where did this come from?"

"I don't know—it's your birthday. I was just wondering what giving birth was like, and then I thought about our names. Were you born with green eyes and me with yellow?"

"Highly unlikely. Mom likes jewelry, and amber and jade seem to be what she wears most often. Don't overthink this. I'm sure there wasn't a deep-seated thought process when we were named. Mom is easy to read. I bet she wears jade tonight."

We both laughed.

I wanted to bring up the idea of self-defense courses with Amber. I decided to do it after the birthday party. It was time to go home and get ready for dinner.

I paid the bill and got up. "Let's go. We don't want Mom to have a heart attack if we're late."

Chapter 32

The hostess led Amber and me to the back room at Stanley's. The large banquet room was divided into six sections, separated by planters filled with glossy greenery. Mom and Bruce were already there and waved when they saw us approach.

Mom stood up. "There's our birthday girl! Hi, honey."

Our mom, Ann Sommers, was dressed nicely tonight. She wore a summery sheath and had her shoulder-length black hair pulled into a sleek ponytail that just skimmed the back of her neck. She wore her signature plum-colored lipstick, which we always had to wipe off our cheeks after a kiss.

Amber and I exchanged glances and smiled. Mom wore jade jewelry tonight, obviously in honor of my birthday. She kissed me then moved on to Amber. I pulled a tissue out of my purse and wiped my cheek.

Bruce looked like Bruce. He always wore a plaid cotton shirt when they went out. He never tried terribly hard to impress anyone. His shirts were dangerously snug around his ever expanding midsection, and he usually wore jeans that looked uncomfortably tight. His short gray hair looked the same as always, although it did appear to be thinning more every time I saw him.

Amber and I said hi and sat down. We didn't want his hugs that would last too long while he pressed himself against our chests. I made sure Amber sat between Mom and me so Bruce wouldn't have the opportunity to accidently brush his knee against hers.

"Let's order a few drinks and catch up. After that, we'll eat, then you can open your presents," Mom said.

"I'm thirty-one, Mom. I don't really need presents and a cake."

"Nonsense. As long as I'm alive, my kids will have birthday parties. Maybe someday I'll even throw parties for my grandkids."

Amber and I rolled our eyes.

"In due time, Mom. So, we looked at condos today and found a beautiful one available in Ashbury Woods. It's a fairly new complex on the south side of town. I just might put an offer in on it tomorrow."

"That sounds wonderful, honey. Here comes the waitress. Let's order."

Prime rib was Saturday night's special, and we all ordered it. I couldn't remember the last time I had prime rib, a baked potato with sour cream, and steamed vegetables. Hot bread and butter was delivered to the table first.

Mom and Bruce each drank their usual—a Brandy Old Fashioned. I grew up in an era where all adults drank them.

I was sure anyone over sixty in Wisconsin still did. The memories of my youth returned, and I smiled. I recalled sneaking around at dinner parties, plucking the speared maraschino cherries and orange slices out of our guests' Brandy Old Fashioneds and gobbling them down.

"Excuse me. I'll be right back." Mom pushed back her chair and headed to the nearest waitress. They whispered to each other, and Mom returned to the table.

"That was subtle," I said, jokingly.

"Fine—whatever, I gave them the cake when we walked in. They're going to cut it and bring it out with thirty-one lit candles on it. Yay! You can open your presents after that."

I laughed. "Sure, no problem."

The waitress arrived with a cart. The candlelit sheet cake, already cut into three-inch squares, was placed in the center of our table. "Happy Birthday, Jade" was written in brilliant fuchsia lettering on white frosting.

"Hurry. Make a wish and blow out the candles."

I smiled, closed my eyes, and wished that we'd catch this sick killer. I blew out the candles.

The marble cake was moist and rich, and one piece was more than plenty. The gold-colored carafe of coffee was filled twice. While I opened my gifts, Bruce told us the most recent off-color jokes he'd heard at work.

The waitress appeared at our table one more time. She carried a bottle of wine cradled in her arm.

"Did you order wine, Mom?" I asked.

The waitress spoke up before Mom could answer. "This is for the birthday girl."

"Thank you, but I don't think we ordered it," I said.

"It's from the gentleman at the bar, ma'am. He said to tell you Happy Birthday."

She handed me the wine bottle, swaddled in a white linen tea towel to catch the drips, and walked away. Amber again reminded me of the fortune cookie.

"Geez, Sis, your fortune cookie keeps coming true. Remember what it said? 'A stranger will present you with a gift.'" Amber went on to tell Mom and Bruce how I'd received a floral arrangement at work last week.

I turned the bottle to look at the label. It read, *Sweet Melissa—Sweet Sparkling Red Wine.*

"Son of a bitch. Don't touch this bottle." I ripped my badge out of my purse and leaped from my chair. I grabbed the waitress by the arm, startling her. "Show me the man that ordered the wine."

"Excuse me?"

I flashed my badge at her. "I'm a cop, now where is he?"

"Oh dear—right this way, he's at the bar."

I raced through the main dining room and into the bar, with the waitress on my heels. "Which guy?"

"Oh—that's odd, he's gone. He was standing next to that stool, right there." She pointed to a barstool that a young lady had just sat down on.

"Do you see him anywhere?"

The waitress scanned the bar. "Sorry, I don't."

I approached the woman that had just sat down. "Excuse me, ma'am, you're going to have to get up." I raised my voice above the crowd. "I want this entire bar cleared right now. Sorry, it's a police matter." I told the bartenders not to touch anything and to get the manager out here. I turned to the waitress again. "I'll need the man's description, and do you have camera surveillance outside?"

"Just at the door. It doesn't go out into the parking lot very far."

I glanced around, my eyes darting from corner to corner. "What about these cameras at the bar."

"They're fake and only used as a deterrent so people don't get too crazy. This is a nice establishment."

"All right, don't go anywhere."

"But ma'am, I have tables to wait on."

"Not anymore—stay put. This is a police matter."

I made a call to the North Bend police dispatch and headed back to the banquet room.

"Mom, Bruce, Amber, you're leaving now. Amber, go home with Mom. I have a policeman on the way to escort you home safely."

"But—"

I interrupted my mom, "No buts. You're going home and lock the doors behind you. Don't let anyone in. Do you understand me? Take everything with you except that wine. Don't touch it. Mom, please don't argue with me. Amber, you're in charge—now go wait in the vestibule. The police officer is on his way."

I called Jack. "I need you at Stanley's now. The killer was just here. Get Kyle and Dan. I need them too."

Chapter 33

Hurry—go before you're seen! The voices had come to life once again.

He laughed and exited through the deliveries driveway. "What? Now you're concerned about my welfare? Aren't you always telling me when I should kill somebody?"

Dime peeled out of the driveway and was long gone before the first officer arrived. He chuckled as he imagined Jade's expression when she looked at the wine label. He wished he could have seen her face.

How appropriate was that? I couldn't have gotten any luckier if I had tried. A fitting birthday gift if I do say so myself. I wouldn't want you to become too complacent on your birthday, Sergeant.

He'd timed it just right. Today, Jade and her sister were supposed to look at condos with Melissa—poor Melissa. She was incapacitated and couldn't make it.

Dime knew Melissa's absence had to have bothered Jade. It was part of her training as a detective—she couldn't help herself. He doubted if her mind was entirely focused on her birthday party anyway.

Bingo! What a brilliant idea the wine was. Now she'll be frantic, wondering what happened to the Realtor.

That little hint, the subtle nudge, would send the entire city of North Bend into a tailspin. Everyone that had to leave the restaurant would be talking about it. The search for Melissa would begin soon—he'd planned it perfectly.

Melissa had been dead for four full days already, and she was most likely beginning to stink, especially in that closed-up barn. Blowflies laid eggs on corpses soon after death, and the eggs turned into maggots in no time. Dime was sure Melissa must be a mess by now. He grinned at the thought.

I have to come up with an idea for her to be found in the next day or so. It's time for the sergeant to get busy.

Dime drove home and went downstairs. He got comfortable on his wooden chair with his notebook in his lap and a Stella Artois on the side table. He turned to the dog-eared page for Melissa and filled in more information. He'd be starting a new page soon.

He thought about Melissa's briefcase and the information that lay inside. He got up and walked to the bookcase. With his strong body pressed against its heavy weight, he pushed it aside and reached into the wall. He felt the briefcase handle and pulled it out. Back on the chair, he rummaged through her paperwork. He knew what he was looking for. Somebody had to be in charge of maintaining that property. If the current owners ever hoped to sell that estate, the grounds would have to look pristine. He remembered the lawn appeared due for a cutting when he was there last Tuesday.

The name of the lawn service has to be in here somewhere, he thought.

He read over the listing sheet, then checked a few others. It appeared that the same lawn service was retained for all of the upscale properties that were vacant. A sly grin crossed his face as he checked the names of the male Realtors at Realty World. He randomly picked one, reached for his burner phone, and made the call. He knew he'd get a recorded message on a Saturday night—it was just what he wanted anyway. He left a message saying Realty World needed a groundskeeper at the property on Oriole Lane tomorrow to freshen things up. A potential buyer was coming to view the estate first thing Monday.

Dime pulled the tab on another beer. He knew he would need several beers to sleep soundly that night. The anticipation he felt in hopes of the groundskeeper finding Melissa was more than exciting. He took the stairs to the first floor, shut off the basement light, and went into the living room. He turned on the TV. His favorite crime thriller was just beginning.

Chapter 34

I saw my family off and spoke to the manager while I waited for Jack. I knew we wouldn't find any evidence left behind. Our killer was smarter than that. Plus, this bar and restaurant was crowded. I was certain the bar countertop had been wiped down too since the killer had left.

"We need the restaurant closed, sir. I know this is an inconvenience, especially on a busy Saturday night, but there's no alternative."

The manager wrung his hands and groaned. "I understand, but I don't even know how to go about doing that. People are waiting for their meals and—"

"Sir," I interrupted, "whatever is ready to be served can go in doggy bags. Whatever hasn't been started isn't an issue. Give the customers rain checks, I don't care, just get them out—now. I have a forensic team on their way, and any chance of finding evidence could be destroyed the longer people are here."

Jack, Kyle, and Dan arrived and entered through the front door. By now the place was nearly deserted. The manager, bartender, and the waitress remained in the building with me.

"Jade, are you okay?" Jack asked when he saw us sitting at a table in the main dining room.

"Yeah, I'm fine. Jack, this is Leanne Frank, the waitress that spoke with our guy, the bartenders, Fred Stevenson and Mike Williams, and the nightshift manager of the restaurant, Brian McKinney."

They shook hands.

"These two fellas, Kyle and Dan, are our forensic team. Leanne, Fred, and Mike, I'm going to need you to show these two everything you remember. Show them exactly where our guy stood, if he sat, what he touched, if he ordered a drink or food for himself, if he held a plate, a glass, a utensil, pulled the barstool out, and so on. I'm sure you get the idea."

Leanne, Mike, and Fred nodded and began with Dan and Kyle at the bar.

I pulled Kyle aside, leaned in, and whispered to him. In public, I didn't want to use the name "Dime" too often, fearing the media would sensationalize the story and start using "Dime" as the killer's moniker.

"The wine bottle is sitting in the banquet room. As far as I know, it was only handled by Dime, the waitress, and me."

"Got it, Jade."

"So, what do you know so far?" Jack asked.

"The only thing the waitress and bartenders remember was that he wore a baseball cap and dark green–lensed glasses. They couldn't tell his hair or eye color, and with such a crowd at the bar, they couldn't tell how tall he was. Apparently, he was shoulder to shoulder with everyone else standing around. They thought he wore a black hoodie, and they didn't see his pants."

"Yeah, a dark hoodie over his head would look out of place in a nice restaurant like this. He'd stand out more by wearing it up—smart to wear a baseball cap instead." Jack looked around and pointed at the cameras.

I read his mind. "They're fake."

"Damn it. Okay, let's take a look at that bottle."

We got up, and I led the way to the banquet room. We walked up to the table and took a seat.

The bottle remained where I had left it, still swaddled in the tea towel. The towel was wet, and the tablecloth beneath the bottle was damp.

The room had been bustling with families enjoying their Saturday night less than an hour ago. Now the empty space felt ominous.

Jack leaned in and read the label out loud. "Sweet Melissa—Sweet Sparkling Red Wine." He whistled, ran his fingers through his hair, then squeezed his head between his hands. "If that isn't a clue, I don't know what is."

I agreed. "We need the manager to pull up a list of how often this wine is purchased from the wholesaler, how often customers request it by the glass or by the bottle. Is it on their drink menu? I've never even heard of it. How would Dime know they sell it here?" I motioned for Brian to come over. I wrote all my questions in my notepad and tore out that page. "Brian."

"Yes, Sergeant?"

"I need you to take care of this immediately." I handed him the piece of paper and continued my conversation with Jack.

"My question is how did Dime know you'd be here tonight?"

"I don't know, Jack, but I do know one thing, we just might have a serial killer on our hands."

Jack squeezed my shoulder. "We'll get him, Jade. You can count on that. Right now, we need to focus on Melissa. You said she hasn't been heard from since Tuesday?"

"That's right. According to Adriana, one of the Realtors, she received a text from Melissa Tuesday night saying she had a family emergency. Nobody from the office has heard from her since. I tried calling Melissa this morning, but her mailbox was full. Adriana said her appointment calendar and her briefcase were gone."

"What about her family? Is she married, does she have anyone in North Bend or Milwaukee?"

"Apparently not. It sounds like her family lives somewhere else. I think Adriana said Iowa. That means she could have easily driven there."

"But if it was an emergency, she probably would have flown. We'll check the airlines. This clue with the bottle might just be a hoax to ruin your birthday. I don't know, Jade, but we have to cover all angles. What about gloves? Dime had to pay for the wine even if he didn't actually touch the bottle, right?"

"That's true—hold on." I called out to Fred and Mike,

the bartenders, to come over. "Who actually spoke to our guy?"

Fred answered, "I did."

"How did he pay for the bottle?"

"Um… it was prepaid over the phone with a credit card."

A surprised look furrowed Jack's brows. "A credit card? We need to see the receipt on that right away."

"Sure, I'll go find it."

"There's no way he'd be that careless. It must be a stolen card," I said.

Fred returned a few minutes later with a credit card receipt. "Here it is. The bottle was ordered at five thirty today. We billed it to a Melissa Mately's credit card."

I pressed my palms into my eyes and shook my head. "Thanks, Fred. We'll need a copy of that receipt." I waited until he was out of earshot to continue. "Well, Dime is definitely making a name for himself. I doubt if we're going to find Melissa alive, if we find her at all. If that's the case, he'll be officially on the record as a serial killer."

Kyle and Dan joined us at the table and looked at the bottle.

"Should we process the bottle now, Jade?"

"Sure, go ahead. It sounds like he didn't touch it, but it's protocol. I don't know what to do about this restaurant. With the volume of patrons here tonight, is it even feasible to waste time trying to lift fingerprints that may belong to hundreds of people?"

I looked from face to face—their expressions were all the

same. It didn't matter if Dime was in the woods or in a bustling restaurant—he never left a trace of evidence.

"Has anyone called the lieutenant?" I asked.

Jack answered, "Yeah, I did on my way in. He's expecting the four of us in his office first thing in the morning for a briefing."

Chapter 35

A crew of three groundskeepers arrived at the estate on Oriole Lane at nine a.m. One man sat atop the oversized riding mower and addressed the large areas of lawn that needed cutting. Another pushed a self-propelled mower. His job was to trim the lawn in all of the tight spots, around trees and flower beds that the large mower couldn't get close to. The last man operated the leaf blower and cleaned off the walkways, porch, deck, and the driveway area nearest the garage.

A strange scent seemed to linger in the air near the barn, and Joseph, the man pushing the hand-operated mower, noticed it. The riding mower that Andy sat on was moving at too fast a clip to catch the scent. Harry, the man blowing the leaves and debris from the hard surfaces, had his own force of moving air, making the odor unnoticeable.

With the front porch and sidewalk done, Harry moved on to the garage area. He adjusted the slipping shoulder straps, wiped his brow, and began blowing debris. The row of windows on the garage doors fell right at eye level.

The zinging sound of a stone hitting the garage door caused Harry to turn. He hoped it hadn't left a mark. He turned off the blower, set it down, and walked over. The sun pouring through the row of windows caused something to catch his eye. Harry peered in, cupping his hands against the glass to block the sun at his back. A gold Infinity sedan was parked inside. He rubbed his chin in thought. The place was supposed to be vacant, and he was under the assumption the owners had moved to another state. *What the heck is a car like that doing here*? He flagged down Joseph, the man using the push mower.

"Hey, man, come and take a look. There's a high-end car in the garage."

They both peered through the garage windows. Harry again, just to confirm what he'd really seen a few minutes ago.

"That kind of car shouldn't be parked in there. Something isn't right, plus there's a really foul smell coming from the barn area. Do you think somebody abandoned an animal in there and it died?"

"Hang on." Harry went back to the porch area and looked at the front door. The lockbox was on the handle. He gave it a tug—it was locked. "Something about this smells fishy to me."

"It's worse than fishy, man. Let's take a look in the barn."

"Isn't it locked?" Harry asked.

"Nope. No reason to lock it if it's empty. Let's get Andy over here. We all have to agree before we go in there."

Andy had just finished the backyard and was driving the riding mower toward the tractor shed to cut a perimeter around it. He heard yelling and caught a glimpse of waving arms. He turned and headed in their direction. He disengaged the mower blade and turned the key to shut down the machine.

"What's up?"

"We might have a problem," Joseph said.

Andy swung his leg over the seat and dismounted the mower. "What is that supposed to mean?"

"Come, take a look." Harry led the way to the garage and looked in for the third time. "What do you make of that?"

"There's nobody here, is there?" Andy asked.

"Nope. The house is locked up tight, and according to our contract, the owners moved out of state. At least that's the way it's written on our service agreement. I don't think it's legal for the Realtors to keep a vehicle here. They're the only ones with access to the house or garage," Harry said.

Andy chewed on that information for a minute. "Yeah, we better give them a call."

Joseph paused. "What about the barn?" He stared at Harry.

"What's going on with the barn?" Andy asked.

"There's a really bad smell coming from it, and a car like that in the garage? It doesn't feel right."

"Smell?" Andy's eyes darted around. "You mean like meth lab smell?"

"No, not like that—like death."

The three cautiously checked all of the house doors and peeked through the windows. They didn't want to be surprised by anyone who might be there that wasn't supposed to be. When all seemed safe and they'd found no evidence of anyone lurking around, they headed toward the barn. The odor got stronger as they approached.

"Holy crap, I smell what you mean," Andy said. He covered his nose with his sleeve and shoved the barn doors open. The stench overwhelmed them, and they backed out.

Joseph vomited against the side of the building. "I'm not going in there. I think we should call the cops."

Chapter 36

We gathered around the small corner table in the bull pen. A pot of coffee was halfway through the brew cycle, and it wasn't going fast enough for my liking. I gave it a glance—six more cups before the beep would indicate it was full. I had all of four hours of sleep last night. My mind was in constant motion, running like a gerbil on a wheel—as usual. My eyes burned, my brain was a ball of fuzz, and we had nothing to tell the lieutenant.

"So, you missed him by a couple of minutes, Jade?"

"I guess so, sir, but I wouldn't have known it was him even if I was sitting at his side. We don't have an actual description. All we have is a general idea of his size and that a weird-acting guy was sitting at Eddy's Tap for a few minutes."

The lieutenant leaned back in his chair, causing it to creak, and focused his eyes on the ceiling. He let out a long sigh. "Let me guess—no cameras at Eddy's Tap?"

I answered. "Unfortunately not."

"What about forensic evidence, guys? Do you think

there's a gopher's chance in hell of coming up with anything at Stanley's?"

"In all likelihood, sir, not really," Kyle said. "According to the staff, there were a good forty people in the bar area and fifty more in the restaurant that probably sat at the bar prior to eating dinner."

Dan added, "From what the bartenders and the waitress could remember, our guy didn't order or handle anything."

"No video of the bar area?"

"Nope."

The lieutenant filled his cup and took a gulp. "This is a nightmare, a damn nightmare. How did he know where you were last night, and why would he target you, Jade?"

"Sir, I have no idea. I'm guessing maybe to create more fear within our own department. Maybe he only picked me because I'm female. He could have thought I'd be more intimidated by him than a guy would."

"Well, until we catch the maniac, I'm putting a deputy on you twenty-four, seven. Got it?"

"Yes, sir."

"When the media gets wind of this—"

Peggy, our weekend dispatch officer, interrupted, "Excuse me, boss, there's a call on line two. They said it's urgent, and they wanted to speak to the person in charge." Peggy closed the door behind her as she turned and left.

"Give me a second, guys." The lieutenant picked up the receiver and pressed the button for line two. "Hello, this is Lieutenant Clark speaking. How can I help you?"

The lieutenant abruptly sat up straight, his back

involuntarily stiffened. He motioned for a pen and paper. I grabbed both off my desk.

"Yes, the address again. A gold Infinity and you said the listing agent is who? Got it. Don't touch anything and don't leave the scene. We'll be there in fifteen minutes." He hung up. "Son of a bitch, get Peggy back in here." Clark stood and headed for his office.

Dan ran out of the room and grabbed Peggy. She came back in as the lieutenant was strapping on his shoulder holster. "Sir, what can I do for you?"

"Peggy, call every patrol unit that's east of town." He handed her the piece of paper. "Get them to this address yesterday—go."

"Gear up. Let's roll. Something suspicious is going on at a property listed by Melissa Mately. Somebody ring up Jason and Doug. Tell them they're on call."

"Boss, the gold Infinity is her car." I swore under my breath as we strapped on our hardware.

"Let's move. Can this weekend get any worse?" The lieutenant was out the door before the rest of us.

Jack looked at me as he holstered up. "I'm afraid it just might"—he looked at the clock—"in about fifteen minutes."

We jumped into the first cruiser in the lot and took off. Ten minutes later, we passed Eddy's Tap along the highway as Jack drove east, our lights flashing and the siren singing. He had the gas pedal pressed to the floor.

My head spun back to look at the bar. "Shit, didn't Mike Cole say that weird patron was at Eddy's on Tuesday evening?"

"That's exactly what he said."

"And Adriana said Melissa hadn't been heard from since Tuesday night, correct?"

"Yep. So you're thinking our killer was on his way to the house on Oriole Lane to meet with Melissa and stopped at Eddy's first for a beer?"

"It makes sense to me. He had to pass the bar anyway. That guy has to be our killer."

"He stops and has a casual glass of beer before he kills someone? That's more than twisted."

As Jack drove, I secured my hair into a ponytail with the elastic band on my wrist. "Jack, everything about this psycho is twisted. We're going to have to interview Mike and Abe again. There has to be more about him they remember."

Jack exited the highway and turned left onto Oriole Lane. About a half mile up the road, we found the long driveway with the For Sale sign in front of it and turned in. The driveway widened near the garages, offering a good number of parking spots. The groundskeeper's vehicle was near the walkway at the front of the driveway. Four sheriff's patrol cruisers sat behind and to the right of their vehicle. We rolled in with the forensic van and two unmarked black cruisers.

"Boys, what do we know?" Lieutenant Clark asked as he got out and slammed the car door. Jack and I exited our car right behind him, and Kyle and Dan were already at the back of the van, grabbing their supplies.

"Lieutenant, there's a suspicious smell coming from the

barn. The garage has an abandoned vehicle inside," Deputy Silver said.

"Okay… Deputy Lawrence, stay behind and get the groundskeepers' statements. Somebody call the realty office now. We need to get this house opened up. Jade, get on it."

"Yes, sir."

"Okay, let's go."

"Sir?"

"Yes, Deputy Silver?" Clark stopped and turned.

"The smell is *really* bad."

"Got it."

I called Realty World and talked to the first person that answered the phone. Apparently, Leon Erikson was the lucky recipient of my call. I told him to get to Oriole Lane now. It was a police matter, and in twenty minutes the front door would be broken down. I hung up, and we followed Kyle, Dan, and the lieutenant to the front of the barn.

With everyone gathered, Kyle and Dan passed around the jar of Vicks before we entered the barn. The sickening odor was intense. Each person reached in, pulled out a glob of Vicks, and dabbed it under their nose before entering.

The deputies entered first with the rest of us right behind. Silver hit the lights as he passed through the door. He called back to keep the doors open. To the left and right were box stalls, most likely for horses. A tack room stood twenty feet ahead to the right of us. Since we had no idea what to expect, the deputies had their guns drawn as a cautionary measure. Jack, the lieutenant, and I followed Kyle and Dan into the tack room while the deputies kept a watchful eye for any movement on the rest of the barn. The pungent, rotting smell made our eyes water, and our gag reflexes kicked in even with the menthol salve beneath our noses.

"There's been a scuffle in here," Dan said, pointing out the disturbances in the straw strewn about. "Look over here." We hugged the edges of the room to the opposite wall, trying not to disturb the scene. Dried blood spatter and strands of blond hair were stuck to the rough-hewn boards. We gave the wall a long look then left the tack room—it needed to be processed.

Lieutenant Clark nodded ahead. Two deputies hugged the left stalls and two hugged the right as we inched forward. The odor was getting thicker with each step. The deputies peeked over every stall gate as they got to it, their guns at the ready.

Something odd caught my eye at the third stall on the left. I whispered and pointed. The deputies nodded and approached what looked to be leather tied around the gate slats.

Deputy Silver knelt down and peered between the slats. "Holy shit." It took him a second to process what he'd just seen. He stood and looked over the gate. He waved us forward, then backed away so we could get through. Dan and Kyle peered over the gate with the lieutenant on their heels.

"Son of a bitch." The anger spewed out of the lieutenant's mouth.

Jack approached, looked over, and held up his hand for

me to stop. "There's no need for you to see this, Jade. It's pretty bad. Silver, call Doug and Jason. Get them out here now."

"Yes, sir, I'm on it."

"Jack, move aside. We have a job to do. I can't let personal feelings get in the way of our investigation," I said.

Kyle climbed over the gate first, and Dan handed him the camera. Kyle took close to twenty pictures before allowing us to climb over and join him on the side where Melissa sat tied to the gate and bridled.

We spent a good amount of time studying the way she was propped against the gate, the bridle in her mouth and the leather strap that had likely choked the life out of her wrapped around her neck and the gate. I wondered if there was significance to her being bridled. Her mouth was swollen, and her eyes bulged from bloat. The skin was beginning to turn a shade of grayish green. Looking at her was difficult, but we needed to get into the head of this madman. Why was he so devious and angry, and what did these innocent people do to make him choose them?

"Come on. Let's get some fresh air and let Kyle and Dan begin processing this barn. Doug and Jason should be here soon."

We went outside to talk to the groundskeepers. The sight of an approaching vehicle caught our attention. The car, a newer sporty orange Camaro, had magnetic ads for Realty World on each door. I assumed it was Leon Erikson.

"Officers, what's going on?" he asked as he parked behind the row of vehicles and rushed toward us.

I extended my hand. "Mr. Erikson? I'm Sergeant Jade Monroe"—I nodded to my left—"and my partner, Detective Jack Steele. We're from Washburn County Sheriff's Department."

Jack shook his hand.

"Mr. Erikson, we need to get inside the house right away. It's a police matter."

"Yes, ma'am, let's go." Leon entered the code for the lockbox, opened it, and pulled out the house key. He unlocked the heavy oak door and pushed it forward.

"Sir, you'll have to wait outside with Deputy Lawrence. Deputy, interview Mr. Erikson and find out when Melissa was here last and with what client."

"Yes, Sergeant. Sir, please step this way. Let's find a place to sit."

Jack, two deputies, and I entered the house with our guns drawn. We split at the end of the foyer, the deputies taking the first level, Jack and I taking the staircase to the second floor. I heard the deputies call out as they cleared each room. We cleared the second floor, checked each balcony and closet. The four of us cleared the basement level together before we entered the garage.

My breath caught in my throat when I saw the gold Infinity parked in the third stall. Jack pushed the button for that garage door. It lifted, allowing more light into the garage. With gloved hands, I opened the driver's side door and looked in. Nothing seemed amiss, and the seat appeared to be in the correct position for someone Melissa's height. A struggle hadn't taken place in the car.

"Doug and Jason are here," Jack said when he saw them come up the driveway and park the coroner's van next to the forensics van.

Doug approached the garage. Jason followed behind him. "Sergeant, Detective Steele, what do we have?"

Jack stepped out of the garage and responded while I popped the trunk. I went to the back of the car to give it a look. "We've got a body in the horse barn, and it looks like she's been there for a while." Jack nodded toward the outbuildings. "It's the one on the right."

"Okay, Jason, back the van over to the barn as close as you can," Doug said as he turned and walked toward the barn alone.

Jack stuck his head in the trunk. "See anything unusual?"

"No, nothing that looks out of place. We should call for the flatbed. We aren't going to drive Melissa's car back to the evidence garage."

"Good idea. May as well get a head start on it. Kyle and Dan can give the car a quick once-over before they load it up. They'll likely take a few photographs here too."

Chapter 37

Doug and Jason spent a good half hour in the barn. Jack and I talked to the lieutenant near the cars as we waited. I explained to him that the oddball in Eddy's Tap Tuesday evening was more than likely our killer. He had to have been on his way to the house to meet up with Melissa under false pretenses. Pretending to be an interested buyer—especially of a home worth as much money as the house on Oriole Lane— would be a great way to lure a Realtor out there alone.

"Don't you think common sense flies out the window at the chance of a hefty commission? And who would imagine a killer using that as a ruse? Scary and dangerous people are most often pictured in bad neighborhoods, not here," I said.

"Sounds logical. Do you think you got everything you could get out of the bartender and the man at the video poker machine?" Lieutenant Clark asked.

"Not sure, sir, but they're both getting a second interview."

Doug and Jason walked out of the barn and headed our way.

"What can you tell us?" the lieutenant asked.

Doug shrugged. "Pretty gruesome, if I do say so myself. Body appears to be a female in her thirties. It looks like she's been here around five days according to the maggots. Rigor has passed. The quantity of facial lacerations and contusions may have been enough to render her unconscious. COD was likely asphyxia. Her tongue is swollen and protruding, but I found decomposed paper in her throat, and this"—Doug held out a dime in the palm of his hand—"under her tongue."

"Son of a bitch." Lieutenant Clark ground his fist into his eyes. "Okay, bag everything up and give it to Kyle and Dan. I'll call the North Bend PD and see if their forensic lab can spare Peterson and Gundrum. I'm sure our boys could use the help. Monroe and Steele, get back to town and round those fellas up again. There has to be more they can tell us."

"You got it, boss. We'll head out now," I said.

Jack backed our car down the driveway and out to the road. With the number of vehicles at the house, there wasn't room to turn around.

"Do you think my family is safe, Jack? Last night couldn't have been personal, could it?"

Jack exited Oriole Lane and merged onto the highway heading back to town. His expression told me he was concerned.

"I don't have any answers. Fred told us the guy ordered the wine at five thirty. You guys got to the restaurant at six thirty. That means he didn't follow you there. He already knew where you were going."

"The only thing I can think of is he may have been at Left Field and overheard Amber and me talking, or he knows Amber works at Joey's and heard her telling a friend what we were doing Saturday night. I swear my brain is ready to explode."

"Yeah, join the crowd. I think you should call Amber and update her. She's a big girl, and if she really wants to be a cop someday, she's going to have to know what kind of people are out in the real world. We'll ask the lieutenant's opinion once he gets back at the station. Maybe you and your family ought to hole up together for the time being."

"I'm going to give Amber a quick call and tell her to stay at Mom's house until I get back to her later. Somebody will have to let Realty World know it was Melissa we found. Leon has no idea why he came to the house, just that it was a police matter."

Jack pulled into the station and parked. "The deputies can take care of that. I'll tell them to track down her next of kin too. We have plenty on our plates already."

We entered the bull pen, and I dropped to my chair. My notepad was still on my desk where I'd left it Friday night. I flipped the pages to Mike Cole's interview and read through the information again out loud. "I'm going to call him right now."

Mike answered on the third ring. I heard the TV playing in the background. It sounded like sports.

"Hello."

"Mike, Sergeant Monroe calling from the sheriff's department."

"Hello, Sergeant. Hang on one second."

He left the phone, and I heard the TV volume go down.

"Sorry about that. I have a habit of turning the volume up too high when I'm watching basketball. I guess it comes from having the bar TVs muted most of the time. Sometimes I actually like to hear the play-by-play action. I'm recording it, so we're good. Okay, what can I do for you?"

"Mike, it's about the guy at the bar on Tuesday. Is there anything else you thought of since we spoke? Anything, even if it seems insignificant, might help us catch our killer." I stared at the notes again from the interview we had conducted at Mike's apartment. "I'm not necessarily saying the man at Eddy's is him, so please don't spread that rumor. We're just checking every possible lead we can get."

"Sure, I understand. Hmm… I did think it was odd that he mumbled to himself, almost like he was talking to somebody. The guy gave me the creeps. Oh yeah, and he cracked his neck like three times in fifteen minutes. That's really all I can think of, Sergeant."

I wrote the additional information in my notepad and thanked Mike. I felt Jack's searing stare as he stood next to the beverage station. I looked up.

"Well? And do you want some coffee?"

"Yes, please." I shook my head as if to clear the thoughts that were stirring in my mind. "He added that the weirdo at the bar also mumbled to himself and cracked his neck a few times."

Jack laughed and dragged his fingertips through his hair.

"Damn, that sounds just like Doug."

"Ya think? Whatever… people mutter all the time, at least I do, and I crack my neck. All this damn tension settles in my shoulders and neck. I've cracked it so much lately it sounds like popcorn popping."

"Yeah, me too."

My desk phone rang. "Hello, Sergeant Monroe, how may I help you? Deputy Silver?" I glanced up at Jack and mouthed a thank-you when he brought a fresh cup of coffee to my desk. "Yes, either Adriana Cruz or Leon Erikson, the Realtor that opened the house for us. Somebody has to know something about Melissa's next of kin. Neither of them has names or phone numbers of her family? All right, get her address then. We'll search her house. I'm sure we'll find something there. Thanks." I hung up.

"What did he say?" Jack dropped down into his desk chair.

"Nobody at Realty World has information on Melissa's family except that some relative lives in Iowa. Her purse, cell phone, and appointment calendar are missing. According to Adriana, Melissa normally kept all of that in her briefcase. I think we should call the boss. He can get Billings and Clayton to go through Melissa's house."

Jack agreed. "Relax for a few minutes. I'll call the lieutenant."

Jack's conversation with the lieutenant was short. They were just finishing up at the house, and the lieutenant was heading back to the station. Kyle, Dan, Doug, and Jason were on their way back too with the body in the van and the car on the flatbed. Two deputies stayed behind, and the North Bend PD offered us assistance with forensics. Their investigators had already arrived at the scene. The lieutenant said he'd make the call to Clayton and Billings and get them over to Melissa's house right away.

Jack's desk phone rang a few minutes later. Brian McKinney, the manager at Stanley's, was calling. "One second, Brian." Jack put his hand over the receiver and told me who it was. "Brian, I'm going to put you on speakerphone so Sergeant Monroe can join the conversation. Go ahead and tell us what you have."

"Sure thing. Anyway, Sweet Melissa Sweet Sparkling Red Wine has its own website. Apparently their products can be ordered directly from their site by wholesalers, retailers, restaurants, and private individuals. Our daytime manager takes care of orders, so I spoke with him."

I scooted my chair next to Jack's desk to make sure Brian could hear my questions. "Brian, it's Sergeant Monroe here. Does your daytime manager order directly from the website or a wholesaler?"

"Since we don't have a ton of people asking for that wine in particular, we order a case at a time off the website. Sweet Melissa is on our wine list, though, which shows up on Stanley's website along with our menu."

"Got it. So what you're saying is, it's a dead end? You guys order directly from Sweet Melissa, plus anyone can look online to see your wine list from Stanley's website?"

"Sorry, Sergeant, but that's really it in a nutshell."

Jack thanked Brian and hung up.

Chapter 38

Lieutenant Clark buzzed himself through the security door and into the bull pen. He turned the wand on the blinds—the glaring afternoon sun had already come around the building.

"Jade, I need you to gather your family together later and have them stay at your house for the time being. I'll station two deputies on your residence, one during the day and one at night. It's all we can spare. We have to find this maniac, even if it means working around the clock."

"We still need to come and go, boss. We all have jobs."

"Understood, and I'm sure you'll explain to your family how important it is for them to watch their backs at all times. If anything seems off or someone looks suspicious, I expect an immediate phone call to the officer I'm assigning to you. I want your family members to have his contact information. I'd prefer it if everyone took time off and stayed put, but that's your call."

"I want to work, Lieutenant. We need everyone on this case, don't we?"

Lieutenant Clark sighed and scratched his neck. "You're right, we do. First things first, though, we need to give a press statement. There's too much speculation out there. We want folks to be safe and keep a diligent watch on their surroundings. We have no idea who this killer is targeting. Right now, we have to come up with the best profile we can to give to the press. It's going to be tough since we have no witnesses to anything. I'm calling Clayton and Billings in to help us brainstorm. I'll have a couple of deputies take their place searching Miss Mately's house."

Clayton and Billings arrived at the station at two thirty. The five of us sat in the lieutenant's office with the door closed. We wracked our brains trying to come up with a suspect profile to give the media.

The lieutenant pulled the white board and easel out of his coat closet. I couldn't remember the last time he used it.

On it, he wrote each victim's name, the chronological order of the murders, where the bodies were found, and the cause of death.

"Okay, it's fair game here guys. Throw out everything you know." He waited.

"It seems that our murderer uses something related to the deceased to kill them," I said.

"Good point, Jade. So what is that telling us?"

"That he's an opportunist, he doesn't want anything traced back to him, or he's done his homework," Jack said.

We all chewed on that statement.

"He's strong, has endurance, plus he must have a certain amount of charisma to get Elise and Melissa's attention. But he has a few quirks too. Apparently, the bartender at Eddy's said he cracks his neck and mumbles to himself," I added.

The lieutenant nodded. "Good to know. So he has some physical quirks, he's strong, smart, and careful." Clark wrote it down.

"He takes the victims' personal belongings—cell phones, wallets, and so on—to make our job more difficult," Clayton said. "Everyone is killed in a remote area where there are no cameras."

"Isn't it odd that he would bring Morris all the way to Washburn County, though? Melissa lived in town, yet she was found outside the city limits. Elise worked in North Bend, but he made sure she was killed out in the country too. For some reason, he wants his victims to be outside the city jurisdiction and in our hands, the county sheriff's department," I said. "Think of it, that has to be the reason, or why would he bring Morris here instead of leaving him at the crime scene in Milwaukee?"

"So he's taunting the sheriff's department in a way?"

"He has to be, and he leaves that damn dime so we know it was him. You know, I just realized something. It holds true for Elise and Melissa anyway."

"Go on, Jack," Lieutenant Clark said.

"We talked about this a few weeks ago with Kyle and Dan. We were trying to figure out the connection between Morris and Elise, then Kyle had mentioned that it might not be a connection with Morris and Elise at all. Maybe the killer is trying to get somebody's attention. He could know this person was friends with Elise or Melissa. These are targeted acts to get this person to sit up and take notice."

Each of us stared at the white board, giving that statement some thought.

"He's doing a damn good job, but I don't see where Morris fits in with any of this," I said.

Clayton spoke up. "Okay, let's take Morris out of the equation. Maybe he was just someone the killer wanted to hone his skills on. Bad luck, wrong place, wrong time, that sort of thing. Did Elise and Melissa know each other?"

"Nope. Melissa wasn't on Elise's list of friends or acquaintances. She certainly wasn't Elise and Perry's Realtor. They've lived in the same house for over ten years."

"Then there's only one person it could be," Billings said. "The connection between them is Jade."

"What?" I suddenly felt ill and reached for my chair. I had to sit and give that statement some thought.

"You might be on to something, Billings," the lieutenant said. "Jade, Elise was your yoga instructor, Melissa was the Realtor you were working with, and now, somehow the killer knew you were going to Stanley's and it was your birthday. He wanted to shake you up personally and taunt you with the bottle of wine. I think we're getting somewhere."

"But why me?"

"Who knows, but maybe if we put you under the microscope, we'll be able to profile our killer," Jack said.

The lieutenant raised his eyebrows. "Okay, let's go with that theory. Jack, take the lead."

"Sure. What if the killer has a beef with people in law

enforcement? Maybe he's a misogynist, for Pete's sake, or what if he doesn't like authority figures, as in a female sergeant." Jack entwined his fingers behind his head as he leaned back in his chair. "Let's put it all together. He doesn't like women in law enforcement that have authority over people. That fits Jade perfectly."

"And because he doesn't like me, he's killing people? That sounds like a stretch, Jack. Don't you have to have killer tendencies to begin with?"

Billings added, "Maybe he does and we just don't know it. Since he's killed three people that we know of, we can already consider him a serial killer, but now he's a spree killer too. Somebody like that is even more difficult to track."

The lieutenant sat down. He had already paced in front of the white board for the last half hour. "Okay, so we're dealing with a psychopathic spree killer. That's really going to go over well with the public." The lieutenant let out a groan. "All right, what about age, married or single, local or not? What about employment?"

"I'd put him between twenty-five and fifty because he's strong enough to overpower people. He has enough intelligence to catch women off guard through his charm or through a ruse. He must be single to come and go at night. I'd even go so far as to say he knows how law enforcement works. He can hide in plain sight, and he always covers his tracks. He's never seen on video, and there's never a speck of trace evidence left behind." I looked at everyone and waited for input.

"Okay, I think we have a good enough profile to hold a press conference. I'll set something up," the lieutenant said.

The phone rang on Clark's desk. "Hi, Peggy, what do you have? Okay, put her through."

The boss talked to Deputy Lawrence for ten minutes while he jotted notes. He hung up.

"They found an address book at Melissa Mately's house. Lawrence just spoke with Melissa's mom in Iowa and told her the news. Apparently, the last time Mrs. Lawrence had any communication with Melissa was Tuesday around six p.m."

"Sounds like it must have taken place while she was driving to Oriole Lane," Jack said.

The lieutenant responded. "Well, I think we have our first actual lead. The mother said Melissa texted her. Here is the text her mom received, verbatim."

The lieutenant began to read. "Hi, Mom, I'm on my way to show a really expensive property. This man, David Ingles, and his family are moving here from Philadelphia. It sounds promising. I'll keep my fingers crossed. Maybe I can come and visit sooner than I thought. Love you."

I nodded. "That's the type of ruse we were talking about. Nobody from Philly is committing these murders. He led her on that he wanted to see the house. How could Melissa resist? The commission would be huge if she sold it." I groaned at the image. "She went out there voluntarily and was probably really excited about it."

Lieutenant Clark picked up his phone and called downstairs to Todd in the tech department. "Todd, I need you to do a criminal database search in Pennsylvania and Wisconsin for a David Ingles. Hell, make it a nationwide search. We can always narrow it down once we get the results."

He hung up, then picked the phone up again and called Susan Adams, who wrote the sheriff's department press releases. He got her voice mail. Like most of the administrative staff, she didn't work on Sundays. "Susan, Lieutenant Clark here. I need you to write a press release on the North Bend killer first thing in the morning. Meet me in my office at ten o'clock, and I'll go over everything with you."

The lieutenant checked the time on his desk clock. "Okay, it's almost five. I'll let Doug know to get the forensic dentist in here tomorrow. We aren't going to let anyone make a visual identification of Melissa in the state she's in. I'll keep in touch with the mom. Everyone, go home, get some rest, and we'll start with fresh eyes in the morning. Jade, call your family, tell them to grab what they need, and get to your house. I'm putting Collins on your home beginning at six o'clock. Once he's in place, I'll have him give you a call so you have his contact number."

Jack and I walked out to the parking lot together. There was a chill in the air. The breeze coming from the east off Lake Michigan made me shiver.

"Cold or nervous?" Jack asked.

"Both I guess. I'm looking forward to the time when I can say I live in a sleepy little town where nothing happens."

"I hear you. If you need—"

I interrupted Jack and smiled. "Thanks, but I do wear a gun, you know, and I'm a pretty good shot."

"Yeah, you're a tough one, Jade Monroe, I'll give you that. Actually, I was going to say if you need to talk."

I nodded. "Thanks, partner. Jack?"

"Yeah?"

"You're welcome to hang out at my place with us. Amber said they were bringing dinner over."

"Thanks, but I'll take a rain check. I feel like turning in early tonight."

Chapter 39

Dime started a new page in his notebook. He wrote the person's name on a folder tab and pulled the sticky backside off. He pressed the tab against the outer edge of the notebook page.

"There, that's perfect."

He had been following his next victim for a few days. Now that Melissa had been found, the cops would be busy trying to keep the community calm. He'd have free reign to carry out his next act while they were preoccupied with her. He knew his next victim's routine pretty well, and he'd put his idea into motion soon. There was no way he'd give Jade Monroe time to rest.

The radio played his favorite blues channel as he relaxed on that wooden chair in the basement. The local news broke in and interrupted the music. He took a sip of beer and listened. He couldn't help smiling. The breaking news stated that a body had been discovered in a barn near the small town of North Bend. A well-known and respected local Realtor was found dead earlier today just east of the city. The name wouldn't be released until the next of kin was notified.

He laughed a full belly laugh. *Found dead, huh? Put your generic, nondescript spin on it if you want. We wouldn't want to start a citywide panic, would we? I'll admit, it would be fun, though, if John Q. Public really knew how she and the others met their demise.*

Dime rose and walked to the bookcase. He gave it a forceful shove to the side, then pulled his chair over and sat. With a beer in his hand, he smiled into the gaping hole in the wall then took a sip.

Chapter 40

I was more than angry. I couldn't save the lives of two women I knew and cared for and one young man I had never met. They had no say in their demise. They were just innocent victims. Dime couldn't be left on the streets much longer. I was sure he'd strike again.

I pulled into the garage and lowered the overhead door before getting out of my car. Amber, Mom, and Bruce should be here soon, and I needed to set up the guest room for Mom and Bruce. My mental energy was spent, yet I had to explain a few things to my family. They would only get the generic version—nothing more. Some information needed to stay quiet. Only law enforcement knew the way Dime killed his victims and what he used as a calling card. That bit of information had to stay within the sheriff's department.

I fed Spaz and the birds. They all got hugs and kisses, yet I probably needed the affection more than they did.

Amber said they were picking up dinner from Tony's and would be here by six. She ordered two large pepperoni-

and-black-olive pizzas and three two-liter bottles of Coke. I poured myself a much-needed glass of wine and waited. I looked at the mantel clock on the shelf above my TV. The six o'clock chimes would sound any minute.

The key turning in the front door got my attention. I needed to put on my confident-sergeant face and ensure my family we'd all be fine.

"Hello, sweetheart." My mom entered first and hugged me. Bruce followed with the pizzas and set them on the breakfast bar. Amber came in last, carrying the mail that had been sitting in my mailbox for who knew how long.

"Here's your mail, Sis. I guess my change of address hasn't kicked in yet. Looks like you got a few birthday cards mixed in with the bills."

"I'll look at them later. Let's eat. I don't remember if I've eaten anything since breakfast."

"Let me get the table set up. You just relax, honey. Amber, will you pour the soda and get out some plates?"

"Sure, Mom."

Spaz wrapped his tail around Amber's legs and meowed while she set the table. Amber chuckled. "You'll get plenty of attention after dinner, crazy cat."

After we ate, I explained the situation to my family. It was in our best interest to remain in the same residence for now. We didn't have enough extra deputies to put on both houses, and although I didn't feel that I was in immediate danger, I did agree that for whatever reason, Dime might be targeting me.

Our evening consisted of me showing my family a few

tactical maneuvers if they were ever caught alone and off guard. I explained to Amber that I was signing her up for self-defense courses soon. She would need to know some moves anyway if she was serious about eventually becoming a cop.

"I'll even take the classes with you, Sis. It never hurts to brush up on self-defense training."

"Thanks, Jade. That's something I was always interested in learning. Now I have no excuse to put it off."

"As long as we're on the subject, I want you to think of the type of personal handgun you'd like. Maybe tomorrow night we'll look at a few online. I'll explain which are my favorites for women and why. A pistol is going to be my gift to you for wanting to go into law enforcement. You may as well get an early start on learning how to handle your weapon. Actually, going to the gun range and practicing is a lot of fun."

Amber's eyes lit up. I could tell she would be a good cop in time, and I was proud of her.

"I'm really looking forward to it, Jade. Thanks."

"You're welcome."

We all turned in after the ten o'clock news. There was a brief segment about a woman being discovered in a barn at a residence that was for sale, but since we hadn't disclosed any details to the press, they didn't have much to report. We said good night, and I closed my bedroom door, brushed my teeth, and climbed into bed. I hoped my family would sleep well. I was exhausted.

Talking to someone other than Spaz, Polly, and Porky

during my morning routine was nice. Bruce had already left, so Mom, Amber, and I ate breakfast together. Since Amber didn't have classes until eleven o'clock, she took over the cooking detail and made each of us an omelet and toast.

"I have to go. Both of you, check in with Deputy Richards if, and when, you leave. He replaced Collins at six this morning."

"Jade, you didn't look at your birthday cards that came in the mail," Amber said as she loaded the dishwasher.

"Oh yeah, guess I forgot." I dropped the accumulated mail in my lunch bag with intentions of chucking most of it. I'd look at the birthday cards and pitch the junk mail if I had a chance during lunch.

Just as we'd thought, there wasn't anyone in the nationwide criminal database named David Ingles. That name alerted twice, once in Kentucky and once in Oregon, but only for traffic violations and unpaid parking tickets.

We gathered in an interview room at ten o'clock with Susan Adams to go over the key points for the press conference being held later in the afternoon. Our brief description gave Susan an estimate of age, weight, and height. We added the few quirks the perpetrator had, and the fact that he might wear a dark-colored hoodie. We ended with a plea to the public to call the North Bend sheriff's department or police department immediately if they saw anyone or anything that seemed suspicious.

"Okay, Susan, use that information to put something together. Let me take a look at it before we go live. Let the media know the press conference will take place at three o'clock at the front entrance to the sheriff's department."

Susan perused the notes she'd taken. "Sure thing, Lieutenant. I'll have this ready for you to look over in an hour."

"Want to go out for lunch, Jade?" Jack asked.

"Thanks, but Amber made me a sliced deli turkey sandwich"—I looked in my canvas lunch bag—"oh, and a banana. I think I'm going to like having my little sis around."

"I bet you will. No problem. I'll grab a sandwich from the vending machine."

I sat at my desk, pulled out my sandwich, banana, and my mail. I wanted to eat before anything went haywire. So far in the last two weeks, I had lost seven pounds.

"What's that?" Clayton asked as he gnawed on a caramel chocolate bar.

"Just my mail from the last few days. I haven't even thought about it lately. Amber saw it wedged in the mailbox and brought it in for me."

"How does Amber like living with you?"

I chuckled. "I'll let you know once life is normal again. Right now, living in the same house with my mom and Bruce is far from normal." I bit into my sandwich and flipped through some of the mail. Three pieces of junk mail were pitched before I got to the first birthday card. I tore it open and grinned at the card. My aunt Abigail, Mom's sister, in Tallahassee, Florida, had sent birthday wishes my way. The front of the card showed two birds sitting on a branch. I could tell this was one of those musical birthday cards, and when I opened it, the birds whistled out the Happy Birthday song. I laughed at its unique tackiness. "Gotta love Aunt Abigail," I said as we all chuckled.

"Got another one?" Jack asked.

"I guess so. It doesn't have a return address, though." I had an eerie feeling as I slipped my finger under the envelope seal and slid it across. Inside was a birthday card showing a cat lying on a couch. The resemblance to Spaz was remarkable. I breathed a silent sigh of relief and opened it. I stared at the handwritten words in large block letters: SPAZ IS QUITE A LOVABLE CAT. I'D HATE TO SEE ANYTHING HAPPEN TO HIM. DO I HAVE YOUR FULL ATTENTION NOW, SERGEANT?

A dime was taped beneath the words.

"The card…" My voice caught in my throat.

Jack and Clayton jumped from their chairs. I motioned for them not to touch the card.

"It's from him. The son of a bitch sent me a birthday card."

Chapter 41

He waited at the far end of the apartment parking lot for Lance. He could have had a lot of fun with the sergeant's ex-husband in a more secluded area along his jogging route, but Dime wanted Lance found soon. *Gotta strike while the iron is hot*, he thought.

Sergeant Monroe wasn't going to get any rest. Dime looked forward to breaking her, putting her in her place and taking her down. She already reminded him too much of his overbearing mother.

He chuckled, remembering the press conference that had been broadcast earlier. "The media really tore into her and the lieutenant. She got plenty of heat from them. The entire sheriff's department did. And they don't have the slightest idea of who I am or how to catch me—idiots!"

Dime watched through the windshield—nothing yet.

The voices came to life as he thought about Lance. *Killing this idiot will be a piece of cake. He'll be exhausted after his run and have no energy to fight back. He'll be putty in your hands.* Dime laughed loudly as he sat low in the driver's seat of his Jeep. "I know, right?"

Street lamps lined the sidewalk every thirty feet, leading to the apartment complex. He knew exactly where he would strike. Lance ran the path at River's Edge County Park, then crossed the street, ran two more blocks, and ended his run at the apartment. He'd cut through the area where the Dumpsters were lined up, then take the sidewalk to the main entrance of Cassie's apartment building.

Do it by the Dumpsters. It won't take long for somebody to find him there.

"Yeah, that's my plan. Don't worry. I know what I'm doing," Dime said in response.

He hit the button on the side of his watch to check the time. "He should be showing up soon. Another idiot, out for a nighttime jog when there's a madman roaming the streets—he deserves death. Taking her ex down will be a great blind side for Sergeant Monroe—she definitely isn't expecting that." Dime laughed and rubbed his hands together in anticipation.

A movement across the street caught his attention. Lance was walking the last few minutes of his jog. He had to cool down.

You'll be stone cold soon enough.

Dime chuckled at the voice talking in his head. He responded, "I'll admit, your quips are pretty damn clever."

The Jeep door opened quietly. Dime had sprayed the hinges earlier to make sure they didn't squeak. He pressed his body tight against the building, staying in the shadows. The hoodie concealed his face, and black gloves covered his hands. The sound of footsteps got closer. Dime peeked around the Dumpster, Lance was ten feet away and looking down at his Fitbit.

Dime thumbed the button on his knife as he stepped out of the shadows, plunged the switchblade into Lance's midsection, and gave it an extra twist for good measure. Lance grunted and fell to the ground. About to hit Lance with another blow, Dime was alerted by the sound of a side door opening. He retreated into the darkness and climbed back into his Jeep. He pounded on his steering wheel as he looked in his rearview mirror. He pulled out of the parking lot but not before the couple found Lance on the ground and saw Dime driving away.

"Son of a bitch!"

The plan was interrupted and didn't turn out as he wanted. Dime pounded on the dashboard and steering wheel again as he drove to the safety of his house and basement.

Chapter 42

I found it difficult to focus while Amber and I looked at handguns online. I promised her we'd check out a few, but I couldn't get that birthday card and taunt out of my mind. I wouldn't tell my family about that, especially Amber, since the message involved Spaz. Somehow the killer knew about the cat. Jack had taken the card downstairs and given it to Kyle, but we all knew there wouldn't be any fingerprints on it. The postmark showed it was mailed from North Bend on Thursday.

We sat at the desk in my bedroom, Polly and Porky happily chirping in the corner of the room. The door was closed so Spaz couldn't sneak in. Dinner was over, and the kitchen was cleaned up. With my mom and sister in the house, I barely had to do anything. Mom and Bruce relaxed comfortably on the couch, each with a glass of wine, watching a made-for-TV movie.

My cell phone rang at nine o'clock—Lieutenant Clark was calling. My heart thumped triple time just from seeing his name on the screen. I knew it couldn't be good. I looked at Amber.

"Jade, I'm not leaving, just answer the phone."

I picked up on the third ring. "Lieutenant?"

"Jade, get to St. Joseph's Hospital right now. Apparently, Lance was stabbed tonight. Jack is on his way. I'll meet you there."

I jumped from the desk and instinctively put on my shoulder holster. I loaded the magazine and holstered my weapon. I put my chained badge around my neck.

"Jade, what's going on?" Amber's eyes were filled with fear.

"I have to go. Lance is in the hospital. He's been stabbed."

"I'm going with you. Don't waste your breath arguing with me either."

"Fine, let's go."

I told my mom that Lance had been injured and Amber was going along for moral support. I had to ask him a few questions at the hospital. In reality, I had no idea if he was conscious or near death.

"Oh no, honey. Are you sure you don't want Bruce and me to go with you?"

"No, Mom, please just stay put. We have to leave now."

Amber and I reached the hospital in fifteen minutes. Jack and the lieutenant were waiting at the nurses' station in intensive care. We rushed toward them.

"What do we know?" I asked.

"He'll make it, Jade. Luckily the knife didn't hit any organs. He's already out of surgery and in room three." Jack nodded to his right. "According to Cassie, Lance went on his evening jog like usual. The next thing she knew, the neighbors were pounding on her door, saying he was lying outside and covered in blood. That was a couple of hours ago."

"It didn't occur to her to call me, or any of us, earlier?" I said, spewing the words.

The lieutenant put his hand on my shoulder. "All we know is she called the North Bend PD. Of course they dispatched an ambulance, even though it wasn't their jurisdiction. By the time I got word, Lance was already in surgery."

"When will he be coherent enough to talk?" I asked.

"The doctor said he was already coming out of anesthesia. He'll let us know when we can ask Lance a few questions. Let's wait in the visitors' lounge. Amber, how about helping me get coffee for all of us?" Jack suggested.

"Yeah, sure."

"Is Cassie in the room with him?" I wiped my eyes with the back of my sleeve. "Lieutenant, do you think it was Dime?"

"Yes, Cassie is in the room waiting for him to wake up. I'm not sure about Dime. I dispatched the closest deputies to the area to secure the scene and to interview everyone at the apartment building. Kyle and Dan are on their way."

After we'd had three cups of coffee each, the doctor finally entered the lounge. He sat and spoke to us.

"Lieutenant Clark. Always a pleasure, detectives." He shook our hands and gave Amber a smile. "Mr. Keller was lucky tonight."

I let out an audible sigh of relief.

The doctor looked my way. "Detective Monroe, you're Lance's ex-wife, correct?"

"She's a sergeant now," Amber said.

I ruffled my brows at her to hush. She looked down.

"Yes, I'm his ex-wife, but his attack may be part of an ongoing investigation. We'll need to question Lance if he's awake. I'm sure you're aware of the killer in the community. Lance might be able to tell us something."

"I understand. Luckily his injuries weren't life threatening. The knife just missed his intestines and hit his left oblique muscle instead. He's stitched up, but he's going to be sore for a few months. He needs rest. I'll give you fifteen minutes."

I thanked the doctor, and he left. "Amber, you're going to have to wait out here."

"I know. That's fine."

"I'll sit with her. You and Jack go ahead," Lieutenant Clark said.

We passed the nurses' station and turned left at the first hallway. Room three was on the right. The sliders were closed, and the curtain was drawn most of the way. I opened the door and pushed the curtain aside to see Cassie sitting on a chair next to Lance's bed. I nodded at her while grimacing through my teeth.

Jack spoke first. "Ma'am, we're going to have to question Lance privately. This is a police matter."

"I'm not leaving."

"Excuse me?" I cocked my head to the right. "Detective

269

Steele just said this is a police matter, meaning we're investigating something. Either you leave voluntarily or you leave on a gurney—take your pick." I stared at her and smiled.

"Whatever." She kissed Lance's cheek, huffed, and pushed past me.

"Bit—"

Jack coughed, interrupting what I was about to call her.

I approached the hospital bed. "Lance? Can you hear me?"

His eyes fluttered and finally focused on me.

I forced a smile—he looked weak.

"Jade, what are you doing here? Where am I?"

"You're in the hospital, man. Lance, do you remember anything?" Jack asked.

"Jack?"

"Yep, I'm here."

"Lance, tell us what you remember. You went out for a jog, right?" I sat in the chair that Cassie had been on earlier. Jack stood with his notepad out.

Lance pointed to the cup with ice water. I handed it to him, and he drank from the straw.

"I went for my normal jog after dinner. It was almost dark when I got back."

"Do you remember what time that was?" I asked.

"Um." He coughed and took another sip of water. "I remember looking at my Fitbit. I think it was almost seven thirty, maybe a little later."

"Then what happened?" Jack asked.

"I don't know. A shadowy figure came out of nowhere. I tried to turn, and then I felt a sharp pain in my side. That's it. I must have passed out."

Jack continued, "That slight turn probably saved your life. So between then and now, you can't remember anything? Not the people around you, the ambulance ride, arriving here, nothing?"

"Sorry, but no."

I looked up at Jack and shrugged. "Okay, I guess that's all we need, then. I hope you recover quickly, Lance."

"Jade?"

"Yeah?"

"Why do you think someone did this to me?"

"I have no idea, but we're going to find out. Take care of yourself."

We met up with Amber and the lieutenant again in the visitors' lounge.

"What do you think, boss? Should we head over to the apartment building?" I asked.

"No, let's just go on home. Kyle called and said there wasn't any evidence at the scene."

The lieutenant gave each of us a direct look. We knew he meant no dime was found, but he didn't want to give that detail away in front of Amber. He continued, "The deputies interviewed everyone at the building. The couple that found Lance said an SUV of some sort pulled out of the driveway right when they walked out the front door. They couldn't tell the make, color, or plate number because the exit was obscured by the large apartment sign and shrubbery. They said the red plastic on the right taillight was broken. The brake light flashed clear when the vehicle turned out of the parking lot. That's really all they had."

"We can add that information to our profile if it actually was our guy."

"Could it have been a botched robbery by someone else?" Amber asked.

"Doubt it. Lance didn't have anything with him except his Fitbit."

Chapter 43

We parted ways with Jack and the lieutenant outside in the hospital parking lot. Amber and I headed home in silence.

"Why are you so quiet?" she asked.

"Just thinking how a grown man wasn't even able to defend himself. Even though Lance and I aren't together anymore, I'd never want anything to happen to him."

"But Lance didn't see it coming. He was blindsided."

"So were the other victims. I guess the element of surprise works in our killer's favor."

"So you think it was him for sure?"

"I don't know, Amber. Lance survived, but maybe it was just dumb luck. The attack was likely interrupted by the couple coming out of the building. When do you work next?"

"I have off until Friday night. Why?"

"Good, I'll make a call. We're going to start your self-defense classes tomorrow night."

I pulled into the garage, and we stepped into the quiet house. All of the lights were dimmed. Mom and Bruce had obviously turned in since it was close to midnight. In a whisper, I said good night to Amber and went to bed. I lay there feeling as if the safety of our city rested entirely on my shoulders. This killer was targeting me through other people, and I didn't know why. Tomorrow, I'd start my own profile of Dime. I'd dig into his psychotic mind and try to figure out the connection he thought he had with me.

Throughout the week, we'd gone over everything we had so far. Nothing was found at the apartment complex or the barn where Melissa was killed. We concluded that the lack of the signature dime at the apartment was only because the killer was interrupted. The attempt on Lance's life was going to be attributed to Dime, just like the rest of the attacks.

We addressed the public again, asking for help in apprehending the killer. We stressed that if anyone noticed a suspicious person or activity going on, for them to call either the North Bend PD or the sheriff's department. We were also looking for an SUV with a possible broken right taillight.

I called every auto repair shop in the county. So far, nobody had brought in an SUV that needed the right taillight replaced.

A call came in from Melissa Mately's mother on Thursday. She thanked us for confirming through dental records that the body found at the barn was indeed Melissa's. Her request to have Melissa cremated and the ashes sent to Iowa was honored. I spoke to Perry Adams too. He informed me that Elise's funeral would be held on

Saturday at Myram & Frank Funeral Home here in town. I told him that a few of us would be there.

Friday during lunch, I went downstairs to the tech department and asked Todd to pull up the driver's license photos of the two David Ingles in Kentucky and Oregon on his computer. I studied their faces and noted the height, weight, and age of each man. Their descriptions didn't match the profile we had put together of Dime. I closed out the program and returned to the bull pen.

Jack and I finally left for the day at five o'clock and headed out the door. "Do you want to go somewhere for a beer? Amber is working tonight, and Mom and Bruce said they were going out for dinner and a movie. It's just going to be Spaz, Polly, and Porky keeping me company otherwise."

"Sure, I don't have any plans."

"Good, I need your take on a few things that have been bothering me anyway. I'd rather keep my personal opinions just between you and me for now."

"Yeah, sure." Jack gave me a concerned look. "Are you okay?"

"I'm not sure. Something has been weighing heavily on my mind. Let's go somewhere quiet where we can talk."

"Chelsie's?"

"Yeah, I'll follow you."

A crunch sounded under my shoe as I neared my car. Instinctively, I turned and looked back to see what I'd stepped on.

"Jack, come here and check this out."

Jack was in his car and ready to leave when he heard me call out to him. He got out.

"What do you have?"

I motioned him over. "Take a look." I knelt over what appeared to be broken pieces of plastic. Jack joined me and picked up a shard.

"This looks like taillight plastic."

"I thought so too. Is there any way to tell what kind of vehicle it came from?"

"Probably if it was larger and had a model number on it. These few shards are pretty small." Jack scanned the parking lot. "Todd's car is still here, and so is Kyle's. Let's get their opinion."

We went back inside and took the stairs to the lower level. Both men were closing up their respective doors for the night.

"Hey, guys, I thought you left," Kyle said.

"We almost did until I stepped on this." I held up a piece of red plastic about half the size of my pinkie finger. "Is there any way to tell what kind of vehicle this came from?"

Kyle took it in his hand, Todd came over and inspected it too.

"Looks like a piece of taillight plastic. No numbers on it and no definite contour. I don't think it's possible, Jade."

Kyle looked at Todd, waiting for his opinion. Todd shrugged.

"If we had a model number, I could run it through the database. It's unlikely we could find out anything with a piece this small. Is that the largest piece you have?"

"Unfortunately yes. How about parking lot video?"

Todd raised his eyebrows. "That could take forever. It's a public lot, Jade. A lot of cars come and go, and people park anywhere they want. We don't have any set time frame to look at?"

"No, sorry. I'm just thinking out loud. Okay, good night, guys. Hopefully I won't see you until Monday."

I told Jack I'd follow him, and we left. Chelsie's was a quiet bar and grill at the intersection of Main Street and Poplar. I wanted to avoid the loud, Friday night crowd so we could do some private brainstorming. Nothing else seemed to be working.

The waitress approached our table. "Hi, folks, what can I get you?"

"You hungry?" Jack asked.

"Yeah, I guess so."

Jack asked for two menus, and we each ordered a beer.

"You and Amber started the self-defense classes a few nights ago, didn't you?"

I grinned. "Yeah, she's a quick study, that's for sure. If I'm not careful, she'll kick my ass soon."

"Doubt it, but the class is a good idea. You never know when a self-defense technique might save your life."

I agreed. I began telling Jack about my concerns as we sipped our stouts. We'd already placed our food orders.

"When did all of this craziness begin?" I asked to get the conversation going.

"Three weeks ago that we know of."

"Right. I got promoted from detective to sergeant in

criminal investigations last month, and a week later the bodies started popping up in our jurisdiction. The whole female-authority thing has been stuck in my head since we put together the press release." I rubbed my temples. "I'm afraid my mind has been going nonstop since."

"So what does your gut tell you, Jade?"

I looked around. "I'm afraid to even say it out loud."

Jack took a gulp of beer. "You think Doug is good for this, don't you?"

I nodded, afraid my voice would crack. I cleared my throat. "Apparently you do too. What do we really know about him? I mean other than him being the ME for years."

"I know he's a loner and has a chip on his shoulder about his ex-wife. He's antisocial outside of work, yet he's a good medical examiner. He's always on time and at the scenes. His whereabouts are usually accounted for."

"We don't know what he does when his workday is over, though. Have you ever been to his house?"

"Never, have you?" Jack asked.

"Nope, and he's lived there forever. I believe that's the house he was raised in."

"The house belonged to his folks? Where are they now?"

"No clue. Doug does drive an SUV, you know."

Jack checked the time on his cell phone. "It's seven thirty. By the time we're done with dinner, it will be after eight. Do you want to do a drive-by of his house? Maybe he'll be home."

"Sure, but we can't just knock on his door without a reason."

"We don't have to. If his vehicle is parked in the driveway, we can at least check to see if the taillight is broken. We have to tread lightly. Doug is an odd duck, for sure, but we have absolutely nothing on him. We can't ruin someone's reputation based on him being weird and antisocial. He's still a very competent ME."

"I know, but things are coming together that can't be explained. He cracks his neck and mutters. He's probably the right build and strong enough. He's kind of weird and short tempered at times, and he'd definitely know how to avoid detection."

"True, but other than the weird and short tempered part, that could easily describe me."

The waitress brought our meals, and we ate quickly—we had someplace to be.

Chapter 44

Since neither of us had ever been to Doug's house, we had to go back to the station to find his address. I pulled the door handle and entered the bull pen, Jack right on my heels. Jamison and Horbeck sat at their desks, doing busywork.

Jamison looked up from his desk when we walked in. "What are you guys doing here?"

I kept quiet, figuring Jack would take the lead. He responded for both of us as he cut through to the file room.

"We just need to check on an address. Brainstorming, you know?"

He didn't want to get into a conversation with either of the detectives. They might ask too many questions.

Horbeck's ears perked up. "Really? Need some help?"

I made small talk to keep both men distracted. "Nah— we're good, thanks. Slow night?" I peered over Horbeck's desk to call his attention back my way.

Horbeck leaned back in his chair, almost lifting the front wheels off the floor. "Yeah, quiet so far. I hope it stays that way. There *is* a full moon out tonight, you know."

I grimaced. "Ugh, don't remind me."

Jack returned and gave me a nod. "See you guys later."

Jamison smirked. "I hope not."

We headed back to the parking lot. I looked up at the bright full moon just because Horbeck mentioned it. I hadn't even noticed earlier, and now I hoped it wasn't a bad omen.

"How are we going to do this? Neither of us can leave our cars in the lot. Somebody might wonder why we aren't inside."

"Yeah, good point." Jack scratched his chin. "Follow me to my house. We'll leave your car there."

"Got it."

Jack's house was less than ten minutes away. He lived in a three-bedroom bungalow on Hawthorne Street. Most of those homes were built in the forties, and they looked nice and cozy. The neighborhood was quiet with mostly single people or empty nesters living there.

Jack stopped in the street and waved me around him. He opened his window and called out, "Park in the driveway. That's fine."

"Okay." I pulled in, parked, and got out. With a tap on the key fob, the car beeped, the lights flashed, and it was locked. I climbed into the passenger seat of Jack's Charger, and we were off, heading south to Jackson City. The drive would take only fifteen minutes.

"Here's his address." Jack handed me the slip of paper he'd written it on. "Plug it into your cell's navigation in case we ever need it again."

We took the exit ramp into Jackson City. The navigation led us down several streets. We followed Main Street for five blocks, turned left onto Adams Street and another left onto Temper Way. According to the navigation, his house was the sixth one on the right.

Streetlights were few and far between. We were close to the edge of town, with a city park between Doug's house and the vast country farm fields to the east. Jack drove slowly, watching for Doug's address.

"It should be the next house on the right." Jack pointed and lowered his head to look out the passenger side window as he drove slowly forward.

I felt as if I needed to whisper even though it wasn't necessary. "The house is dark," I said, whispering anyway.

"Maybe he's already in bed."

I checked the time. "It's only nine fifteen. Maybe his car is in the garage."

Jack parked three houses beyond Doug's and got out.

"Where the hell are you going?" I asked, my voice becoming raspy. My mouth felt as dry as the desert—I needed water.

"Wait here. I'm going to look through his garage windows to see if his car is inside."

"Fine, but hurry and stay in the shadows." I unbuckled my seat belt and turned to see him running toward Doug's house. My neck was stretched to its limits as I watched over my shoulder. The lack of streetlights didn't help my anxiety. By the time Jack passed the second house, I couldn't see him anymore. I waited and watched my surroundings.

The sound of running footsteps getting closer told me Jack was returning. I watched until I saw him again and breathed a sigh of relief.

"Anything?"

"Nope, he isn't home."

"Damn it. I'll remember to check the taillight on his vehicle Monday morning, that's for sure." I refastened my seat belt, and we headed back to North Bend.

"Do you want to come in?" Jack asked when we reached his house. "It seems like your mind is going a hundred miles an hour."

"It is. For some reason, the name David Ingles sticks in my craw. I don't know anyone with that name personally, but something is definitely off."

"We can do a little more detective work over a beer. Come on in."

"Okay. I probably can't sleep anyway."

I had been in Jack's house only a handful of times and chuckled to myself how neat and clean he kept his home. His mother had taught him well.

"Beer or coffee?" He headed into the kitchen and stood by the refrigerator.

"Better make it a beer unless you have decaf. I don't want to be awake all night."

"No decaf in this house. I only drink leaded."

I smiled. "A beer sounds great."

Jack reached into the refrigerator and pulled out two stouts from the door rack. I noticed a few items on the shelves, but most of the refrigerator was empty.

"You fasting?" I asked, giving him a small grin.

"Yeah, probably as much as you are. You look like you've lost a few pounds."

"Hmm... thanks for noticing."

Jack handed me a can and a glass, then sat down across from me at the kitchen table.

"A can and a glass, just like Dime ordered his beer at Eddy's." I popped the tab and listened to the hiss of the cartridge in the can. The thick, creamy head was my favorite part of this rich, dark beer.

"Okay, so what bothers you about the name David Ingles?"

"I'm not sure. I don't think it's actually the name that throws me. I need to write things down as we talk so I don't lose my train of thought. Got any scratch paper?"

"Sure." Jack rose and went to the first drawer at the end of the kitchen cabinets. "Does everyone use the end drawer as their junk drawer?"

"I do. I think it's mandatory."

He handed me the pad of paper and a pen, then took a seat in the chair next to mine. I wrote down the name David Ingles. I remembered that neither of the driver's license photos of the two guys in the system looked at all like our suspect might look. I wrote Doug Irvin below David's name.

"That's it! I know what's been bugging me this whole time. The initials are the same." I slid the sheet of paper over to Jack.

"Son of a gun, Jade, I think you're on to something.

Wait a minute." Jack took the pen and added ME, as in medical examiner, after Doug's name. "What do you think? Doug Irvin, ME. Use his initials only and see what you get."

I wrote them out and got DIME. I dropped the pen to the table and rubbed my forehead. "Jack—Doug's the killer. We have to do something, but how are we going to prove it? His name and title don't automatically make him a killer. We have to run this by the lieutenant."

Jack checked the time—eleven o'clock. "First, we have to get our ducks in a row. We can't present this to the lieutenant yet. Let's make an outline of sorts. We need to compare Doug to the vague descriptions of suspects we got from people. We need a motive too. If we call the lieutenant half-cocked and try to present our weak ideas as evidence, we'll lose Doug as a suspect. It's only circumstantial at best." Jack grabbed two more beers. "Let's get busy. We need enough to go on or we'll never get a warrant to search his house."

Chapter 45

"Do you think this is enough to present to the lieutenant?" I squeezed my temples and handed Jack the sheets of paper we had compiled over the last few hours.

We had put together a profile and possible motive, making Doug our most probable suspect. We carefully went over every bullet point we'd listed and added what we'd used as our basis for the information.

"I think this should do it, but what we really need is to see his vehicle."

"He couldn't have replaced that taillight yet unless he left the county. I called every repair shop in Washburn County and told them to flag all SUVs that come in to have the right taillight replaced. They're supposed to call us immediately, and I haven't heard anything yet."

"He either fixed it himself or it's still like that, that is, if Doug really is the killer."

I looked at the clock again—two a.m. "Do you feel confident enough to call the lieutenant?"

"Yes, do you?"

"Absolutely." I pulled my cell out of my purse, ready to dial the lieutenant, when it rang. "Hang on, it's Amber. I told her to call me every night she closes Joey's, especially since she had that scare with Sean last week." I picked up. "Hey, Sis, how was your night?"

"Busy. I made a ton of tips tonight. I swear I'm giving up on men, though."

I chuckled. "Really, why's that? You're young, beautiful, and have an outgoing personality."

"Thanks. Anyway, remember that guy I said has been hanging out here lately? The older guy that I thought was crushing on me?"

"Yeah, I remember you mentioning him. Did he replace you already with someone closer to his own age?"

"Worse than that. The jerk sat here for the last four hours schmoozing me up, taking up all of the time I could have been gabbing with the regulars, plus he was the last one to leave. I just wiped down the bar and saw that he left a measly dime as my tip. What an asshat!"

"Son of a bitch! Amber, lock the doors and don't leave. Do you hear me? Lock the doors now!"

"What's going on, Jade? You're freaking me out."

I heard Amber through the phone line, talking to someone.

"Hey, why are you still here? The bar is clos—"

Our call abruptly ended.

"Amber? Amber, are you there? Amber! Shit, Jack, Dime or Doug or whoever the hell it is has Amber."

Jack was already on his cell, talking to the night dispatch,

Bob Kennedy. "Bob, get everyone on patrol out to Joey's Sports Bar and Grille now. Ten thirty-nine, tell them to move! Put out a BOLO on a red Jeep, back right taillight could be broken. We may have a possible ten thirty-one in progress involving Jade's sister, Amber Monroe. Have Jamison and Horbeck get out there too. Call the lieutenant. Jade and I are on our way."

The normal fifteen-minute drive to Joey's from Jack's house took eight. Luckily this time of night, the streets were nearly empty. I tried Amber's phone over and over, but she didn't pick up. I tried to think—did she always keep it on silent, or did it actually ring? I couldn't remember. I hoped it was on silent. If Dime heard her phone ring, he would surely take it away and destroy it.

We saw the red and blue flashing lights from blocks away. We pulled into Joey's parking lot. Five cruisers were already there along with two black sedans. The lieutenant pulled in right when we exited Jack's Charger.

I ran to Jamison. "What do we know?"

"Sergeant, Jack, Lieutenant. We cleared the building, and there's nobody inside. Looks like a scuffle took place, though. Chairs are knocked over, and there's broken glass everywhere. I hate to say it, but Doug's Jeep is out back by the Dumpsters."

I ran to the back of the building, knowing my worst fears would be realized. Doug's Jeep was parked twenty feet away from the back door, beyond the garbage bins. The motion sensor light above the door flicked on when I ran past. The rear of his vehicle illuminated just enough to see that the right taillight was broken. I entered the back door, then rushed through the hallway where the restrooms were and into the main bar area. Everyone had already gone inside the building to find out what had transpired there.

I nodded when I looked at Jack. "Doug is definitely Dime."

Lieutenant Clark ground his fist into his eyes. "How could we have a psychopath right under our noses and not realize it? Son of a bitch. Jade, what does Amber drive?"

"She has a 2012 gray Prius but I don't know the plate number. We need everyone at the station. Her cell isn't turned off, so Todd and Billy can ping it and triangulate the location, can't they? They can pull up her license plate number too."

"Already on it, Sergeant. Hopefully she keeps her locations on or they aren't going to get anything," Jamison said. "Todd and Billy should be arriving at the station any minute now. They said they'd call as soon as they had their asses planted in their chairs."

"Does anyone know where he may have taken her? Has Doug ever mentioned a place, somewhere that holds memories for him—anything?"

I searched everyone's faces for something, any clue to Doug's whereabouts. I needed to know where he took my sister. The lieutenant's phone rang—it was Todd.

"Okay, hang on, Todd. Jade, what is Amber's phone number? The guys are ready."

I gave Clark the number, and I paced as we waited.

The lieutenant stayed on the line until Todd came back

on. "Yep, okay, we're on it." He hung up. "They're in Jackson City."

"He took her to his house?"

"Apparently so. Okay, once we hit the city limits, we go silent. Got it, everyone? We don't want to alert him we're coming. We already know what he's capable of."

We nodded.

"Let's roll."

Jack and I jumped into his Charger and led the way. Five cruisers, Jamison, Horbeck, and the lieutenant followed Jack's car. We exited the ramp into Jackson City, and the cruisers turned their lights off and silenced their sirens. If we had any hope of getting Amber out of there safely, we had to take Doug by surprise. If he knew we were coming, all bets were off.

We parked at the end of the block and got out. The cruisers fell in behind us, and Lieutenant Clark rounded us up.

"Okay, gear up. I want everyone wearing vests. We're going in hot and quiet."

We approached the house and peeked through the garage window. Amber's car sat inside.

"All right, listen up. We know they're here. First, we'll surveil what we can through the windows. Deputies, do a quick sweep. Check every door. See if we're lucky enough to find something unlocked."

"Got it, Lieutenant."

Deputies Schmitz, Taylor, Drury, and Ryan checked every window and returned back to the front of the garage where we waited.

"No sign of movement, sir, and no sounds. There doesn't appear to be an alarm system either. All doors are locked except the double cellar doors. We're pretty sure we can breach the house through the patio doors, though. It doesn't appear that there's a pole in the track. We'll lift the door and push it aside."

"I can do that," I said.

"Okay, Jade, you and Jack take the patio door. Deputies, cover the garage entrance and the cellar door. Horbeck and Jamison, head to the front. I'll go with you. Jade, we'll wait for you to get inside and let us in. Everyone, take your positions."

Jack and I ran around to the back of the house. Together, we pressed our hands firmly against the patio door glass and lifted straight up. The panel cleared the locking mechanism and slid to the side. I peeked my head in, looked around, and listened. The door opened to the kitchen dining area. Straight ahead, beyond the kitchen looked to be the living room. I could see the TV and the front door from my position. The house was dark. We stepped inside, hoping the floors didn't creak. Our guns were drawn, and Jack pulled out his flashlight. I followed Jack through the kitchen to the door leading into the garage. We had no idea if anyone was in there. We stepped into the darkened area. He aimed the flashlight at Amber's car. It was empty. Jack unlocked the side door, allowing Schmitz and Taylor in. I had Schmitz call over his shoulder radio for Drury and Ryan to hold their positions at the cellar entrance. Back in the house, I rounded the kitchen and crept to the front door. I let Jamison, Horbeck, and the lieutenant in. We cleared the first floor.

The lieutenant whispered to us, "Did you locate the basement door?"

With a nod, I motioned with a hand signal for them to follow. We grouped by the basement door and listened. A male voice sounded below us. Doug was down there doing who knew what to my sister. My heart raced, but I needed to keep my composure. We had to get Amber out of that situation. I carefully turned the knob and eased the door back toward me. The basement lights were on. I checked the stairs—they were covered with dirty old carpeting. That would help silence the sound of our movements. I took four steps down and knelt when I cleared the basement ceiling. I peeked around the corner, assessing what lay ahead of us.

Doug stood near a bookcase, his back toward me at the far end of the room, muttering something I couldn't understand from my distance. I saw Amber sitting in a wooden chair. Her mouth was gagged, and her hands and legs were tied to the arms and feet of the chair. Her forehead was bloodied. Her eyes darted toward me when she saw our movements. I motioned for her to stay calm.

Doug remained unaware of our presence as he paced in front of the bookcase. We swept in with guns drawn. He spun when he heard us. In two strides, he was at Amber's throat with a knife.

I called out, my gun's red laser sights on his forehead. "Doug, you don't want to do this. Put the knife down. Step away from Amber. She's done nothing wrong."

He laughed and spewed out his hatred for me. "There you go again, Sergeant, giving orders. Do you have any idea how sick I am of women like you? You're just like my mother, rest her soul." He laughed again. "You think you call the shots, bossing me around, telling me what to do. You stupid bitch would have been next, but your sweet sister was ripe for the picking. You see, not only do I hate women who think they have some type of authority, but I also hate shrinks. Isn't that what this sweet, innocent girl is going to school for? You're going to be a shrink, aren't you, Amber?" He jerked her head back by her hair and held the knife tighter against her throat.

"Are you really prepared to die tonight, Doug?" I walked closer to him as I talked. "One shot—that's all I need. Let her go, now!" I couldn't look Amber in the face. I had to keep my eyes and weapon zeroed in on his forehead.

The lieutenant spoke up. "Doug, we can get you the help you need. Back away from Amber. She's an innocent woman."

"There isn't a woman alive that's innocent." Doug sneered and held his position while he pressed the knife harder against her neck.

I saw blood dripping beneath the blade.

The sound of a crashing door behind him made Doug turn. I had a split second to act. I squeezed the trigger.

Chapter 46

He lay on the floor dead, and the nightmare was over. I holstered my gun and rushed to Amber's side. My hands shook as I tried to untie her.

Jack reached out to me. "I got this, partner. Take a breath. Amber is safe."

I wiped my eyes and pulled the gag from Amber's mouth while Jack released the ropes from her arms and legs. She broke down and sobbed against me.

I held her tight. "I got you, honey. You're going to be okay."

The lieutenant called the Jackson City EMTs, and they were en route. Amber had a gash on her head that needed to be attended.

She was loaded up in the ambulance to be taken to St. Joseph's Hospital, the same place where Lance was still a patient.

I stood at the back of the ambulance. "I'll be there soon, I promise. You're safe now, Amber. I'll call Mom and have her meet you at the hospital. I have to take care of a few things here, but I'll be there as quickly as I can."

She held me, afraid to let go.

"Guys, take good care of her. I'll be there shortly."

"Yes, ma'am. Let's go." I watched as the ambulance drove away, then I went back to the basement.

"How did Drury and Ryan know when to break in the cellar door?" I asked.

Taylor responded. "I held back so Doug wouldn't hear me on my radio. I knew they were positioned just outside the door. It didn't look like we were going to talk Doug down. The lieutenant nodded, and I gave them the go-ahead to kick in the door."

"Thank you—all of you." I sighed and took a deep breath.

We finally had time to look around. Kyle and Dan were called in to help. I stuck around for a short time as the guys gloved up and began processing the basement. I wanted to check on Amber soon and knew I'd be whisked away for my formal processing too. I quickly scanned the basement, trying to figure out Doug's mind. A wall to our left was covered in corkboard. Newspaper articles about my promotion from detective to sergeant were pinned to the board. Clippings from every case I had ever been on, and every newspaper photo that had me in the shot, were pinned to the wall. Several pictures had my face slashed. Old yellowed newspaper clippings showed Doug's ex-wife being presented with awards as she advanced in her career. Several more newspaper articles dating back to the mid-nineties told how Betty Irvin had abruptly left her job in family medicine and moved away. Her only child, Doug, had stayed in the family home to continue his college education. He was studying pathology.

"What is this stuff?" I asked as we all stood there staring at the wall. Goose bumps popped up on my arms as I read a few of the articles.

"Looks like Doug was a sick man," Taylor said.

We continued through the room. The bar was covered with rows of prescription bottles. A still cold Stella Artois sat on a side table. Doug's body lay on the floor next to it.

Jack rubbed his head. "This place gives me the creeps, and what was he doing by that bookcase?"

We walked over to take a look. The floor beneath the bookcase was scraped as if it had been moved numerous times.

"This is interesting. Drury, give me a hand," Jack said.

We stood back and watched as Jack and Deputy Drury put their backs into it and pushed the bookcase to the side. Behind it was a large opening in the wall.

"What the hell?" Lieutenant Clark said. "Let's take a look in there."

With our flashlights lit, we found Melissa's briefcase with a bag of bloody clothes. Elise's cell phone was there along with a wallet, knife, and cell phone belonging to Morris King in a bag with more bloody clothes and a bloody tarp.

"I guess this is where he stashed everything," Jack said. "Hang on, there's something farther in. Anyone have a brighter flashlight?"

Jamison handed Jack his. Jack wedged himself farther back. We could see only his feet as he inched his way in.

"Holy shit."

"What's going on? What did you find?"

"There's a bag of bones and a skull back here. They're human."

Chapter 47

Our appointment with Dr. Candace White was at ten a.m. Jack and I were led into her luxurious office on Milwaukee's east side overlooking Lake Michigan. The view from her eighteenth-floor office was magnificent.

"Detectives, please have a seat. Coffee?"

I nodded and thanked her.

She poured two cups and placed them in front of Jack and me. She already had a cup of her own on her side of the desk. She returned to her leather office chair and sat.

"Yes, Doug Irvin was a patient of mine for nearly ten years. I'm sorry to hear of his passing"—she gave us each a saddened look—"and his actions. He was quite a troubled soul and quit coming to see me in February."

"What was Doug diagnosed with?" I asked.

She shrugged. "Just about everything, I'm afraid. He was so volatile. I knew if he stopped taking his meds, something horrible could happen. I had no idea he was Washburn County's ME, but in hindsight, he was really a brilliant man. He was quite capable of doing just about anything.

That's the problem with psychopaths—they can live among us and appear very normal. Classic examples would be Ted Bundy and the BTK killer. Doug's main problem was he hated women, a true misogynist. He told stories of how his mother used to berate him, tie him to a wooden chair in their basement and beat him. According to Doug, he'd spend hours down there, many times without food and the ability to use the bathroom. He'd mentioned how he soiled himself and received beatings because of that too. If any of this was true, he did live a very horrible life growing up."

"Could you explain why we always found something in the mouths of his victims?" Jack asked.

"Typically that's symbolic. I would imagine it was his way of silencing people—as in his mother."

"Wasn't there a father in the family?" I asked.

"He never spoke of one. He said his mother moved away when he was nineteen, but by then his mind was deeply disturbed. He was on a very strong regimen of antipsychotic drugs. Doug was an anomaly in a way. Not only was he a psychopath, but he also had delusional disorders causing borderline schizophrenia, hence the drugs. He said he heard voices in his head."

I glanced at Jack. "Maybe that explains the muttering. He could have been communicating with them."

Jack nodded. "Weren't his treatment or prescription bills ever sent to his insurance company?"

The doctor shook her head. "Doug told me he didn't work. He said he'd inherited quite a sum of money when a relative died. I imagine he didn't want a paper trail. He paid for everything by money order."

We thanked the doctor and left.

"What are the odds that the bones behind the wall belong to Doug's mom?"

Jack looked at me as he pulled out of the parking garage. "I'd say 100 percent. The DNA results should be back tomorrow. Kyle and Dan will let us know."

"I feel bad about missing Elise's funeral, but Perry understood. He was so relieved that this nightmare is over and he has justice for Elise." I smiled at Jack. "He thanked us for the flowers."

"That's nice. I guess Jason will take over all of the ME duties until another one is hired."

"Well, I hope things stay slow for a while. It will be a welcome change to say we live in a quiet little community again."

"Do you want me to drop you off at home?" Jack asked.

"Why don't you join Amber and me for lunch? She'd love it."

"Are you sure?"

"Absolutely. You have time before you need to get back to the station."

"Are you rubbing it in?"

"Why? Because I took a week off to spend with my little sister? She can either spend the week with Mom and Bruce as she heals or she can spend it with me. I think you know which one she chose. Anyway, she suggested the Washington House."

Jack grinned. "You know the offer is still on the table. I

can rough Bruce up if you want."

"Nah—that's okay, but what are you doing over the weekend?"

Jack raised his eyebrows and looked at me. "Why?"

"Because we really need a big strong guy to help us move."

Jack chuckled as we got out of the car. "You've got a deal as long as you're buying lunch today."

He put his arm around my shoulder. "Come on, partner. I see Amber waving at us."

THE END

Thank you for reading *Maniacal*, Book 1 in the Detective Jade Monroe Crime Thriller Series. I hope you enjoyed it!

Now that you've read *Maniacal*, move ahead and dive into *Captive*, Book 2. You can find it at http://cmsutter.com/.

Stay abreast of my new releases by signing up for my VIP e-mail list at: http://cmsutter.com/newsletter/

You'll be one of the first to get a glimpse of the cover reveals and release dates, and you'll have a chance at exciting raffles and freebies offered throughout the series.

Posting a review will help other readers find my books. I appreciate every review, whether positive or negative, and if you have a second to spare, it is truly appreciated.

Again, thank you for reading!

Visit my author website at: http://cmsutter.com/

See all of my available titles at: http://cmsutter.com/available-books/

Made in the USA
San Bernardino, CA
25 September 2017